THE STAMP OF TREACHERY

By

Tony Buckingham

ISBN-13: 978-1530137947
ISBN-10: 1530137942

DEDICATION

I wrote three books after I sold my company Bonham, in 1997. The first, *The Grave Digger's Apprentice*, was an amusing account of how we started Benham. The next two, *The Stamp of Treachery* and *Valentine's Day*, were both murder mysteries and I had plans to develop them but despite a major publisher taking an option on *Valentine's Day* (they wanted changes) I started a new company that suddenly needed all my time.

I meant to continue later but alas I have Idiopathic Pulmonary Fibrosis so I would like to dedicate both books to the NHS. Starting with the Royal Brompton and Toby Maher for putting me on Pirfenidone which I think has given me an extra year of life, Adrian Morris my local consultant, Dr Farrow my GP, Gemma, my lung nurse, plus all the wonderful district nurses thanks for everything.

***

But the person to whom this book is really dedicated is Cath, my wife of fifty years, who didn't realize when she said, "In sickness and in health," she would be a carer for 24/7 for years. Without her I would never have completed these last two books. My thanks to her are more profound than I can express.

CONTENTS

PART I

JOHN RICH

Preface

It was the same recurring nightmare. As always I woke sweating, yet cold at the same time, with that dreadful question screaming inside my brain:

Could I have averted the tragedy?

Was I in some way to blame for the train of events that led to so many deaths?

I should have been more aware of what was going on, in that respect I was responsible. In my defence, I was still very worried about Beth's health and there was nothing in the world more important to me than her. My great friend, Chief Inspector Sandy Neil, tells me I'm not untypical. Apparently most businessmen don't want to think about dishonesty or theft. They normally blame themselves for any business failings.

As I lay there in the dark, keeping as still as I could to avoid waking Beth, I came to a conclusion. I'd try to write the whole messy business down on paper. Perhaps that would help. I thought perhaps I'd get you to read it, then ask you to tell me honestly – was I in any way to blame?

Well, how should I begin? I think you need to understand the people involved before you can judge, but to be fair to them, I'll let you tell them about it in their own words.

Mark Cheshire

Chapter 1

"There seems to be a discrepancy in the books," said the small bald-headed man who had been sitting at my dad's desk for the last few hours. He wasn't very impressive and the back of his well-worn, dark, shiny suit was covered with flakes of dandruff. He was very pompous and spoke with an annoying, slow emphasis.

"That's impossible," replied my dad confidently. "I don't make mistakes, book-keeping is my strength. You must have got it wrong."

"I'm sorry," he continued, "but I'm sure I'm right. I've checked and double checked; there'll have to be a proper investigation."

"That's bloody stupid," the old man ranted. "How can we continue with business with all sorts of people in the shop? What would it look like? You've got it wrong. They're all right – I know they are."

I wished I could share his confidence. However, I'd been here before. Shop after shop, town after town; it was always the same. Some dour little man would check and find my dad's pathetic attempt to hide his dishonesty. I'd been to eight schools before I was eleven. It was difficult at times to remember my new surname. At least I was always John, I suppose that was something. Today, standing in that grotty, nasty little newsagent's, I was John Rich, failure son of a real failure father.

The bald-headed git continued his accusations.

"As you see, there is no mistake, the figures don't add up and there is a sizeable discrepancy. If it was a small one I'd let it go, but this just isn't on – I'm very sorry. It's probably something very silly – the investigating accountants will find it quickly enough. Don't worry."

"Well I do worry. I've never had anything like this happen to me before. It makes me feel quite ill just thinking about it. I think I'd better sit down." At this point he staggered to a chair and sat down very slowly. *A nice touch*, I thought. Although it was a well-rehearsed routine he carried it off very well. I hadn't seen it performed for nearly a year and I thought that he sounded a bit more convincing this time.

"Well I'm not suggesting that you've purposely done anything wrong," said Baldy kindly, "not for one minute. It could be a mistake. Don't worry, we'll sort it out. I'll have to take the books with me as it's Friday. Anyway, nothing can be done until Monday so I suggest you put a notice in the shop window that you'll be shut on Monday, and probably Tuesday, due to staff training or ill health, whichever you prefer. We should be finished by Wednesday." He smiled reassuringly.

"Well, you're the boss," said Dad, in the way he always did when he had been caught out. "But I think the company'll be annoyed losing two days' takings for no reason. I'll be writing to the company myself."

"Well you have that right. Well, goodbye Mr Rich – we'll see you on Monday."

Oh no you won't, I thought. *We certainly won't be here on Monday.*

"Yes, I suppose you've got to do your job," continued Dad. "What sort of time will you be here on Monday?"

"About 10 o'clock. Goodnight." With that, the bald git left and my father sat with his head in his hands.

I came slowly down the stairs and through the shop, picking up a Coca-Cola and a couple of bars of Cadbury's chocolate as I went. After all, we wouldn't be here on Monday, it was help yourself time.

"So, where are we going this time?" I asked with heavy sarcasm.

"Don't be so bloody cheeky, boy. It's not my fault. We weren't due for an inspection for another year. It's just bad luck."

"All right, but where the bloody hell are we going this weekend? It would be nice to know. After all, it's my life too."

"I don't know, but we'll be off by Sunday. I'll find somewhere, I always have." Although he said this confidently his face didn't seem to be quite so optimistic. I'd always been amazed about the way he kept getting jobs with large companies. It was obvious they didn't check very carefully.

"Well, I'm out then," I said. "I'd like to say goodbye to a few of my mates before we go."

"Yeah, you be careful to tell them that your grandma's ill. We've got to go and look after her. Don't say anything about the investigation," he told me worriedly.

"Do you think I'm stupid?" I shouted. "I've been through this before – many times, if you remember, so I do know what to do."

"Yeah, all right. You go out and enjoy yourself. I'll sort this lot out."

I felt gutted. I was used to moving suddenly but for once I'd started to settle in. I liked Mexfort. It was small and friendly. But what the hell, I'd soon leave home and have a place of my own. I wasn't going to be a failure like my father. I'd take my chances and be someone. But before we left I had one last thing to do. I'd been going out with Jenny for a month or so. Going out was probably the wrong way to describe our relationship. She wasn't the sort of girl you wanted to be seen with, if you know what I mean. She really was a bit of a dog. She was nearly twenty, a lot older than me, and was grateful for the attention I gave her. I hadn't as yet gone the whole way but if I was to succeed in losing my cherry, it had to be this weekend. We, so far, had done everything possible in the dark of the Astoria cinema – I'd regularly walked home with wet trousers – after Jenny had pleasured me for the second or third time during the evening. And in turn I had explored every inch of her ample body. She'd never get her picture in a magazine but she certainly liked what I did during those darkened cinema evenings. Where could we go so I could experience the ultimate of doing 'it' properly? With these serious thoughts on my mind, I phoned her from the coin-box phone by the Post Office.

"Jenny, is that you?" I asked. Her voice seemed somehow different.

"Oh John, I'm glad it's you – I'm feeling a bit low and could do with some company."

"Fancy the flicks?" I asked, knowing that she'd know what I meant.

"Great," she replied, sounding more normal. "I'll see you there in fifteen minutes."

This was our usual arrangement. I never went to her place. She never came to mine. We always met behind the cinema in the car park and went in through the back entrance. It had been her idea but it suited my book. I didn't really want to be seen too much with her in public.

The Astoria cinema had seen better days. In its heyday it must have been something. Thick-pile red carpets, marble statues, impressive windows, glitzy mirrors and long, impressive stairs up to the balcony seats. It was built like a palace in the thirties, but fifty years later it was more like a slum. The carpets were threadbare, the statues chipped and broken, the mirrors dirty, the steps uneven and the windows black with years of grime. Old posters showed stars of the past; Garbo, Bogart, Valentino. Resplendent in popular black and white fade. Graffiti artists had added glasses, moustaches and beards to the reachable ones, adding that general effect of decay.

Jenny arrived slightly late and flushed. I didn't bother to ask what was wrong. I was only interested in Jenny for one thing. I'd never bothered about her personal life.

"Let's go in, shall we?" I said, taking her hand. "We don't want to miss anything, do we?"

I bought our tickets and led her to the far end of the darkest row. Not that I needed to worry. Very few people went to the Astoria – even when it was a blockbuster of a film. Tonight's offering, 'Van Ryan's Express', was not exactly a new film and Frank Sinatra was not going to appeal to the youth of Mexfort.

As soon as we'd settled in I started kissing her with great passion. Jenny might be a dog in the daylight but in the dark she was incredible. I worked my hand into her blouse and opened her bra, giving me ready access to her very large breasts. I always found it amazing how her nipples grew with my attention. It seemed absolutely incredible. I don't know why because if I equate it to my own equipment it would seem very small beer.

I'd hardly got started when the B-picture ended and the lights came on. We quickly adjusted our clothing and I went to get an ice cream. It was our usual ritual. I often wondered if Jenny preferred the ice cream to sex. She certainly seemed to enjoy it more. Perhaps that was why she was so large. We sat and watched the advertisements. We never talked much – I wouldn't really know what to have said. Sex was all we had in common and that was all we required from each other. When I looked up, I was startled to see that Jenny was crying. It gave me a start. I'd never seen her cry. It never occurred to me that she could.

"What's wrong?" I asked.

"It's my mum," she replied, still crying. "They rushed her into hospital this afternoon. I don't know what to do. My dad left us years ago and I'm all alone."

Mum in hospital. Dad left home, what the hell were we doing in a grotty cinema when there was the luxury of an empty bed waiting at her home?

"Come on, darling," I said. "You don't want to sit in a cinema. Let's go back to your place in case the phone rings. There could be a message from the hospital for you. I'll walk you back."

I hurried her out of the cinema. It was drizzling when we hit the street, the rain shimmering against the early evening winter darkness. It wasn't the most beautiful road in the world. Rubbish was stacked up all along the edges due to some sort of industrial dispute between the council workers and the government. The vile odours coming out of the garbage didn't help the romantic flavour of the evening. Not that I was interested in romance. I was only interested in one thing that night. I was determined that nothing would stop me. Jenny seemed detached. She wasn't really with me as we slowly walked back to her house which was situated on the poorer hillside of the town. As we climbed the hill, the houses gradually got less and less attractive. The gardens were just rubbish tips with abandoned supermarket trolleys and bits of old cars forming the principal decoration. Eventually, we turned into a shabby house with a door which had once been green, but now was a dirty colour, punctuated with cracks where the wood was rotting. Jenny opened the door and a foul smell of burnt cabbage hit me.

"Sorry about the smell," she apologised. "I left the pan burning when I heard the news and I haven't been able to get rid of the smell."

"Never mind the cabbage," I said, as I helped her to remove her coat. I realised at that point I'd never seen her without her clothes. Mind you, I'd never seen any girl naked except in Mayfair or at the flicks.

"Do you want a cup of coffee?" she asked.

No, I don't want coffee, I thought. *Just you in the bedroom.* However, I thought I'd better play it cool just to be on the safe side.

"No, I'm all right. But I could do with a drink, if you know what I mean."

"Well we ain't got much, we don't keep it in the house now Dad's gone. But I think we might have some whisky." She went out, leaving me alone in the front room, which was small and shabby, with a collection of furniture that wouldn't look out of place in the Salvation Army shop in Castle Street. There was a picture of a couple on their wedding day on the sideboard. I was looking at it when Jenny returned.

"That's my mum and dad," she told me proudly. "He was all right till he took to the booze."

"When did he leave you?" I wasn't asking out of politeness, but because I ought to. She started to cry. I didn't want to upset her, that might prevent my big night.

"There, come on," I said, putting my arm round her so I could play with her breasts. "I'm here, come on." I started to kiss her. She responded immediately and before long I was working away at her breasts. Her breath quickened. *Softly, softly, catchee monkey,* I thought – kissing her as I unbuttoned her blouse. Eventually, I reached behind her to release her bra so I could play gently with her nipples. I took one into my mouth and sucked. It felt strange. But she certainly seemed to like it. I switched to the other breast as my hands moved slowly down her thighs. I touched the vital spot. I rubbed my hand up and down, her breathing got heavier and heavier. I started kissing her again, violently this time and opened the zip at the top of her skirt. The skirt fell to reveal a not very sexy pair of panties. They were, I noticed, very wet, as if she'd peed herself. My hand went back down again and I pushed my fingers into the crack as I kissed her breasts again.

"Let's go up to your room," I suggested, and led her slowly out of the room and up the stairs. The room was very small and strangely innocent. A large Paddington Bear was on the bed and around the room were pictures of horses, ponies, and a very large poster of Abba. I pushed Jenny onto the bed and removed what was left of her clothing. There she was, naked and ready. I was out of my clothes in a flash and tried to mount her.

"I can't get it in," I complained.

"I'm a virgin," she confessed. "I've never done it before."

Oh, great, I thought. I was hoping she'd be able to help me. "That means we've got to break the thingy," I said. "You'd better open your legs wider." I was getting more and more excited. I pushed and eventually the inevitable happened, I climaxed. This was certainly not how I imagined my first time.

"Oh, sod it," I shouted. "I've been and bloody come."

"Ugh, it's all sticky," Jenny complained.

While I was waiting for my erection to return I thought a bit of finger work would be sensible. I pushed in first one then two fingers and finally tried my thumb. Jenny was in seventh heaven. After a few minutes of this playing I was up and ready to try again. This time I was prepared for more effort. I pushed again.

"Stop it, you're hurting," moaned Jenny, but I was in no mood to stop. I gave one last push and broke through. Jenny screamed but I took no notice. It didn't take me long to come off. It wasn't particularly good, but I'd done it with a girl at last. Jenny was crying.

"What's up? Didn't you like it?" I asked.

"No, you hurt me and I'm sore."

"They always say it's no good for the girl the first time. Give me half an hour and I'll see if I can do it better."

When I pulled out there was a lot of blood. I was worried I'd really done some serious damage. She looked at my worried face and laughed.

"Don't worry, I think you've started my curse. It was due. I'll go and clean up. Help yourself to some more whisky."

I got dressed and went downstairs. I went into the kitchen and thought about making myself a cup of tea. I opened a teapot and saw that there was a lot of money in it.

"Stupid place to keep money," I said as I helped myself to a five pound note. I wandered out to the dingy parlour and poured myself a large tumbler of whisky and sipped it. *I'm a man*, I thought. *I've had my end away. I'm no longer a virgin*. I was very pleased with myself, particularly as I wouldn't have to see Jenny again. It couldn't have worked out better for me. At that point the phone rang.

"Hello," I said, "can I help?"

"Is that Miss Redmond's house?" It was a man. The voice was rather posh.

"Yes, you've got the right house."

"Is Miss Redmond there please?" the voice enquired.

"She is, but she's a bit busy at present. I'm a friend, can I help?"

"It's a bit awkward – it's about her mother. I'm afraid she's dead."

"I'm not bloody telling her that. Phone back in about thirty minutes."

"Thank you for being so helpful. I will call back and if you can do anything to help cushion the shock, I'd be very grateful." With that, he put the phone down.

Christ almighty, I thought. *She ain't gonna be happy when she hears the news.*

"Who was that on the phone?" called Jenny from upstairs.

"Nobody, just a bloke selling double glazing. I wound him up a bit – for a laugh – you know what I mean. I'm afraid I've gotta go now though. My dad's got some problems and I said I'd help him. I'll see you around. Thanks for everything. I'll let myself out. You needn't come down."

I went out into the dark. It was still raining, but now I didn't care. I ran down the road beating my fist into the wind. It had turned out to be a good day after all.

I didn't go straight home. I knew my parents would be rowing as usual so I headed into town to play some pinball and, if possible, to say goodbye to my mates.

Chapter 2

The Yellow Strike café was just off the High Street, on Crofton Street. It wasn't much to look at, but it was a magnet for the young of Mexfort.

"Hi, John," said Buffer as I entered the place. "I ain't seen you around for a while – what you been up to?"

"Well, you know, this and that and a bit of the other. Usual sort of thing."

"I'd like a bit of the other myself."

I should think he would. I suppose he could get lucky on a very dark night and, providing he took her down a coal mine, he might score. Otherwise he was far too revolting even to think about it.

"Hello, John," came a female voice from the back of the room. That sounded distinctly interesting. I walked back to investigate.

"Oh hello, Gail. What's going on?"

"Nothing, as usual. Nice if there were."

Gail was in my class at the Councillor Clark Comprehensive on Breacon Way. It used to be the grammar school but it got changed a few years ago. We've all got to be the same nowadays. She was fairly good looking in a young way. She hadn't got the figure that Jenny had but then again she wasn't carrying the excess baggage. I'd always quite fancied her, but Jenny was a better bet for what I wanted. Perhaps I could work a double my last weekend in Mexfort.

"Doing anything tomorrow night?" I asked nonchalantly.

"Neh, bugger all to do anyway."

"How about the flicks? Alien's on if you fancy being scared to death," I teased.

"Okay. Where are we gonna meet? Outside the Astoria?"

"Yeah, about seven. Do you want a coffee?" I added, thinking that this was looking distinctly promising. A nice end to the week.

"No thanks. I can't stay. I gotta get home. See you tomorrow."

With that she left by the back door. I couldn't see any sensible reason to stay so I decided to face the unpleasantness at home.

When I opened the front door, it was obvious that the row was still in full swing.

"Are we ever going to stay in a town more than a year?" My mum was in full cry. "You never get anything right, not even thieving. I don't know why you bother – you're pathetic. It isn't even as if you do much in the shop. You just take the money and chuck it away at the betting shop. You're bloody sick – that's what you are. A bloody loser, that's all you are, a bloody loser." She turned to me. "Well, don't just stand there, John. Do something useful, start packing. You don't want to end up like a no-hoper like your father, do you? No, you're a good boy. You got more sense. At least you got my brains. Him, he wasn't born with any."

Throughout this racket, my father just sat with his head in his hands. He looked a beaten man. His face was white as a sheet. She must have been going on at him, solid, for hours.

"Just look at him sitting there. He hasn't got an idea in his stupid head. I dunno why he bothers, he's useless. Where are we going this time, Clever Dick? Where's our next port of call? North, South, East or West? Better make sure we haven't been there before though. How many times is it now, twelve? What a bloody loser!"

Dad groaned. He launched to his feet and suddenly it was as if a monster surged out of his mouth. A horrific, dark, black-red serpent. It just kept coming. It was as if his whole insides were spewing out. It was the most horrible thing I've ever seen. He collapsed on the floor while my mother screamed and screamed. I rushed to the phone and dialled 999.

"I need an ambulance, please. Quickly, my father's dying, I think." They told me the ambulance would be there in a few minutes.

We waited for what seemed hours until it arrived and they stretchered my dad off to hospital.

It seemed impossible that he could live. My mother just sat wailing in the corner of the room like some wounded animal.

"Come on Mum, we'd better go down to the hospital to find out what's happening," I said as confidently as I could.

"He's going to die," she wailed. "I've been a bitch. I might have killed him. I didn't really mean it. I love your father." She'd certainly made a good job of hiding it. But then people were strange.

"Come on, you haven't done anything. He's got something dreadfully wrong with him," I said, trying to reassure her.

"He's going to die. I know it. We won't even be able to bury him."

"What do you mean, not able to bury him. Surely we're not that poor?"

"It's not the money – it's that dreadful strike. They've got bodies stacked up in the old meatstore. Even the gravediggers are on strike. It was on the news last night."

Of course I knew about the rubbish but it never occurred to me that the gravediggers would stop burying the dead. So much for the common band of the workers.

"He won't die. You know only the good die young, and he's certainly not one of them. Come on, let's go to the hospital."

We trudged off to catch the bus at the bottom of our road. It seemed a pity we couldn't take Dad's Cortina, but neither of us drove.

It was steadily drizzling outside and it got colder as we stood waiting. Eventually the lights of the bus emerged from the gloom and we were driven to the Victorian monstrosity which was the hospital. It seemed dirty, which I thought was wrong. I said as much to one of the other visitors as we sat in the cold, lifeless waiting room.

"It's those bloody strikes," came his reply. "Porters, cleaners, even the nurses are all on bloody strike. The whole country's grinding to a halt. They said on the news we'll be poorer than Albania, the way we're going."

We all sat quietly awaiting news from the main part of the hospital. Eventually Florence Nightingale came to see us.

"Mrs Rich?" she asked.

"Yes, I'm Mrs Rich," replied Mum.

"Your husband's had a very serious internal haemorrhage. The trouble is that it happened about five days ago, but he either didn't know about it or he was too frightened to admit it. It's going to be touch and go but he's probably going to be all right. He's a very sick man, and I'm afraid he'll be in hospital for a long time."

"Can I see him?" asked Mum quietly.

"No, he's unconscious now, but he should be ready for a very short visit tomorrow evening. There's no point in staying, so I'd go home. Leave your phone number and if there's any major change we'll phone you."

"There, I said he'd be all right," I told Mum as we returned home.

"It's all right for him, isn't it? He's in hospital. What about us? We've got to face the investigation on Monday," she said in despair.

"Oh Christ, I'd forgotten that. Well, we'll just have to bluff it out – I'll stay home from school if you like."

"No, thanks. You're a good boy, but I'll just tell 'em I know nothing. With him in hospital they won't be too bad, will they?" The words were spoken more in hope than with much confidence.

Lying in bed that night, I reflected life had become very complicated. I'd expected to be out of Mexfort by Monday so I wouldn't have to see Jenny or Gail, let alone the investigation team. It looked like we'd be here for a long time, so I had to make up my mind what to do.

I certainly wouldn't mind going on with Gail, but I couldn't keep both of them going. Thinking of what I'd like to do to Gail, I fell asleep. I had a dreadful night. I woke up very early next morning just as it was getting light. I got dressed and crept downstairs. For about the first time in my life, I took Mum a cup of tea.

"What's all this? Turning over a new leaf?" she asked. "Will I get one every morning now?"

"I doubt it. It's just that I couldn't get back to sleep. I kept having nightmares. Dad will be all right, won't he?"

"Of course he will, he's too bad to die, you said so yourself. What are you going to do with yourself today?"

"I've got a job at the market. It doesn't pay very well, but at least it's some money. I did have a sort of date this evening. I ought to cancel it and come with you to the hospital."

"Don't do that – I doubt if you'll be allowed in. No, you have your date. Is she nice?"

Nice wasn't exactly what I had in mind but I suppose she might be nice to me, but Mum wouldn't want to hear that. "I think so, she's in my class at school."

"Well enjoy yourself. You're only young once."

I certainly hoped I would enjoy myself. It would be nice to explore a new body. *I wonder if she does go the whole way?* I thought. Only one way to find out, though.

Down the market I worked for a pig of a man called Warts. His real name was Smith but as his face was all lumpy everywhere; everyone called him Warts. He paid virtually nothing and all the casual workers reckoned he expected them to steal so he wasn't going to overpay us.

"Don't pinch more than five pounds a day," I was told by Jake, another of the Saturday boys. "Just take the odd fifty pence, never ever take a fiver. You might get away with a quid, but be very careful."

I'd taken his advice and stolen my pound each time I worked there. It was bloody hard work though, loading those spuds into the trays. Those sacks were very heavy. You wouldn't believe how many potatoes were sold during a day. The most I counted was eighty sacks, and that was just potatoes, and there were the carrots and the onions as well. In between we served customers, which was where we could pilfer a bit of the loose change. As you took the money you transferred fifty pence into your other hand, went off to get another bag of potatoes and pocketed the cash as you went. When you had a break, you wrapped the coins up into a handkerchief, so that they didn't jingle.

I preferred serving the customers. The women liked me and I enjoyed the back-chat.

"What do you cost to the pound, love?" asked a middle-aged woman in an artificial leopard-skin coat.

"More than you could afford," I replied cheekily.

"Do you deliver?" asked another suggestively. I knew she wasn't talking about vegetables!

"Depends when you want anything delivered and what, if you know what I mean." I flashed her my cheeky smile. It never fails to get them going.

There was one particular lady, a cut above the average, who I really fancied. Pretty in an expensive sort of way, a good dresser, well-spoken and she had a really good figure. Very slim with fabulous blonde hair. I had a few good dreams about her, I can tell you. She was always very nice to me and smiled the sort of smile you could die for. It was interesting how she always seemed to buy her vegetables when I was serving.

"Is the asparagus good this week?" she asked me, flashing that gorgeous smile of hers.

"I wouldn't bother if I were you – they're a bit iffy, if you know what I mean."

"In that case I'll have the calabrese then – yes, that piece will do – and four zucchini please."

I picked out the best courgettes I could for her. I loved the way she called them zucchini. Apparently it was the Italian.

"Are they firm?" she asked.

I looked straight at her small but perfectly formed breasts. *I should say so,* I thought.

"I really want them soft so I can have them tonight."

I realised she was looking at the avocados. *Christ, just think of opening that blouse and exposing those,* I thought lustfully.

"I'll find you some ripe ones. How many do you want?" I asked.

"Two would be fine and thank you for being so helpful. I suppose I couldn't ask you a favour, could I?"

She said this softly. I immediately thought of the favours I could easily do her.

"'Course, what is it?"

"I'm an artist and I'd like to draw you. I've been looking at you for some weeks and you've got just the sort of face I'd like to sketch. I'd like you as a model. Would you be interested in another job? I'd pay you well."

Biting back the comment that I'd pay her just to come to the house, I stammered out, "I-I-I'd like to, I could do with the money. When do you want me to come, tomorrow?" *Oh I'd love to come tomorrow,* I thought. *God, would I!*

"No, it'll have to be next Wednesday evening. Can you come about five? Here's my card so you'll know the address."

"I'll be there and I'll be the best model you've ever had."

"I hope so," she said, smiling.

With that, she paid and walked off. I watched her go, daydreaming of me and her. I looked at her card. Georgina Radcliffe. *I love you Georgina Radcliffe*, I thought. I imagined us on some desert island, romping in the blue water stark naked.

"Rich, for fuck's sake get on with some bloody potatoes!" shouted Warty. "You're standing there like a wet Sunday. Move it."

I came back to the reality of a cold, wet November and the necessity of moving tons of potatoes. Wednesday night would be different. I'd be posing for Georgina.

Chapter 3

I got back about six and was greeted by a very upset Mum.

"Dad's in intensive care!" she cried. "I can visit, but only for a few minutes. He's not good. It's touch and go. I just don't know what to do."

I'd never seen Mum look so upset. I had never thought of her as old but she certainly looked it now. It hadn't been easy for her. Dad was a compulsive gambler – he'd bet on anything. He did win occasionally but he quickly lost his winnings. The bookies gave him credit, but when he didn't pay they threatened him. He was a weak man so he stole from the shops he managed. It was always the same story. Shop after shop, town after town. There was my mum, always packing and unpacking and trying to pick up the pieces, never knowing when the knock on the door would herald yet another move. She must have loved him otherwise she would have left him years ago. What a bloody mess their life was. I vowed I'd be different. I would make something of myself. I'd go and see the world. I'd live in a big house with a swimming pool and drive a flash car. I wouldn't be another loser like Dad.

"I'm off to the hospital. See you later, love. There's a casserole in the oven, help yourself."

"Thanks Mum. Give my love to Dad."

I ate a bowl of very uninspiring casserole. Mum was never a great cook but this was poor even by her standards. I washed and shaved, changed my shirt and splashed Brut all over. *I wonder how far I'll get tonight*, I thought as I hurried to the Astoria. *Now I'm going to be around for a few more weeks I needn't rush it, which'll make it easier.*

Gail was already at the Astoria. She seemed very young compared to Mrs Radcliffe. Her clothes were smartish but looked cheap. Mind you, I liked the short skirt she was wearing.

"Hi, Gail. Been waiting long?" I said.

"No, I've just got here. I've been thinking – I don't really want to see Aliens, couldn't we go and see one of the other films?" she asked, smiling at me.

"There isn't mush choice. There's Van Ryan's Express. I don't know about you but I ain't going to Bambi, that's for sure, so if we're going to go anywhere it better be Van Ryan's Express." *Sinatra again*, I thought. *But who cares? I don't really want to see the film anyway.*

"I'd like that," said Gail, smiling at me. A smile that really didn't begin to stand up against Mrs Radcliffe's.

I bought two tickets and was very pleasantly surprised to find the auditorium almost empty. I guided us to the back of a dark row, putting Gail against the wall so nobody could see what we were doing. We started kissing. She wasn't very good at it. Jenny was far better – she had more practice. I put my arm round her shoulders and casually started to stroking her. I gradually worked it so I could play with her nipples. She seemed to enjoy it but she didn't react in the same way as Jenny did. I bought my other hand into play and opened on both sides at the same time. It was amazing the difference between the two girls. Whereas Jenny's breasts were large, Gail's were the opposite. I assumed it was because of her age and that they would grow as she got older. I dropped my hand onto her leg and started to work upwards.

"No," she said firmly, pushing it away and at the same time removing my hand from her breast. "I want to watch the film."

I'd never seen Van Ryan's Express before and was surprised how good it was. During the film I made another couple of excursions into forbidden territory and had some success. *Another night, perhaps,* I thought. By the time Van Ryan was shot trying to clamber aboard his train, I'd certainly established a base for further exploration.

I walked Gail home, stopping for many long kisses. I arranged to take her out again in a couple of days. My dreams that night were far more interesting. Not only was I making up to Gail but also to Mrs Radcliffe. It was fantastic. I woke up to find my pyjama trousers soaking wet. I supposed that's what they meant by wet dreams.

*

Dad's condition had deteriorated during the night and Mum phoned to say that she had decided to stay at the hospital for the whole day. I lay in bed most of the morning reading a battered copy of Mayfair that I hid in my wardrobe. I got myself a fried egg sandwich for lunch and spent the rest of the day reading the News of the World, watching television and waiting for Mum to get back. Eventually at around nine o'clock the front door opened and Mum came in looking very worried.

"How's Dad?" I asked.

"Not good, I'm afraid. It's still very much touch and go. All we can do is pray."

She made us a cup of coffee and we went to bed early ready to face the ordeal of the morning.

*

The next morning I decided not to go to school. I decided I'd wait in my bedroom with the door slightly open. That would mean I would be able to hear everything that happened from the shop. If Mum wanted my help I'd be there and available. As they'd promised, the inspectors arrived at about ten o'clock. There were two of them, the bald one from last Friday and a new one, a rather serious tall man in a pinstriped suit. He seemed to be the boss and did most of the talking.

"Good morning, Mrs Rich, I'd like to see your husband please."

"I'm afraid that's impossible," said Mum, who was almost in tears. "He's in the intensive care wing in hospital."

"Oh, is he? And when did this happen?" said the man, in a voice which showed that he wasn't convinced that what Mum was saying was true.

"He collapsed on Friday evening after your friend's visit," said Mum.

"Oh dear, that's very awkward," said the tall one. "I suppose we couldn't talk to the hospital just to find out how long he's likely to be in there just for planning purposes?" he enquired.

I thought, *The miserable bastard he doesn't believe a word of it. He wants just to check up to see we're not lying.*

"I suppose so," said Mum, somewhat dubiously.

"What hospital is he in?"

"The Royal Victoria."

He dialled the number.

"Ah, good morning. I believe you've got a Mr Rich in intensive care, I wonder if I could speak to somebody to find out how he is?" There was a pause. "Ah hello, yes, my name's Sinclair – I'm Mr Rich's employer and very concerned about him. How is he? Oh. I see. Yes, yes, I quite understand. Oh dear. Yes, it would be, wouldn't it? Thank you very much and give him my best wishes."

Mr Sinclair put down the phone.

"Yes, well this does make things very awkward. Mrs Rich, could I ask you to make us a cup of tea? I'd like to discuss a few things with my colleague here, in private."

Mum went out of the room to put the kettle on.

"Would you shut the door as you go out please, Mrs Rich?"

I slipped down the stairs and put my ear to the door. "This is a little bit awkward. He is very ill, in fact it's touch and go whether he'll live. I don't think a prosecution would make any sense at all under the circumstances. I think I'd better phone the office just to get approval for what to do next."

There was a short pause while he dialled the number and then I was able to hear his end of the conversation very clearly. It was pretty obvious what was being said at the other end.

"Hello, Sinclair here. Yes, we're at the shop. We've got a bit of a problem with Rich though. He's in hospital, seriously ill. Yes, yes, that's what I thought at first but I have phoned the hospital and checked. It's pretty certain – he really is very ill. Yes, I agree, it would be pointless prosecuting. The man might die and we'd look pretty sick if we seemed to be persecuting the widow. But I've checked the lease; it runs out in two months. The shop's never made any money. I think the best thing is to close it. Yes, yes I agree. You'll send a lorry round will you? Yes, I'll wait – and can you send an accountant with it, someone independent? We might as well make out a case just to be on the safe side. Yes, I'll talk to Mrs Rich and explain the circumstances. I don't think there'll be any problems. Yes, I agree. Very unpleasant thing to have to be do. Right, I'll see you back in the office. Fine."

"I've got the tea," said Mum, coming back with a tray. I moved out of sight as she opened the door.

"Oh thank you very much, Mrs Rich, that's very kind of you. I don't take sugar, but Ron here, he likes one. Very nice, thank you. Um – we've got a bit of a problem with the shop, I'm afraid. You probably know it's been losing money for some time and the lease runs out in a couple of months. I'm afraid the company have decided to close it. It seemed the best option. The rent's paid up for the next couple of months, so you and your son can stay until then. I'm afraid you'll have to go in two months, though, when we vacate the shop. I'm sorry about this but it's the best we can do under the circumstances." He looked at her piercingly and there was no doubt about what he meant. "We're not going to re-open this shop. We'll be sending a lorry round this morning and we'll remove all the stock. I'm sorry to have to give you this bad news when your husband's in hospital but I'm afraid it's one of those things."

"What about his money?" asked Mum. "Will you pay him for the next two months?"

"Ah," said Mr Sinclair, "I hadn't thought of that one. I'll have to check with head office and let you know."

They sat drinking the tea and chatting until the lorry arrived for all the sweets, magazines, cigarettes and fancy goods. By eleven o'clock the shop was empty. After they'd gone I came down to join Mum.

"Did you hear all that?" asked Mum.

"Yes, and a lot more when you were out of the room. They were definitely going to prosecute. They've still got a strong case if we're awkward. I think two months rent-free accommodation and perhaps two months' pay isn't too bad."

"Yes," Mum replied, "it's certainly better than having to do the usual runner. I think I'll go down to the Council today to see if I can get some sort of accommodation when we have to leave here. We should get good benefits if we're being evicted." She sighed and reached for a cigarette. "Well, at least that's over. Let's just hope your father pulls through."

I could hardly wait until Wednesday evening came. I had a bath, shaved, did my hair nicely, put on plenty of Brut, put on my smartest clothes, admired myself in the mirror and then left to keep my appointment, feeling nervous, as if I was going to do something important, like meet a new boss.

Mrs Radcliffe's house was very modern. It was on the new estate to the north of the town. It had a wrought iron bell-pull next to a large Victorian coach lamp and the whole house looked imposing and expensive. I could see myself reflected in the glass on the front door. I hardly recognised myself. I had just started to wear contact lenses and it made a huge difference. I'd always hated wearing glasses. I had grown quite a bit lately and I had taken to wearing my brown hair quite long. I thought I was looking good. I straightened my jacket, smoothed my hair, then pulled the bell. Mrs Radcliffe opened the door. She was dressed in what looked like a dressing gown but I assumed it was her working overalls.

"Come in," she said. She sounded pleased to see me! "I've being looking forward to drawing you. Let's go straight up to my studio."

Her studio was in a converted spare bedroom. An easel stood at one end with various paint boxes, packets of paper, paintings and sketches in various forms, some finished, some unfinished. There was a spare bed in one corner.

"Did I ask you to bring your shorts?" she said. "I'd like to draw you as a sportsman."

"No, you didn't mention shorts," I said nervously. If I'd been wearing shorts I knew I wouldn't be able to disguise how I was feeling about Mrs Radcliffe.

"I suppose your pants will be fairly decent," she said. "Can you strip down to your pants then? I'll go out and make it easier for you."

I took off my clothes and was grateful that I'd had a bath and put on clean underwear. As Mum always said, you should always wear clean underwear – you never know when you're going to be knocked down and taken to hospital. I sat on the bed trying to disguise the erection I was developing, hoping that it wouldn't be too obvious.

Mrs Radcliffe came back, looked at me and smiled a sort of knowing smile. She came right over to me. It was at that point that my further education was started. Some people go to Oxford or Cambridge to get a degree. In my case I went to Mrs Radcliffe's academy and became an expert on what pleases a lady. I was putty in her hands. Mind you, not for long. Her hands were exceptionally talented.

That afternoon was followed by many others during the next few weeks; she was the professor and I was the very willing pupil. It was every teenage boy's fantasy – a beautiful, sophisticated woman teaching me all about sex. It was certainly not romantic, it was all done very clinically. She knew exactly what she wanted and she made sure that I followed her every instruction. We did everything I'd ever read about in Mayfair and a lot more, and I was disappointed when eventually, after about three weeks, she told me one evening that her husband was coming back the next day and we'd have to stop meeting. She gave me a very nice sketch of myself and wished me all the best for the future. It was all very strange but I'll always be grateful for Mrs Radcliffe. I'd already started putting some of the lessons to good use. Gail was the first of many girls to benefit from Mrs Radcliffe's kind instruction.

As I arrived home Mum seemed to be in a much better mood.

"Is Dad better?" I asked.

"No, there's no change there but at least I've found us somewhere to live. My sister's got a flat in Clacton-on-Sea; she said we can use it and pay a very low rent. It's on the sea so it'll be nice for your father to recuperate in."

Mum spent most of her time at the hospital now, waiting whilst the doctors fought to save Dad's life. They kept giving him blood transfusions but as fast as they gave him more blood, he haemorrhaged again. In the end, he suffered brain damage and the last time I saw him, he didn't even know me. I hardly recognised him either; he had turned into a frail old skeleton of a man. He never saw our new home in Clacton. He never left the hospital. He suffered a heart attack late one evening. Mum was with him and held his hand at the end, which gave her great comfort.

The funeral was a sad affair, very few people turned up. Mr Sinclair of the company came, which I thought was a nice touch. The vicar got Dad's name wrong in his speech. The pallbearers dropped the coffin just before it went into the grave and in all, it was a disastrous funeral. The day after the funeral we packed our meagre possessions and Mum and I moved down to Clacton-on-Sea for a new future.

*

I decided not to go back to school and as soon as I got down to Clacton-on-Sea I started to look for a job. It was a time of high unemployment and of course I hadn't got any qualifications. The only thing for me, apparently, was work experience and a year's training scheme where you weren't working for the company but there was every chance they'd take you on when you had finished your training.

I was sent for an interview with the managing director of a stamp and coin company that ran a mail-order business from offices on the High Street. At first I had to wait in the secretary's office. Mind you, I didn't mind as she was gorgeous and I sat thinking what I would like to do to her if I got the chance.

Eventually she took me in to see the boss, a very tall, kind-looking man. He was smartly dressed in a light grey suit and I suppose older women would say that he was handsome. Once he started, he surprised me by doing most of the talking, rather than asking me questions. He asked me if I played cricket and I told him I had done at school and liked it very much. This seemed to go down well. I also told him I had collected stamps as a child. Mr Cheshire, that was his name, seemed pleased with this too. He stood up, smiled at me and told me he would give me a chance. I was to start the following Monday.

Great, I thought as I went on home. I'd got my foot on the first rung of the ladder of success.

PART II

MARK CHESHIRE

Chapter 4

An optimist sees that a glass of beer is half full; a pessimist thinks it's half empty. I just want to drink it and get on with whatever I'm doing. My wife, Beth, reckons I should be called Previous as I always want things done before they happen. If I were a child I'd be described as hyperactive. After all, why do one thing when you can do two at the same time, or even three? I'm full of home-spun wisdom, though again, Beth would say I was full of something completely different!

I should never have been a businessman; my father's dream was that I should play cricket (for Surrey) since you ask. I was tall and strong and had double-jointed thumbs which made me perfectly designed to be a fast in-swing bowler. My father was cricket-mad and had put me down for membership of the MCC on the day I was born. I've no idea what he would have done if I'd been a girl. He would never have taken to rounders.

My first real panic came just after the O-levels when I found that I'd done rather badly. It was, as far as I was concerned, a nuisance to have exams during the peak of the evening cricket season. I might have failed most of my exams for lack of revision, but on the other hand I had two medals and a large silver cup for the best bowling figures of the season. Unfortunately, they didn't count as qualifications for my future. I was sent for by the Headmaster and given clear alternatives. I could either leave and try to get a job with very few qualifications behind me, or go into the Remove and get stuck in.

The idea of going out to work just didn't appeal, but luckily it was not the cricket season so I knuckled down and managed to get a further seven O-levels by Christmas to add to my original three. I then passed my A-levels and went to a fashionable new university on the south coast. I chose it mostly because I fancied three years by the sea, and there was a county cricket ground not too far from the campus. In the back of my mind I still fancied being a professional cricketer.

By the time I got to college, I'd had quite a few girlfriends and I thought some were reasonably serious, but when I met Beth, I realised all of them had simply been just good friends.

It's funny how your whole life can change so quickly; one minute I was eyeing up the talent at the Saturday night hop, the next – *wham!* – I was in love. I know it sounds stupid, the sort of thing that only happens in soppy love songs, but in my case, it was true. I saw this small girl with long blonde hair and I was immediately attracted. I couldn't honestly tell you why. She was gorgeous, but lots of other girls were just as attractive. Perhaps it was that she looked vulnerable, so small against all the others that she brought out my masculine protective instinct. I can still remember her looking at me with her piercing blue eyes when I at last got up the courage to ask her for a dance. After that, we were inseparable, that is, other than after the weekly rows, when we had the obligatory forced absence followed by the passionate making-up.

Beth was incredibly intelligent, although she'd learned to hide it as it frightened off most men. She had the uncanny knack of being able to put her finger on the root of a problem which, to most people, looked too complicated. This skill was to help us enormously in our future business. But that was looking ahead. At that time I was still working to be a professional cricketer.

The first turning point in my cricket career was during a match between my club team and a County eleven.

"They want to have a good look at you," said Tommy, our cunning old fox of a captain. "Do the business and who knows? You could be in the county team next month."

Tommy always knew how to get the best out of players. He was a natural motivator – he could read me like a book. He didn't let me open the bowling, which annoyed me more than I can tell you. I always opened. How was I going to get into the county team if he didn't let me show what I could do? By the time he called me into the attack I was extremely angry. I understand now of course, it was all part of his physiological game plan.

"Cheshire, this is your big chance. The ball is swinging, the pitch is nicely damp, just bowl as you do every game for us and you'll be in that county team."

They say you need a slice of luck in life and I have to admit I was extremely lucky to start with. My first ball was bad, luckily the batsman wasn't used to rubbish and in his excitement to score a six, he mis-hit and got caught. The next man in was the opposing captain, fresh from scoring a ton against the Australian tourists the week before. Everybody offered me advice.

"Pitch it up."

"Keep it short."

"Bowl on his legs, he doesn't like it there."

"Make sure it's outside the off stump, he'll murder you if you stray onto his legs."

"Bowl him a slower ball."

"Put your back into it, let it fly."

In the end, confused with all the conflicting advice, I just bowled it. It was the dream delivery, it moved in the air to leg and then seamed away. He was good enough to touch it. It was easy, really. I went on to take seven wickets and Tommy's prediction came true. I was playing minor county cricket the next month. I caught the attention of the nationals when I played in the Gillette Cup. I was called up for a trial, and was given three games to prove myself. These went well and it looked like I would be offered a contract, and my father's dream and mine would come true.

I had the best girl in the world and my career was looking good; I didn't think things could get better, but I was wrong. The first team opening bowler was called up to play against Australia, his partner was ill and I was asked to play against Hampshire, the county champions.

"I'm so proud of you!" said Beth before the game. "Go and show them what you can do."

It was almost as if I'd saved my best for this big occasion. I got six wickets in the first innings as well as running their best player out. I even scored ten in a low-scoring game. I bagged a further five wickets in the second innings and one national paper asked whether I was a future England player. We only needed a low score to win so as I took Beth out after the second day, I was convinced that as I was always the last to bat, I wouldn't be needed on the last day.

Hampshire were not the champions for nothing. The wicket was helpful and they had one of the world's best fast bowlers. I found myself walking out to the middle with my team needing thirty runs to win. There was no way I could play defensively, I was not a good enough batsman, and so I decided it would be death or glory. I swung my bat like a club and as so often happens, fortune favoured the brave. I struck six fours, admittedly not all were off the face of the bat, but we now only needed six to win. I don't remember much about the last ball; it was short and I saw a chance to hook it for six. I flung my bat at the ball and then all went black.

It was a few days later when Beth told me what

happened. She sat on the edge of the bed and held my hand. She didn't need to touch me to let me know she was there, I sensed her presence immediately she walked into the room. She leant over and kissed me gently.

"Hello, you," she said. "Look what you've done to yourself." Her voice was gentle. I asked her what I had done.

"You sliced the ball straight into your left eye. You were out cold for thirty-six hours in intensive care." Her fingers squeezed mine. "The doctors feared for your life. When you eventually came round the worry was brain damage." Although I couldn't see her face, I could sense she was trying not to cry. Her voice changed as she smiled. "I knew there was no danger of that as you are thick-skulled, and besides, you need a brain to damage!"

I held on to her hand and just prayed that one day I would be able to see her again. I reached out and touched her face. It was wet. I wished I could just hug her, but I had so many tubes in my arms I had to lie still.

The County paid for all my expenses and the Hampshire bowler kept visiting me, even though it wasn't his fault. Eventually after three weeks of grapes and boredom, they took the bandages off for the first time. I realised that I could see very little with my left eye, just blurred outlines against a dark grey background, but I was allowed to go home. The consultant came to see me before I left.

"Mark, you have been exceptionally lucky; a blow like that could have killed you or at the least made you into a cabbage. The good news is that your vision will probably improve gradually, though it will never be as good as it was. You will probably need glasses, but we will wait a few months until the injury has had time to heal completely. There is some bad news, I'm afraid, and you won't like it. We've saved your eye for the moment but you must give up all violent and energetic things, which means no cricket."

He saw my face fall at that news. "I know what this means to you. I was at the ground on the first day and saw you get six wickets, so I do understand but I'm afraid you have no choice."

It was hard to take in; I'd opened the door to my future career and had it slammed in my face before I'd even started.

As one door closes, another often opens. My dream of playing professional cricket died and I was forced to re-examine my life. I don't know what I would have done without Beth. She was the one thing I could always depend on. It was her strength that helped get me through. Gradually, I realised that life had to go on. Luckily I still had a year left at university, so I flung myself into my studies. It was difficult at first, but as my sight improved and the headaches became less frequent, I really got interested in the work. Considering my two wasted years, I was delighted to leave university with a 2.1 degree in sociology.

After our three-year honeymoon, we decided to make it legal and we married and set up home in Clacton-on-Sea. Beth got a post at the local Grammar School. I joined the council and got a job as a social worker. I soon found out that disappointing as my injury was, it was nothing compared to what had happened to many of the youngsters I had in my care. It was a real eye-opener to go into their homes, hear their sad stories and understand what bad luck really was. In many ways these experiences made me a far better person, but it did make me more vulnerable as I always looked for an excuse for bad behaviour.

We hadn't been married all that long when Beth caught a nasty virus. It took her a long time to get her strength back and she no energy for anything but her work. This meant that I had lot of time on my hands in the evenings and at weekends with nothing to do, so I started a business based on my hobby, stamp collecting. My idea was that it would pay for my own collection.

At first I made up display boards with packets of stamps mounted on them. These I placed in local shops. They, in return, got thirty percent of the take with no risk. At my peak, I had over fifty shops selling my stamps and covers. It was extremely hard work, but sales were good and I ploughed all the profits back into the business.

I can still vividly remember those cold wet Saturdays. I had to somehow visit at least ten shops, checking and replacing the stock which had been sold, invoicing and collecting the money that was owed to me. In most cases it was a fairly straight forward job, but in some cases, getting the money was like getting blood out of a stone.

I don't know why, but it always seemed to pour on Saturdays. Monday to Friday would be fine, but as soon as Saturday dawned, down came the rain. Despite the weather, I enjoyed those hectic Saturdays. I felt I was achieving something and success is a powerful stimulant.

It certainly made a change from my depressing social work. I had to keep reminding myself that I was dealing with the unfortunate minority and that not all lives were so sad. It did tend to wear me down, seeing so much suffering and feeling so powerless to do anything about it.

I found that envelopes bearing new stamps, dated on the first day the public could buy them, were popular. These first day covers, as they were called, soon became the major part of my business. Each shop was selling an average of twenty envelopes a time which meant that I was selling over a thousand first day covers for each new stamp issue. Friends, neighbours, and colleagues at work also bought them and soon I had over two hundred local customers as well. The business grew quickly and it was obvious I had a potential winner on my hands. As a great friend kept telling me, I had a tiger by the tail. The question was, should I give up my safe, pensionable career and take the ultimate risk, putting my fate in my own hands? Beth and I talked it over and she made the final choice.

"Look, we can live on my teaching salary while you get things going. If you can do as well as you are just working part-time, then think what you could do if you put all your efforts into it. After all, this is the time to try it. There's only us to worry about and if things go wrong, you can always get another job."

That's how the Cheshire Stamp Company came about.

Chapter 5

I should never have made us work so hard, but when you first take the decision to leave safe employment, the fear of failure drives you on. We had a mortgage to pay and because I had no track-record in business, naturally the banks were not very keen to lend to me. This meant that money was always tight, particularly just before each new stamp issue. The Post Office insisted on cash with order, and I do mean cash. They wouldn't accept cheques and so I had to draw the money from the bank and walk it over to the Post Office. I always had the nightmare that one day I'd be mugged, would have no money to pay for the stamps and so would be ruined. We were allowed to have the stamps a week before the issue date so we could get them stuck onto the envelopes, but if we failed to get them to the relevant Post Office, which could be in anywhere from Land's End to John o' Groats, then the Post Office would refuse to postmark them and again we could be ruined. Although we paid for the stamps a week early, our shop customers, who took most of our covers, didn't pay us for at least six weeks. They had to wait for their customers to pay them first.

It was frightening watching for the money to come back in so we could buy the next stamps. I know that Beth worried even more than I did about it, but she never showed it, remaining apparently calm through even the worst crisis. During our early days, we regularly worked a twelve-hour day as well as exhibiting at stamp fairs on Saturdays and Sundays. These took place all over the country and involved driving thousands of miles – one year we drove forty thousand miles! It was, however, the heavy lifting that caused Beth's problems. In my own mind, I'm sure that this was the prime cause of Beth's dreadful miscarriage. The guilt of being so selfish preyed heavily on my mind.

Gradually we began to see the light at the end of the tunnel and hoped that it wasn't just the lights of the oncoming train! By the time Beth became ill and had to give up her job, the company had turned the corner and was making good profits. We were no longer working from our back bedroom and had moved into purpose-built offices in the town. They were a little too big for us to start with, but as our orders increased and we took on staff to help us, we soon filled all the available space to overflowing. Among the staff who joined the company at that time was Charles, who soon became head of my accounts department. He originally applied for a job as a book-keeper, saying on his application form that he'd been a bank manager. I assumed it was a small bank but I was wrong. He had in fact been the manager of a Lombard Street bank, but that was before he got a promotion to become Area Manager of the City Branches and finally he joined the board of one of the major five banks. Charles was an impressive grey-haired man with a neat grey moustache. He had an air about him of tremendous confidence and stature. He was so confident that if no-one made the tea he'd make it himself and take it around the entire company, and even give it to the work experience lads. He was like that. He was always called Mr Cox by the other staff and commanded tremendous respect. Although technically he worked for me, I never quite saw the relationship in that light. He was more like a father to me and I enjoyed having the benefit of his superb intelligence around to discuss ideas.

As space was getting tight, Beth and I decided that it would be a good idea to open a shop, which would give us more room for our stock and, hopefully, be self-financing. Beth refused point-blank to work in the shop. She said she was temperamentally unsuited to sitting alone most of the day sorting stock. I knew that I couldn't tie myself down there either; I needed to be out and about to keep working the business, so I hired a man I had known for years. He was a keen stamp collector and small-time dealer, and he jumped at the chance to earn his living working at his hobby. The shop was so successful that I set up a second shop in Southwold. Although the town was very small, it was the sort of place collectors would travel to on a day out with the family. This time I employed Jim Smith, a leading light from the local philatelic society to manage it. He had been unemployed for some time as he was not a well man, but he was popular and knowledgeable. Work in a stamp shop was ideal for him, not too taxing.

I thought things were looking good. I'd even bought myself the car of the year, a green Rover, which was ideal for taking the stock to the provincial stamp shows. We appeared to be getting our lives back on track when we were hit by two separate disasters.

I was having one of those days from hell. I was naïve enough to think that things couldn't get worse when Jim phoned me from Southwold. He was in obvious distress.

"Mark, I don't know how to say this," he started.

"Well, do your best," I replied irritably. The events of the morning had meant my patience was not quite as it should have been.

"We've had a theft." He dragged the words out reluctantly.

"Not shoplifters again!" I replied. It was one of the problems of all stamp and coin shops. We were always plagued by shoplifters, both amateur and professional. "What have they taken this time?"

"No, not shoplifters. Someone has stolen my display rack with all the best stock in it."

"What!" I shouted. "The whole rack! No shoplifter could do that, surely? It's too big. You'd have seen it going out of the door!"

"That's what I'm trying to say. We've had a burglary over lunchtime. There's no sign of a break-in though. I can't understand it. It's almost as if they had a key."

I sensed that he was close to breaking point. He was almost crying down the phone.

"OK, Jim. Calm down a bit. Have you sent for the police?"

"Yes, I did that straight away, Mark. They'll be here soon, I hope. I just don't know what to do."

"Well for a start, you had better try to work out

how much we've lost."

"That's fairly easy. I've only just done the stock-taking. We haven't sold much out of that rack. I reckon it was at least thirty thousand pounds."

"Thirty thousand pounds!" *Oh God,* I thought. Grabbing at straws, I asked, "Retail or cost?"

"I'm afraid it's cost, Mark. Retail would be more like seventy. Wait a minute, I think the police are here. I'd better ring off. Could you come over? I'd be grateful."

"Yes, of course I will." I could see he needed support.

I sat looking at the wall. Thirty thousand pounds was a lot of money.

Hoping that the day had no more unpleasant surprises, I hurried over to the scene of the crime.

The police immediately suspected the shop manager, Jim Smith. They put him through a horrifying interrogation from which he never really recovered. He was not well anyway. At the beginning it really did look as though it could have been him, but I always had my doubts. It had to be an inside job, that much was obvious. There was no sign of a break-in and Jim looked very guilty. He was shifty, sweated a lot, and continually shook when the police asked him questions.

The police talked to all the staff. I realised halfway through my interview that they thought I might have done it for the insurance. There are few things worse than theft, which brings the police poking their noses into your business. They suspect everybody, and their manner is not very pleasant. There was only one member of our staff exempt from the investigation and that was Major Roger Williams, who had recently joined the company. He was a retired intelligence officer looking for a new career and as a stamp collector, he was keen to work with his hobby. Despite being the outsider, he made a good impression when I interviewed him for the position of office manager.

I remember asking him an important question. "You've got no real qualifications for this particular job. Why should I take you on rather than any of the others?"

His reply was a classic. I can always remember it word for word.

"I totally understand your point, and I would certainly feel the same way if I were in your shoes. I'm not exactly qualified; however, I am a very knowledgeable stamp collector. I'd be expensive at first and it would be presumptuous of me to expect to be well paid during my learning curve. I have an army pension so I would be happy to take a smaller salary for the first year on the clear understanding that it would be reviewed if everything goes well. I can promise that should you give me a chance, I would certainly take all the opportunities I get."

I looked at the tall, rugged, ex-army officer, wearing his tweed jacket and grey flannels, shiny brown brogues, short hair and unmistakable military style and I thought, *What the hell!* It could be an excellent move. So I took him on. In retrospect, I learned quite a lot from that load of old army bull.

Roger couldn't possibly have been involved in this theft as he had been driving up to York with his current lover to deliver some first day covers to the Post Office for a special postmark. The police didn't even talk to him at first. The day itself had been very odd. I'd had problems all morning, many of them as it later turned out were caused by Roger's carelessness. I was getting rather ratty by mid-morning and it didn't help to get a very strange phone call.

"Mark. It's Roger. Can you ring me back?" I scribbled the number down as he rattled it off to me. Then he rang off at once.

I didn't like the sound of this at all.

Oh God! I thought. *What's happened? An accident? Have the covers all burnt?* It was one of my worst nightmares. We had no real insurance for such a calamity and we'd be in a catch 22 situation. All we would get from our policy would be what we'd paid, whereas the finished envelopes would be worth five times that. Even worse, the Post Office wouldn't replace them. This would mean that Beth and I were ruined. We had already signed personal guarantees to the bank, and they'd take everything. All these flashed through my mind. I dialled the number.

"Hello, Roger. Don't tell me you've got a problem, that's all I need."

"I've arrived safely and delivered the covers."

"Well, that's something! So what do you want?"

"I'm going to get petrol now. I'll be back late this evening. I thought you'd want me to report. Bye." With that, he rung off and I was left holding a silent receiver. I screwed up the piece of paper I had written the number on and chucked it in the bin. *What was all that about?* I thought. Then another call came in and I had to get on.

*

"Roger's gone batty," I said to Beth as we had our coffee. "I honestly don't know how he got into the Intelligence Corps. Why on earth should I be interested in his petrol consumption? It beats me."

"Perhaps he wants brownie points," laughed Beth. It was nice to hear her laugh again. I hadn't realised how much I'd missed it.

So Roger was the one person who couldn't possibly have taken the stamps.

On his return from York next day he took charge of the whole investigation for us. He questioned Jim again, he liaised with the police, and he even went on regional television on the local Crimewatch programme.

"Anyone buying these stamps is committing a crime themselves," he warned the East Anglian viewers. I had to admit it, his performance was excellent. But in spite of all the publicity, there was no trace of our stamps. As the investigation continued it was obvious that Jim, the shop manager, was innocent. I had never thought he was guilty anyway. He was in a position of trust and could have stolen regularly without being caught. Neither I nor the police thought him to be a criminal. Something was worrying me about the whole incident but I couldn't put my finger on it.

About a week or so after the theft, I had a horrific nightmare. I saw Roger walk into the shop, pick up the display book and come out with it again. It was very vivid and it was repeated in various ways. I woke up sweating and very worried. It couldn't have been Roger, he was in York. Or was he? I couldn't get it out of my head. Supposing he didn't go to York. I told Beth about my dream over breakfast.

"It's silly," she said. "You know he was in York, you phoned him."

"I know, I certainly phoned somewhere but where? I didn't keep the number. I could have phoned anywhere."

"But he bought petrol in York, I've seen the bill. No, it's just a silly dream. Forget it."

Throughout the day the thought kept bubbling into my consciousness. In the end I decided to do something to kill it for good. I reached for the phone and dialled a York number.

"Hello, Will." I was talking to Will Roberts, the head of the Yorkshire postal section. I'd known him for years. He'd be able to help if anyone could. "It's Mark, Mark Cheshire."

"Oh, the stamp king," replied Will.

"Well, not exactly a king, more a jester, I think. Will, I want to ask a favour. It might sound a bit odd but it is important."

"Sounds like a mystery," he said in his delightful Welsh accent. "If I can help, I will. What do you want me to do, back date a few penny black first day covers with May sixth, 1840?" he joked. A genuine envelope postmarked on the sixth of May 1840, the first day of use of the first ever stamp in the world, would be worth a fortune.

"No, I don't think anyone would be fooled into thinking it genuine," I laughed. "No, I'm afraid this is a little more serious. I'm clutching at straws, really. I sent somebody up to the Post Office at York with some covers on Tuesday the twentieth of June. They were to have given them in to the main office. Could I ask you to check if anyone remembers the person who brought them and, if possible, the car that he was driving?"

"Sounds serious, Mark. Sorry for the silly joke but you know me. I'll ask a few questions. I should be able to find out pretty quickly, that's if anyone remembers anything. I'll phone you back."

I tried to get on with the job in hand, valuing a very expensive collection. At about four o'clock I had the return call from Will.

"Well boy, I've got the answers to your questions and I hope they're useful. The covers were delivered by a tall, heavily bearded man who spoke with a Midlands accent. He was with a blonde lady and they drove a red Vauxhall. I hope that's what you wanted to hear."

"Thanks Will, that's wonderful. I owe you. Next time I see you I'll buy you lunch. Do you like vinegar with your fish?"

"Go on with you. I'll see you around," laughed Will.

Will's information was fascinating. Roger was clean shaven, his lover Jill was dark, and they drove a blue Ford. Bingo! My dream was accurate. I must have worked it out subconsciously, but couldn't bring myself even to think about it consciously.

Beth was horrified.

"What a bastard! He must have planned it to the last detail and made sure that Jim was in the hot seat. I honestly thought it was him, he was so shifty when Roger questioned him about it. He sweated so. It must have been worry and fear. I feel awful!"

"Don't blame yourself. After all, Roger was trained in deception by experts," I said as I went off to talk to Charles to see what he thought. Charles was sitting at his desk, humming hymn tunes, happily filling in our VAT return for the quarter. I sat down opposite him.

"I'll come straight to the point, Charles. Have you got any ideas who stole the stamps?" I said bluntly.

He looked at me rather sadly.

"Well," he hesitated, "heaven forgive me if I'm wrong, but there's only one person as far as I can see. When I was at the bank we had a questionnaire concerning thefts. If anyone answered yes to over half the questions then they were looked at very closely indeed. I did the test on the staff and one person leaps out. It's got to be Roger. But I have to admit I haven't a clue how he did it," he said. "What do you think?"

"I agree. I've worked out how he did it." I explained what I'd learned from Will.

"Yes, that's all very well, but I doubt if you'll be able to prove it," said Charles. "So you'd better be careful. We don't mind murder or rape in this country but we do take libel and slander very seriously. I also suspect you'll find this is not the only crime he's committed. You've got to get rid of him, but you're not going to find it easy."

I agreed. Doing it was not going to be easy, I knew. I thought it might be worth trying to find out a bit more about Roger's background so I asked a friend of mine, Peter Pike, if he could find anything about Roger's army career. I had a hunch that we didn't really know much about our ex-intelligence employee.

Peter was nominally a staff sergeant in the intelligence section. I'd always doubted his rank but if he was happy being called a staff sergeant why should I complain? I phoned him and asked him to come round to see us.

"Peter, do you want to swap some information for some bird stamps?" He was a bird fanatic and was never happier than when he was lying, freezing cold, in some God-forsaken spot, watching the lesser spotted twit bird dance its mating ritual. He'd come into my life one night knocking at my front door to say he'd heard we dealt in stamps and asking if I had any which depicted birds. I didn't normally encourage customers to visit my home but as he was there already, and by chance I had bought a collection which probably contained what he wanted, I invited him in. By the end of the evening he'd collected a large pile of stamps in front of him.

Then the cheeky so-and-so tried to pay for them using mandarin liqueur and whisky as currency! I explained that in England we tended to use money, as beads had gone out of fashion. He was somewhat embarrassed, having apparently been in the Far East where barter was acceptable. He was a rugged blond man around six foot tall. Although I was much taller than him, I always felt at least a foot shorter. There was something about Peter that made you feel that way. He was impressive. He was very secretive. He would disappear for long periods and then turn up again as if nothing had happened. Over the years we had become very friendly with him, but we rarely saw his wife Inga, who seemed even more of a mystery.

"What do you want to know?" he said cautiously. "If I can do it legally and if it's something I can do, it's yours."

"I need to know about Roger King's service record and anything else you can tell me about him. For example, why did he leave the army? After all, he had a good rank and must have had a good career ahead of him." He sat fiddling with his pipe. Peter had a thing about pipes, he thought it made him look like Sherlock Holmes. I dreaded the day he'd turn up in a deerstalker, playing the violin. He even collected pipes and had an amazing range, though it seemed to me he spent more time cleaning them than smoking. Maybe that was why he liked them. Eventually he got it pulling well, looked up and grinned at me.

"Is that all? I was expecting you to want me to break the Official Secrets Act at the very least. Well, that shouldn't be a problem. He was in our lot, wasn't he? Right, I'll need his National Insurance number, his previous address and any service details you've got."

"That should be easy. I'll get my secretary to sort it out and give you a call in the morning. Are you living at home at the moment or are you on some mysterious assignment?"

"Ah, so the beautiful Alice is still with you! Why not

ask her to bring the information round to my house? I'm on leave so it would certainly brighten up my morning. Perhaps she would bring me breakfast in bed?"

"Peter! You're an old married man. What would Inga say!" said Beth, pretending to be shocked.

"Not a lot. She's in Essen with her parents, so I'm all alone and lonely."

He sat there, putting on his pseudo hangdog expression hoping for sympathy. All he got, however, was a passable mime of me playing the violin as I hummed a sad song.

Inga was often away for very long periods, as was Peter. I'd often wondered about their relationship. It wouldn't surprise me to find it was an intelligence affair rather than a marriage. Peter was more like a character invented by Le Carré than the sort of chap you normally meet. I was certainly glad to be able to ask his advice.

"You'll have to forget Alice," I said. "Her husband's a giant of a man and very jealous and she dotes on him. Anyway I'm first on the waiting list."

I thought the kick that Beth administered was over the top. It was a bit like a cross between a mule, a donkey, and Nobby Stiles.

"I didn't mean it, honest! I only have eyes, and for that matter, bruises, for you!"

"You'll do the washing up tonight to pay for that, you pig," she threatened.

"Peace, children. There is serious work to be done and I was told as a child that only donkeys kick.

Ouch! That hurt, Beth! Control your wife, Cheshire, she's dangerous! I'm going while I can still walk." He hobbled off dramatically towards the door. "I'll be back in touch as soon as I've had the operation. I just hope my health insurance will pay for it."

Beth grinned at him. "Clear off before I kick the other one and don't try for any dramatic parts in the rep this year, you've no talent I'm afraid, you'll have to stick to limp-on parts."

"What will you do about Roger?" Beth asked, after Peter had finished his Oscar attempt and left.

"Face him with all we know and make him go, it's the only thing I can do." I might have said the words confidently but inside I was dreading the job.

"Would you like me to be there to lend moral assistance?"

"No, it's something I'm going to have to do myself. But thanks for the offer."

I knew perfectly well that Beth would probably do it better than me. She fired my first book-keeper when I was too soft to do it. For such a nice person, Beth was very tough. She was an amazing woman and not for the first time, I thought how lucky I was to have her.

When I went to the office the next day, it was difficult to be in the same room as Roger. My instinct was to confront him and kick him off the premises. However, bearing in mind what Charles had said about slander, I managed to control myself. I drove home slowly, thinking about Beth. She desperately wanted to have children. It did seem unfair that we couldn't have kids when so many silly girls got themselves pregnant every day when that was the last thing they wanted.

Beth had cooked bangers and mash for supper and normally we would have thoroughly enjoyed it, but all we could think about was Peter and what he might find out. We had just settled down for the evening and had opened a bottle when there was a ring on the doorbell. I opened the door and there was Peter beating his pipe on the wall with great concentration.

"That was quick," I said as I let him in. "Coffee? Wine? Or something stronger?"

"Both would be nice. Whisky, or even better, malt if you've got it."

Peter loved malt whisky. He had travelled round the Scottish Islands on one of his many trips, apparently, when he was on loan to the Royal Navy. I never thought it was a coincidence that the Russians were also in the area on a so-called goodwill mission. I poured a large measure of malt into a glass and refilled my glass with the St Emillion we were drinking. Beth glared at me so I filled hers as well and she went out to put on the percolator. We sat looking at Peter expectantly while he sipped his expensive Dalwhinnie malt. He always liked the theatricals.

Finally he put down his glass, picked up his pipe, stretched back in his chair and put on his serious face.

"Well," he said, "there are two reasons why he left the Service, the official one and the unofficial one. Whichever way you look at it though, he left very quickly. In fact, it was within hours. The official version was he was sleeping with the Commanding Officer's wife. He was caught in bed with her and another woman in a three-in-a-bed situation. Needless to say, the Colonel was not over impressed. They had a heated argument and Roger was dismissed for striking a superior officer. It was not the first time he'd been involved with another officer's wife, in fact it was his speciality. Well, that's the official version as far as it goes." Peter leant forward and picked up his glass again; he finished his whisky, topping it up from the bottle that I'd left on the side by him.

"So he hasn't changed much so far as women are concerned," Beth said. "According to office gossip he's sleeping with at least one of our staff. And we know of course he's left his wife and is living with Helen. He's a regular sex maniac. What's the unofficial version then?"

"Well, I'll tell you after the coffee. I like to be theatrical, after all, and according to Beth I need the practice," said Peter with a grin, doing some running repairs on his pipe.

Beth went out to get the coffee.

"Don't start till I'm back," she called from the kitchen, "this is better than Inspector Morse. Peter, I'm sorry if I've put you off acting, I didn't mean it, you're as good as Mark any day." Peter knew I couldn't act to save my life so he didn't take it as a great compliment, he did the obvious thing and ignored it and got back to why Roger left so suddenly.

"I think the unofficial reason is more likely to be what you're interested in. Apparently a large sum of money went missing from the mess accounts. A very large amount. Guess who was in charge of the accounts. No prizes for getting the right answer, I'm afraid. Nothing could be proved of course, and the service wouldn't really want the scandal anyway. My informant tells me there was no doubt he was guilty and he was given three hours to pack and leave. The time factor says that dishonesty is the likely reason for his leaving. I assume he's been at it again. How much has he taken you for?" he asked.

"Thirty thousand pounds' worth of stamps from the shop and probably more from the office," I said. It made me sick to think of it. It had taken us so long to build up that much stock. We'd risked everything. Even our house was on the line and this bastard had just come into the company and helped himself.

"Christ, that's a lot of money. Will you survive?" Peter looked quite alarmed.

"Well, yes, we're insured. In fact I'm seeing the loss adjuster about it tomorrow."

"What are you going to do about it?" asked Peter.

"Get rid of him. We can't prove anything against him easily, but something's got to be done. I'm going to sack him tomorrow morning. Anyway, let's forget it for this evening. Would you like another coffee to sober you up?"

I didn't sleep much that night, I was so angry. I wished I could make the bastard pay for his actions, but without proof, there was nothing I could do except kick him out of our company.

The next morning I called Roger into my office.

"Roger, I'm not going to beat about the bush. I know what's been going on and I want you out of here this morning. I'm not going to give anything –

no redundancy money, no holiday money, nothing. In my opinion you are getting off lightly."

"To be honest, Mark, I'm fed up with stamps and coins. I was leaving anyway, you've just made it easier. But I think you're a little over the top just because that bitch Jane complained." With that, he left, almost breaking the door as he slammed it.

I couldn't help chuckling. I'd left myself wide open for an action for slander by implying he was a thief, and he thought I was so prudish I was talking about adultery! Still, the important thing was that he had gone. I was relieved. I had been dreading the showdown, but at least it was over.

The nice, charming, friendly loss adjuster proved to be as slippery as a snake. Not only did he reduce my claim to twenty thousand pounds, which I reluctantly agreed to in the interest of getting a quick settlement, but then he told me we were grossly underinsured so he further reduced it by twenty-five percent. This meant that I ended up with only fifteen thousand pounds, which was a major blow and I knew it would take a long time to earn the money back.

If that wasn't enough, Beth had gone to a Harley Street specialist to get a second opinion about the chances of her ever having children. She'd arrived back in total despair. The consultant confirmed the diagnosis: she would never ever be able to have a child. Our meal that night was not a happy one. It was as if someone had switched the lights off when we were still reading. We both wanted children desperately.

"We could adopt," I said tentatively. But neither of us were very keen; we really wanted our own child.

"At least one good thing's happened today. We got rid of Roger," said Beth, trying to look on the bright side. "Let's have a drink." A drink was a good idea; two bottles was probably going over the top. A pair of hungover fools did not help solve any problems.

Although I wasn't to know it, two significant things happened over the next few days. During my usual Friday accounts chat with Charles, he sat back, drinking a cup of tea and looking rather worried.

"I know you've got rather a lot on your plate at the moment, Mark, but I think you may have a problem with Ray Mumford. He's not paid us for three months and he owes over twelve and a half thousand pounds. I've written to him and phoned but I'm getting nowhere. Can you have a word with him?" he asked.

"Yes, of course. That's no problem. I must say that I've never taken to the chap. He seems to get far too many rare first day covers for my liking. I just hope he's genuine," I said.

"You don't think he's a forger, do you?" asked Charles, wide eyed. "I thought stamps were very respectable."

"Not really, it's no different from any other business. We get our fair share of rotten apples. I don't know if there's anything in it but my instinct tells me he's a crook. But I'll see what I can do about the money."

I didn't relish the job. I hadn't told Charles all I knew. Reg Knight, one of my customers, was convinced that Mumford was a forger. Poor old Reg, he'd found a hundred fifty-pence stamps which had been printed green in error and had stuck them on first day covers alongside the correctly printed ones. Errors are rare on British stamps and are keenly collected. Reg was convinced he was the only one to have the errors, which meant that these first day covers were worth a lot of money, ten thousand pounds at least. Now there were thousands upon thousands being offered round the stamp trade, mostly by Ray Mumford, and the price had dropped to only six hundred and fifty pounds at the most. Reg was convinced that Mumford had forged these extra ones so he had hired private detectives to try to expose him. For Reg it was a lot of money to lose, which was why he was so angry. Also, like me, he hated forgers and he liked covers. I'd also heard that Mumford was involved with some rather dubious German covers. The whole value of first day covers depends on them being genuine. If Mumford was a forger I'd like to get him caught very quickly as he could really damage the market and with it, my business.

I phoned him up to see what I could do about the money.

"Ray, it's Mark Cheshire here. You seem to have forgotten to pay us. You haven't broken your right hand have you?" I always found you got a better response if you made a joke out of asking for money.

"No," laughed Ray. "Truth is I've bought rather a large collection, I shouldn't probably have done it. It's a bloody good one, about the best I've ever seen. I probably should have sold it to you, you're the expert, but I thought I might be able to flog it quickly. Of course, you've got the customers for this sort of thing, I haven't. How about me coming down and showing you it? If you buy it we can knock the money I owe you off it and put me back into credit."

"Yes, that sounds fine. Come down sometime next week and we'll sort it out."

As I put the phone down, Alice, my secretary, put her head round the door.

"Mark," she said, "you know that we said we would join in the work experience scheme for youngsters? It's not very professional, but the labour exchange have sent a lad along now for an interview. They didn't even give us a call to say he was on his way. Shall I tell him you're too busy?"

"It really isn't good enough!" I said. "I've got so much to get through this morning."

"I know it's not good enough, but he is not quite seventeen and has just moved into Clacton. Apparently his father has recently died and he's left school to look for work. Could you possibly see him?" she asked hopefully, knowing full well I would.

"Oh, all right. Give me five minutes then bring him in. I've got one or two things to do first."

I hated interviews. I knew I was no good at them. I always talked too much.

"Mr Cheshire," said Alice, "this is John Rich, the boy I told you about."

"Thank you. Won't you sit down, John? We work on Christian names here."

I was impressed with John Rich. He was strikingly handsome with a twinkle in his eye. I bet he'd be popular on the exhibition stands.

"Well, tell me about yourself, John."

"There's not much to say. I've got no qualifications as my father was always moving around and now he's dead. I've been told I'll find it very difficult to get any work which is why I'm trying for work experience on the Y.T.S. It's a bit humiliating really," he added.

His voice was rather like a barrow boy's. If you're selling expensive stamps or coins it doesn't help to sound like a market trader. Still, I was sure we could help him to improve this.

"Did you ever collect stamps?" I asked.

"Well, I did like everyone when I was a kid. I quite enjoyed it. I only did British though, I had an album that an auntie gave me. I think I've still got it somewhere."

"What about sport? Do you play anything?"

"Well, I did play a bit of cricket when I was at school. I was in the team and I opened the bowling. Look, I know I've got nothing to prove it, but I'm not a fool. Please give me a chance," he begged.

As it happened I'd already decided to take him on. He seemed a capable lad and I liked helping lame ducks; it made the business somehow have more meaning.

"All right, you can start on Monday. I think you're going to pick up stamps very easily."

I wasn't to know at the time how accurate my prediction was to be.

PART III

RAY MUMFORD

Chapter 6

Ray Mumford was a great disappointment to his father. He believed that the only time his father was pleased with him was when he was born, giving his father a son and heir. At the same time he was not sure his mother was so pleased; she would have preferred a daughter.

Looking back, Ray Mumford really didn't understand why his father thought himself so superior, after all, he was just a displaced person. He had come over to Britain from Hungary before the Russian tanks went in, though he pretended that the family had always been British. That's why he'd chosen a name from the telephone book and changed their name by deed poll. All he ever did was run a poxy little stamp shop in a one-horse town. In some ways he was hoping to live his life again through his son. Mumford's father was always telling him about the dozens of millionaires in the stamp world, saying that there was no reason why Ray couldn't join them. Fat chance! If it was that easy why wasn't he one? It was planned that Ray would learn the trade from his father and take over the stamp and coin shop. They did in fact try it for a short period, but it was soon obvious that they could never work together. However, Ray did enjoy the stamps and decided that he would start his own business, making sure that his was much bigger, better, more successful than his father's.

It had been difficult at first to get his business going. Money makes money and that was one commodity he was short of. Time, though, was in plentiful supply and he worked all the hours God sent. To start with, he visited every stamp and coin exhibition looking carefully through all the dealers' stocks. Many of them had more money than sense; they were so keen on the big deal that they left rich pickings for him. While he was doing this, he talked endlessly to the proprietors about what they wanted to buy. The amazing thing was that, because they were either too busy or too lazy to look round the exhibitions themselves, he found it was possible to buy and sell, even to dealers on neighbouring stands. Another thing that always amazed him was the amount of money the collectors spent. He saw an Arab hand over £300,000 on one stand, and on another a Japanese bought one grubby envelope for £225,000. It certainly made him think that perhaps his dad was right after all.

He decided to move away from Yarmouth, where his overbearing father earned a precarious living from his pathetic little shop. London was the place for him.

He'd soon show the old man what he could do. At first he rented a cheap shop on Charing Cross Station which had a small flat above it. The flat was pretty grotty but the shop was ideal. Thousands of commuters saw it every day. He put up as large a sign as he could, which read:

BUYING AND SELLING STAMPS – RAY MUMFORD, PHILATELIST

It looked classy and it certainly did the trick. Every day people brought him their collections. At first he offered too much for them. He made money, but he realised that if he could buy more cheaply he would make more money. His problem was that he was still short of cash. If only he had capital, he was convinced that he would become seriously rich.

Occasionally he'd go back to Yarmouth and annoy his dad, showing the collections and gloating over how little he'd paid for them. His father always got self-righteous.

"That's theft, boy," he would say, "you could have given them ten times that and still made a good profit."

"Yes, I could," Mumford retorted. "But why should I? They don't have to accept my offer. If they're so stupid that they don't bother to find out what their collections are worth, why should I care? They were happy with my price and I'm happy. What's wrong with that? It's just good business."

"It's wrong," his father would say. "You'll come to no good dealing like that. People will get wise to you and then you'll be in trouble."

"Nonsense, there's plenty more where this came from."

It was very satisfying, winding his father up, and for once feeling he was on top.

Things were going on nicely when, one afternoon in late October 1978, his father had a massive heart attack and died. It was right in the middle of the winter of discontent, when the miners' strike had reduced the whole country to a three-day week. The unskilled public service unions came out in support for the miners too. This meant that rubbish wasn't collected and graveyards and crematoriums were closed. The bodies were stacked up in cold-stores. The labour government called in the army to help, which caused even more strikes and chaos. Typical of him. He'd picked the only time in living memory when you couldn't bury the dead. The funeral was delayed for three weeks and by the time it came round, everyone was thinking about Christmas and didn't really want to go to a funeral. As a result it was even more of a depressing occasion than it should have been.

After the funeral, Ray and his mother went back to the solicitor's offices to hear the will. His mother got the house and all the savings; he was left all his father's stock and the shop lease. He managed to sell the lease and transferred the better stock up to the Charing Cross shop. The rest he put in the next Warwick and Warwick stamp auction.

It was early in 1979 that Mumford received his extraordinary offer. There was a man who came regularly to Mumford's shop, a Mr Gunningham. He was a strange man. He was not very tall and wore his hair very short, trying to cover up the fact that he was going bald. Whatever the weather, he never wore a coat. Ray liked him, particularly as money was clearly not a problem. He always paid in cash, which Ray really appreciated as it avoided VAT and income tax. Ray had nicknamed him The Duck, because as he walked, he sort of waddled with his toes pointing out. He didn't, of course, laugh about this when The Duck was anywhere near the shop, because, not only was the bloke an excellent spender, but he gave the impression of being tough.

They had chatted together on many occasions and Mumford had told him of his plans and ambitions. The Duck wanted to know if Mumford could use a capital injection. Mumford had thought little about it, until one particular grey morning.

Mr Gunningham waddled in as usual and waited patiently until the shop was empty.

"Mr Mumford, I would like to put a business proposal to you." He had a sort of self-taught posh accent.

"Oh yes," Ray replied, keeping his voice neutral. He thought that The Duck would probably want to sell all his stamps back. After all, that was par for the course. Most people who suddenly start collecting and get the bug very badly spend like crazy for the first three years or so, then they get fed up and want to sell it all back. They always expect a huge profit. They don't understand the difference between retail and trade. *A dealer's got to make a living*, Ray thought. He hated that sort. When he told them what he would pay, the collectors often turned unpleasant; they never understood VAT and margins. The thought of telling The Duck this was not one that Ray relished.

"Not here," Gunningham said, "it's too public. Come round to my suite at the Savoy at lunchtime? I think you'll find it'll be worthwhile shutting the shop for an hour or so."

Mumford noticed that he seemed somehow different this time, far more confident, less like a duck.

"All right, what's your room number and what time do you want me to come?"

"I'm in the Blenheim Suite and let's say one thirty." With that, he left Mumford wondering what on earth it was all about.

The rest of the morning dragged. He managed to buy a complete collection of the 1935 Jubilee issue used for twenty-five pounds from a little old lady. He was rather pleased with that. He'd be able to sell it easily for five hundred pounds and that was at wholesale prices. That was the sort of profit margin he liked to work on. There weren't many customers about and those who did come in were a bit of a pain, fiddling about here and there, asking a lot of silly questions. Eventually one o'clock came and he shut the shop and walked slowly round to the Savoy, so as not to arrive too early.

He had never been in the Savoy before. It didn't somehow seem the right sort of place for him, a little bit too plush and expensive. As he walked down the road towards the entrance, a large flunky stood out in front of him. He thought at first he was going to be refused entrance, but surprise, surprise! The door was opened with a cheerful, "Good Morning, sir."

The lobby was large and very grand. He asked at the desk where he'd find the Blenheim Suite.

"Just go up the stairs to the right, sir, and take the lift on the left hand side to the third floor. You'll find the Blenheim Suite up there."

He went up the stairs marked 'Private. Residents Only', and took the lift. The Savoy smelt. It smelt of money and he thought he'd like to smell that way himself. He waited quietly just round the corner, until his watch hit one thirty, before he rang the doorbell.

He was admitted by a tall man servant, who looked a bit as though he were Spanish, but darker skinned. Ray thought he might have come from South America, although he'd never been very good at placing foreigners. The servant certainly had a South American or Spanish accent.

"Good afternoon, sir. Mr Gunningham is expecting you. Follow me, please."

The suite was like a scene from a country house in a movie. It was bigger than Ray's whole flat. He was led along a short corridor into the lounge. It was very plush and he sat down on one of the large, extremely comfortable armchairs. Mr Gunningham came in from the anteroom.

"So nice of you to come, Mr Mumford. Can I give you a drink? Whisky? Brandy? Or perhaps you would prefer a beer?" Carlos opened a cabinet and there was a whole range of drinks there, just like in the films. Mumford hoped he didn't show how nervous he felt.

"No, whisky's fine. You haven't got any dry ginger, have you?"

"I think we can manage that." He poured the drinks and handed one to Ray. "Right, we're both busy men, so let's get down to the reason I've asked you to come here. I've been watching you for some time, Mr Mumford, and it looks to me that you might be the sort of person who can help us. How would you like to have a capital injection of a quarter of a million pounds into your business?" He spoke in a matter-of-fact tone. Ray couldn't believe his ears; a quarter of a million pounds was an enormous amount of money.

"Did I hear you properly? Did you say a quarter of a million pounds?"

"That's exactly what I said, Mr Mumford."

"Well, yes, I mean, it's all very well, but what sort of rate of interest and how long would the loan be?"

"We can offer exceptionally attractive terms, Mr Mumford. None better. In fact we don't want any interest."

"You don't want any interest?" Ray couldn't quite get the hang of this. Why would Gunningham want to give him a quarter of a million pounds without charging interest? He must be barking mad – or something worse.

"No, we don't want any interest. We just want the money repaid over two and a half years at fifty thousand pounds every six months in exchange for you buying stamps from us. There is a slight catch; the money will be in the form of cash, if you understand me."

Mumford was beginning to understand only too clearly. What he was being asked was to launder the money. In other words it was stolen or money that had come from a dubious source. Mumford was supposed to make it respectable.

"It's a lot of cash to deal with," he said. "It's going to involve me in some VAT and not to mention huge problems with income tax."

"There could be one or two problems," Gunningham said, "but I'm sure a man of your ingenuity could work out how to get round them. After all, if you went to the bank to borrow this money to develop your business, they would charge you something like twenty percent interest which is fifty thousand pounds a year. You will get this for free, for absolutely nothing." He paused for emphasis. "But of course if you think it's too much worry, I would quite understand."

Ray did not like the way he looked at him. He had never really realised how sinister he was; more a shark than a duck.

"When would the money be coming?"

"As soon as you would like, Mr Mumford. Tomorrow?"

My God, he thought. *Two hundred and fifty thousand pounds in cash. Just think what that would buy!* Overnight he'd be one of the largest players in the game.

"Right, all right, you're on. What do we do about contracts and papers?"

"Papers? Contracts?" Mr Gunningham gave a sinister laugh. "I don't think we will worry about any papers. We trust you. I'm sure you won't let us down. Obviously you'll realise that should there be any problem, we could not resort to the law. We have our own ways of dealing with problems. Anyway, I'm sure there will be none. Thank you for coming, Mr Mumford, I will organise the transaction. Every six months we will visit your shop and you will write a cheque for fifty thousand pounds, which, as far as the rest of the world is concerned, will be for a good stamp or coin collection. You will not be seeing me again. Carlos will keep me informed of how things are going. Carlos, will you show Mr Mumford out?"

Carlos stood over him. "Come this way please. I will be round tomorrow, twelve noon. Be there."

With that, Ray was back out in the corridor. He was scared, but excited. Things were happening for Ray Mumford! He walked slowly back down to the lift and when he got back to the lobby, instead of going back to the shop, he crossed and went up the stairs on the far side to what was called the American Bar. He went to the bar to order a drink.

"If you'd like to sit down, sir, we'll come across and take your order. There is a menu on the table."

Feeling a bit of a fool, he stumbled back, sat down at a table and opened the menu. *My God,* he thought. *The price of drinks! But what the hell? It's not often you get given the chance to have two hundred and fifty thousand pounds to develop your business.*

The waiter seemed to ignore him so he clicked his fingers to bring him to the table.

"Yes sir, can I get you something?"

Although the man was polite in what he said, it was the way he said it made Mumford feel like mouldy cheese. He thought, *If only you knew, you wouldn't treat me like this!*

"Yes, I'd like a glass of your best champagne, please."

"Certainly, sir."

The waiter went off and returned a few minutes later with some bowls of nuts, crisps, olives, and a glass of champagne.

Mumford sat munching the nuts, drinking the champagne thinking to himself. *YES. Yes, this is what I want. This is what I'm gonna have!*

The following day, on the dot of noon, Carlos came over to the shop carrying a battered old brown suitcase. He waited patiently while Mumford finished with a stupid, fussy customer.

"I think it would be better if you were to shut the shop and we go up to your flat so we are more private." There was something about Carlos that said you don't argue. Mumford put a notice on the door, 'closed for thirty minutes', and they went up the dingy stairs to his flat above the shop.

Ray looked around as if he was seeing it for the first time. The curtains were ill-fitting and torn, the battered armchair stained with generations of brylcream. However, that looked almost clean in comparison to the disgusting carpet. The door of the bedroom was open and as usual Ray hadn't made the bed. To make it worse, a vile smell of sweat filled the air. Dirty washing-up filled the kitchen sink and the whole place looked like a condemned squat. Suddenly he was ashamed of it.

He told Carlos that he'd been meaning to get himself another flat, but that he had been too busy with the shop. He resented Carlos' silent disapproval. Who was he to criticise? Carlos made no comment, he just looked at him with his hard black eyes and said, "Would you like to check the money?"

Mumford opened the suitcase. It was full of bundles of fifty pound notes. He checked one or two bundles and then checked the total contents. It appeared to be all there.

While he was sorting through the bundles of money, Carlos watched him coldly. Then he grinned and looked Mumford straight in the eye.

"Mr Gunningham wanted me to emphasise to you that you are borrowing from a world organisation. I'm sure you would have no thoughts of cheating us but let me tell you clearly, there is nowhere in the world that you would be safe should you consider just taking off with our money. It is very important that you understand our terms very clearly. We don't use the authorities. If anything goes wrong we deal with it ourselves.

The way he explained these ground rules made Mumford realise that the consequences of letting the organisation down would not be pleasant. He had a horrible feeling that it meant murder.

"I have no intention of taking off. I understand what you are saying clearly. I'm going to build a big business." He said this as confidently as he could. "Hopefully I can be useful to you again in the future."

"That would certainly please my masters. I will be back in six months for the first fifty thousand pounds. Be very, very careful. This is a lot of money. Men get killed for far less," Carlos said, and stared at Ray to make sure he understood, then turned and went back down the stairs and left the shop.

Mumford put the suitcase up on top of his

battered old wardrobe and went back to work. All through that afternoon his brain was racing ahead, thinking of what to do next.

Chapter 7

Although the shop in Charing Cross was excellent for buying stamps in, it was not very good for selling; it didn't have the right look to attract the customers with big money to spend. The first thing to do would be get a decent shop on The Strand, and join the rest of the international stamp trade. At the same time he'd keep the old Charing Cross shop going, just for buying purposes. He'd have to employ someone and he thought he knew just the person. Chris Jones was a young, ambitious stamp dealer who'd jump at the chance. Jones was also honest, a bonus in the stamp world. And he'd get himself a better flat. His present place really was the pits.

He found the perfect solution, a double-fronted shop on The Strand with a really good flat above it. It had two bedrooms, a large living room with a dining area and came completely furnished. The previous owner, having had his own personal lease terminated, didn't need it. Unlike some of the other would-be tenants, it didn't bother Ray that somebody had died in the flat. After all, we've all got to go sometime. The rent was a little bit more than he'd intended to spend, but it looked exactly what he wanted. What the hell? He had two hundred and fifty thousand pounds. He paid the deposit and the first three months' rent in cash. Within a week of Gunningham's offer, he'd moved in.

These were good days. He now had an excellent retail presence on The Strand and he got top prices for his stamps. He was buying cheaply at the Charing Cross shop; he could go to stamp auctions and buy extensively. It gave him great pleasure to outbid the established dealers, making Ray Mumford a name to be reckoned with.

He'd also started smartening himself up. He bought a few new suits from the Savoy Tailor's Guild just up the road from his shop on The Strand, along with some expensive shirts and ties. He also visited a second hand car dealer and bought a flashy BMW, getting a very good deal by paying in cash. The dealer was delighted to be able to fiddle his books; Mumford was delighted because it got rid of a bit more of the cash.

Ironically the Charing Cross shop was doing better with the new manager than it ever had with Ray. Chris Jones got on well with the customers and, if anything, was even meaner than Ray was when he bought stamps, which helped the profits at The Strand shop enormously. His margins were fantastically high. Mumford was on his way to becoming rich. If only his dad could see him now!

The first six months went by very quickly and Ray was surprised when Carlos came in one afternoon with a stamp collection for which he wanted fifty thousand pounds. He glanced at it quickly, agreed the figure, and wrote out a cheque made out to a John Green. Thus the first payment of fifty thousand pounds was made.

The price of British stamps was continuing to rise rapidly. It was obvious to Mumford that it was silly just to keep the cash in his flat, when he could put it to good use to buy stock; he could make so much more money with that. Stock was better than cash in the bank, not that he could put it in the bank! At that time mint commemorative stamps of Great Britain were being traded like stocks and shares. Prices were rising rapidly and dealers were making fortunes overnight. Mumford didn't see why he shouldn't get in on the act. He started buying heavily and as the market continued to climb, his paper profits were going up enormously. The Labour government was struggling, inflation was continuing to rise, and because of this the government had brought in Stock Relief. The idea was might have been meant to help manufacturers but it certainly was also a boon to supermarkets and stamp dealers. In effect, it meant that Ray could defer his tax – in other words, pay no tax for the time being, which left him the cash to buy stock and watch his paper profits just grow and grow.

In April 1979, Carlos once again came into the shop. Mumford was amazed how quickly the six months had gone. This time he paid the fifty thousand pounds with a cheque made out to Bill Smith. They were certainly original with their names! The problem was, he thought to himself, that he'd bought so much stock that this payment would put him into the red at the bank. It didn't bother him much, because his fantastic stock was worth a small fortune. He was sure he would soon build up another big cash reservoir.

In May, the electorate finally gave the boot to

Prime Minister Callaghan and his Labour government and to Ray's horror in came a woman, of all things. The country was in the biggest mess in his lifetime and they put a woman in to run it! What on earth did anyone expect Mrs Thatcher would do? The one thing Ray didn't expect her to do was immediately raise VAT from eight percent to fifteen percent. This certainly hurt. It not only hit his profit but it also made some of the investors think twice about buying stamps. In fact it made them think about selling them. Nobody wants to buy on a falling market. Prices fell daily and his paper profits turned into paper losses. Things were so poor, that he had to go to the bank to arrange an overdraft so he could buy the fifty thousand pounds worth of stock he was committed to in October. There was no way he was going to welsh on a deal with those people!

It was pretty obvious by November that the stamp boom was over. Mumford still had an overdraft of nearly fifty thousand pounds and the bank was getting rather concerned. He also still owed a hundred thousand pounds to the organisation. He was beginning to get worried, but as he always said, there's always something waiting just round the corner. He was trying to sell a rare envelope, which had been posted in 1941 by the Germans during the occupation of Guernsey, to a wealthy collector of Channel Islands stamps. The customer was quite rude about it.

"I don't buy envelopes produced by Kurt Bergen."

"Why not? What's wrong with them? This one looks fine to me."

"They're all forgeries. When Bergen fled from Nazi-occupied Guernsey after the allies liberated it, he left with all of the postal equipment and fled to Argentina. He's been selling these envelopes ever since. If you want a hundred – just ask him. The stamps are very cheap and he's got a good supply of old envelopes. He just puts the postmarks on. He's made a fortune."

Without realising it, the man had given Mumford an excellent idea. The one thing that had always fascinated him was the German stamp issues from just after the First World War. During the amazing hyperinflation that hit Germany, money was devaluing so fast that men were paid at lunchtime and they would rush to the factory fence, where their wives would be waiting with a wheelbarrow, which they needed to put the money in, because the banks could not reprint high denomination notes fast enough to keep pace with inflation. So they had huge bundles of low value notes and the women had to rush to the shops to spend it as quickly as they could. By the late afternoon it would probably be worth twenty percent less.

You can imagine the problems for the Post Office. As fast as they issued stamps, they had to double the postal rate and therefore they had to issue stamps of a higher denomination. This week it might be two hundred thousand marks to post an envelope, next week three hundred thousand, the week after four hundred thousand and so on. The result was that mint stamps were now ten a penny, in fact a hundred a penny, but used stamps were very rare. Ray knew that some of the stamps were available mint at five pence but used ones were priced at three hundred pounds.

The German collectors, however, were not fools. They didn't just buy any used stamp – it had to be properly postmarked and this is where his idea came in. Ray knew a little man who was very good at forgery who would help him, so he managed to get hold of a lot of old envelopes and started forging early German covers. At first Ray started putting them in auctions and was delighted to see little batches of them fetching thousands of pounds. He thought he'd extend the idea to other very profitable areas; the obvious target would be rare early British. Very few people collected in first day covers before the war and so to get an envelope dated on the first day the stamps were issued was very difficult. Some stamps probably weren't even posted the day on which they were issued, but if they existed, collectors would love to buy them. And if they wanted to buy them, why not give them what they wanted? It was all so easy.

Mumford also had another stroke of luck. A small part-time stamp dealer in Essex found a sheet of wrongly printed fifty pence stamps. Instead of being grey-black they were green. The dealer rather smartly put a green one and a black one on an envelope and created a hundred rare first day covers. He was selling them at a hundred pounds each. It appeared the reason for the error was the printing press had overheated and it was the heat that had changed the colour. This gave Mumford an idea and he tried ironing a sheet of the black stamps. Bingo! They turned green.

For some time a mate of Mumford's had been giving him preferential treatment at the main Post

Office on The Strand. He didn't do this because Mumford and he were best friends, it had more to do with the five pounds Mumford put with the first day covers when he wanted them back quickly. He could post his covers on the day the stamps were issued and get them back, postmarked, by the afternoon and have them on sale the next morning. Some of the other dealers had to wait weeks or even months and by then, Ray had scooped the market. His mate at the Post Office also found him quite a few stamps with rare errors by checking through the entire Post Office stock. Once he even locked himself in the security store overnight to give himself more time to look. Mumford always rewarded him very well. Judging by his mate's success rate at finding rare errors, Mumford suspected that he had a friend at the printers stealing the misprints. But what the hell? They both made a lot of money out of what was basically printers' waste, including stamps with missing queen's heads, missing perforations, missing colours. The punters loved them. Needless to say it didn't take much for Mumford to persuade his mate to add backdating the envelopes to his activities, so as to create thousands more of the rare green first day covers.

This was the start of yet another profitable scheme. Mumford sold his covers at just fifty-five pounds each and they sold like hot cakes, undercutting Reg Knight, the dealer who originally found the fifty pence stamp green, and he was not very happy. Knight started to be a nuisance and ask too many questions. Ray had thought Knight wasn't very bright, in fact a real no-hoper and so he took no notice. With the forgeries and the fifty-pence greens, Mumford managed to pay the fifty thousand pounds in April. It didn't please his bank manager, who was expecting the overdraft to be paid off. He knew somehow he had to get more money.

*

The big international exhibition at Earls Court in May that year could have been the saving of the stamp world, but in fact it triggered off an even bigger slump. Britain had moved into an economic decline, unemployment was at record levels and stamps were an unnecessary luxury. The stock that Ray had been so proud of was now losing money every day and everywhere he looked he seemed to have debts. It was a good job he had the forgery racket to get him out of trouble, he thought. His Post Office mate had a friend who worked at the other main London Post Office, and who was desperate for money. These were the kind of friends Mumford liked. This friend was yet another who became useful in creating rare modern covers and it gave Ray more Post Office stock to look through, hoping to find further mint errors. He had also had some steel dies made so that he could forge postmarks from Buckingham Palace, Windsor Castle, the House of Lords and Balmoral Castle. If it made him money he'd forge anything. The suckers kept buying and he was very creative with the rarities he created. He'd also noticed the collectors were buying more and more autographed envelopes and with the help of his German forger he found someone who could create excellent forgeries of signatures. Elvis Presley, Neil Armstrong, the Duke of Edinburgh – you name them, he'd forged them. You wouldn't believe how many covers were signed by the entire England 1966 football team. People loved them and Mumford loved the money. Demand never ceased and they were still forging covers when the police raided the premises.

Ray Mumford, his Post Office friends, and a number of others were arrested.

PART IV

JOHN RICH

Chapter 8

A thief's paradise is how I would describe the Cheshire Stamp Company. The Boss, Mark Cheshire, was just too nice and far too trusting. Sure he was enthusiastic, clever and certainly good at what he did, but as for security, it was a bloody joke! I settled in fairly quickly, it was that sort of place. Everyone was a friend. The Cheshires encouraged us all to use Christian names. On the surface, it was one big happy family.

The amazing thing was the number of staff Cheshire employed. I expected a small back street outfit, but his operation was something else and as for the money spent by collectors, it was fantastic. Apparently one film magnate regularly spent over £150,000 every year. It was all mind boggling.

It didn't take me long to spot the first fiddle. The pathetic little wanker who opened the post was nicking the cash. I wasn't certain about this at first, so I watched him. He wasn't even good at it. The notes were moved by 'accident' under some other papers and then, when he was quite sure that nobody was watching, he transferred them to his pocket. To give him his due, the amount he took was not peanuts. I saw him lift some fifty pound notes, so his game had to be very lucrative. I thought he should share his good fortune with others more deserving – like me – so I waited till everyone else had gone home one evening and then confronted him. He loved overtime, well, that's what he called it; I'd say boozing after hours, claiming time and a half, was theft. Still, who's pointing the finger?

"Tim, I'd like to have a word if I may," I asked politely.

Tim was a little jerk who was under the misapprehension he was someone. On pay day, he made all the staff, especially the girls, stand by his desk whilst he wrote out their wage slips. If they didn't queue, they didn't get. They all hated him.

"I'm very busy, John. Can't it wait? I am right in the middle of something at the moment, perhaps I'll find time sometime tomorrow," he said in his usual slow, boring way.

"Nah, it can't. It's about your thieving."

He went a ghastly shade of pale, got up and shut both doors to the office. He came back and sat down quickly. I looked at him, realising that he was really scared of me! *He thinks I might duff him up,* I thought.

"What are you talking about? What thieving?" It really was a pathetic attempt to bluff it out. My old man, stupid as he was, could have taught him a thing or two.

"I'm talking about the fucking money you nick every day and stuff in your pocket. That's the fucking thieving I'm talking about. I thought you and I could have a little talk first to see if we can come to some sort of arrangement before I go to Cheshire. You understand what I'm saying?" I pushed my face right into his. I could smell his fear. He cowered away from me.

"That's blackmail! I'm not standing for that," he stuttered.

"Right then, let's go and see Mark now. Give him a buzz and say we need to see him urgently. Go on! Do it if you dare!"

He slumped further back in his chair. I'd seen the look with Dad. I knew he was beaten.

"Right then. This is what you do. I want two hundred notes per week. You can keep the rest. OK?"

"I don't steal that much, just a few pounds! I could perhaps manage twenty-five pounds," he suggested hopefully.

God! He's pathetic! I thought. I leant over and grabbed his shirt. He was a miserable specimen.

"Look, don't you try to be bloody clever with me. I know, see! Just fucking give me the two hundred or it's up to Cheshire, now. Your choice, Tim."

As I spoke, I shook him violently. He looked terrified. "Let's see what you've got in your pocket now, shall we?" I pulled out the day's take. "Eighty notes, just today! I've been too generous. That's my trouble! I've always been too kind. Well, you owe me a hundred and twenty pounds for this week. Don't let me down!" I pushed him back in his seat and left him to get on with his boozy so-called overtime. I was surprised at the buzz it gave me. I'd never tried to get tough with anyone before. Why on earth did Cheshire bother with a wanker like Tim Peel? I just couldn't imagine. Mind you, quite a lot of the firm were not exactly the brains of Britain. He'd even got a nutter working for him. A genuine hundred percent nutcase. He'd got papers to prove it. I wouldn't have known but for the argument. I'd gone down to the Rose and Crown after work with a group from the packing department. This tosser reckoned the Beatles were the best pop group ever. Stupid! Everyone knows it's Abba. I said, "You're bloody mad!"

He went quite violent, shouting, "I'm not bloody mad! I'm sane, I've even got papers to prove it. That's more than any of you have!" With that, he passed round his discharge papers from the loony bin!

"Well, fair enough, mate. You're not mad," I replied, making a mental note to keep away from that particular nutter.

Sharon had been the real reason for my visit. She was gorgeous. A slim, dark-haired, beautiful girl, with fantastic green eyes. She dressed in virginal white and looked as if butter wouldn't melt in her mouth, but I had a hunch that she was dynamite. She oozed innocence and every male visitor to Cheshire's, of all ages, noticed her. I was determined to bed her as quickly as possible. As it happens, it wasn't a problem.

"How about going on to Stompers, our one and only decent night-club?" I suggested hopefully, glad I'd got away from the nutter.

"I can't. I'm sorry, I'm busy tonight. What about tomorrow? We could do something straight after work, if you like."

"Great! That's a date!" I said excitedly.

About half past four next afternoon, Sharon came into the room where I was working. "Come on, John. I've got to go home first. If we go together, it will be quicker. Come on!"

Cheshire's closed at five, but nobody really checked up on us, so we bunked off. Sharon lived with her parents about five minutes away from the offices. As soon as we got indoors, Sharon changed personality.

"Quick! My parents don't get back till six, so we can't hang about." She started undoing her white blouse as we headed upstairs. I hadn't had a woman since Gail and the contrast was absolutely amazing. Gail was rather wooden and just lay back and enjoyed it. Sharon was incredible. How on earth she looked so innocent was hard to understand.

"I'm on the pill, so you don't need anything," she panted as she dragged me onto her. I was certainly grateful for the individual tuition Mrs Radcliffe had given me, as Sharon was an appreciative partner.

"Oh God, that's good!" she screamed. "Oh yes! Yes! YES!" as she climaxed, it seemed for the tenth time. We used the bed with me on top, her on top, her on the bed, me on the floor and finally with Sharon kneeling on the bed with me standing behind her working my equipment to death. It really was amazing what you could fit into an hour with Sharon!

After that we drifted into a relationship that I mistakenly thought was serious. She could only go out with me on certain nights. I wanted to be with her all the time.

I was quite shaken when I found out she was fucking another bloke and even worse, a member of the Cheshire staff. The bastard was an overbearing Australian, called Wayne. I found out about them one coffee break, when I found them snogging in the kitchen. I grabbed him and bashed him against the wall.

"Don't you fucking see Sharon again, you understand me?" I screamed. Unfortunately, Wayne wasn't like Tim. He kneed me in the balls and smashed his head into my nose. The blood ran down into my mouth and the pain in my testicles was excruciating. It didn't happen like this in the movies.

"Don't ever try that again!" he snarled at me. His Australian accent made him sound particularly vicious. "If I want to fuck Sharon, I'll fuck her. You understand? The fact that half this town is also fucking her doesn't bother me, so why should it bother you?" And at the same time, to ensure I fully understood his meaning, he bashed me up against the wall a few times.

I was bloody furious. I went to the bog and kicked the door. Since I was small I found it very satisfying to kick something when I was angry. As it happened the bog door was not a good idea; it was just a cheap one and my shoe went straight through it. Cheshire wasn't at all amused and stopped the money for a new door out of my wages, so I leaned on Tim and upped my weekly take to two hundred and fifty pounds.

In the end I came to the same view as Wayne. Sharon was just for sex. I would sort out another girl for a relationship when I was ready.

My big problem, however, was Tim. He was looking decidedly ill. He hadn't liked it when I increased my weekly take to two hundred and fifty pounds and I had to tell him a few facts of life.

"Look, Tim. I've got expenses. I need the money. I've also got friends, nasty friends. It's hard to walk with broken kneecaps. You wouldn't want that to happen to you, would you? Course not. Just be reasonable."

This was a bit of a mistake. I had frightened him too much. He had a breakdown and he had to leave work. He also nearly blurted the whole thing out to Cheshire, but Mark was so nice that he just thought the bloke had gone right off his rocker. Still, it was a near thing.

His replacement was one of Cheshire's curly girls, no profit there. But as they say, one door shuts, another opens. Sharon was in charge of the postage stamps. It sounds small beer and that's just what I thought until I looked at it closely. You'd be amazed how much Cheshire spent on letters and parcels each week. Each time he mailed his forty thousand customers, it cost him over six thousand pounds in stamps alone. Throughout the 1970s, investors had spent a fortune on mint postage stamps, hoping to make a killing as the prices went up. Needless to say, they didn't and the investors were left with hundreds of thousands of pounds worth of stamps they didn't want, so they dumped their holdings into the stamp market at very big discounts. Cheshire bought them up to use on the parcels we mailed out to the customers. It was quite normal for Mark to buy fifteen thousand pounds worth at a time at various discounts ranging from fifteen to twenty-five percent. He also had to buy the new stamps from the Post Office at full face value so accounting in the despatch department was almost impossible. Sharon had a small racket going where she stole a few stamps and sold them to her friends. It was hardly worth her bother; it was only worth about twenty pounds a week. I had a much better idea.

I chatted up one of Cheshire's trade customers, a bloke called Colin Grey. He had a shop in a back street in the centre of Birmingham. I went there once with Cheshire when we were on a buying trip. The shop was much cleaner than many stamp shops and had quite a good stock. I thought I might like a shop like that myself one day. He was a friend of Ray Mumford's. I'd met Ray a few times on his visits to Cheshire's office. He was a flash bastard, who drove a large BMW and glittered like a jeweller's shop window. I knew Cheshire didn't like him, mind you, they were like chalk and cheese, Cheshire being so public school and all that and that Ray trying to be, but failing miserably. I quite liked Ray; he knew how to live. If you've got, flaunt it – that was his motto. As far as I was concerned, it was a good one. If you ask me, Cheshire hadn't got a clue and as for some of the no-hopers he employed, he thought he was running some sort of charity.

Well, charity begins at home, so I got a decent little scam going. I stole a thousand pounds' worth of stamps at face value. He paid me six hundred pounds for them and then he sold them back to Cheshire at seven hundred and fifty pounds. The stamps went back into stock, I stole another thousand pounds' worth, and so on. The scheme was perfect. Needless to say, I cut Sharon in for her fair share, ten percent, so she got sixty pounds cash a week, a big improvement on her previous take and with no work involved.

Mark Cheshire called me up to see him. His office was in the next building up two flights of stairs. I thought it a suitable distance away because he never knew what went on. When he came round to check up on us or to tell what he wanted us to do, there was always plenty of time for me to cover up my scams. However, on this occasion I was a bit worried that that miserable scumbag, Tim, had talked.

I'll bloody kill him if he has, I thought, as I went into Cheshire's office.

The room was full of envelopes. The desk was covered with rare covers, piles of cheaper covers were stacked round the walls; he was a fanatic. He lived for his bloody covers. He was an expert on stamps, but as far as people were concerned, he was an idealist. He believed there was good in everyone and he was on some sort of Christian mission. Bloody fool, he didn't know the half of it! He wanted to try living in the real world.

"Sit down, John," he said straight away. I sat down, slightly apprehensive about what was to come. "Did you know you've been here over a year already? I should have called you in sooner, but I've been very busy and you've been doing so well that I forgot. The reason I've called you up is to confirm that you are now working for the firm properly. No more work experience! I'm putting you in charge of the shop and you will be paid £7,500 a year, which is a good starting salary and an excellent rise. I hope that you're pleased. Incidentally, congratulations!" He smiled at me in that pleased way of his. It was a bit difficult grovelling over a paltry hundred notes a week, but I showed willing. There was even better to come though.

"Now you're really on the staff, I want you to be able to do the exhibitions for me and perhaps learn to go on buying trips. You'll need to learn to drive so I have arranged lessons for you starting tomorrow."

"Oh, thanks a million, Mr Cheshire! That's great! I really want to learn to drive now that I'll be able to buy a car when I pass the test. I promise you that I'll take the opportunity and use it well." Too bloody true, it would help me cover up some more scams.

Just then, the phone rang. He picked it up. "Cheshire here." I noticed he always called himself just Cheshire when he answered the phone, not Mr Cheshire like most people. I thought it sounded good, business-like.

"Yes, I wanted to talk to you." His face had completely changed, become suddenly hard. His voice and even his manner had changed. You could see how he had managed to build a business. "The service we are getting is just not good enough. Just wait a minute." He nodded at me to go. I was amazed at the difference in him. He was unpleasant, demanding that someone did something right for change. I could still hear him as I went down the stairs. So he was not always Mr Nice! I'd better remember that.

Chapter 9

I'll never forget my first big evening. The day had gone well; collectors were spending as if money had gone out of fashion. I'd never seen so much cash in my life. People were almost fighting to give us their money. Cheshire was an expert in how to deal with everybody in the most effective way. We had a huge stand and at one end, he displayed only the most valuable stamps and covers under a glass counter; rare penny blacks, thousand pound covers, you know the sort of thing. It was his bait. Once he had a rich punter on his hook, he rarely failed to make a killing. I had to admit that his charm and good manners went down well with the collectors.

In the middle of the stand, he had specially made wooden boxes filled with exciting offers which the collectors could look through and serve themselves. Our job was to make sure they didn't just 'help themselves'. Cheshire seemed to know which ones were thieves and would warn us to watch them carefully. Even then, some were so good at nicking, they still got away with stuff. You've got to give it to them! I expect they liked the challenge.

Cheshire liked the rare and expensive stamps, but he always said that you made most money out of the rubbish. Every time we bought a collection, we probably only wanted ten percent of it. The rest had a value but it was common, all the dealers had stocks of it and it was hard to sell. Cheshire was a real businessman. He gave the collectors really good deals, selling the stuff off in big lots. He never took most of the stamps in a collection off their original pages, he just took the ones he wanted and priced the rest of the page cheaply as a lot. He did special offers on the covers too. £1 each, £7.50 for ten or £50 for a hundred. The more you bought, the cheaper it got. The collectors loved it. I was amazed how many customers bought a hundred. At the end of the exhibition, all Cheshire's expenses were paid for out of his bargain basement. Whatever was left over in the cheap boxes at the end of the exhibition, Cheshire would sell in huge lots at gift prices to small dealers, so we didn't have to take it all back to the office in Clacton. I was well impressed with the operation.

It was hard work on an exhibition stand. Though there were several of us, there were so many customers that we often didn't get any time for lunch, so Cheshire always took us out to dinner in the evening. It had become a tradition.

On my first evening we were taken out to a glittering hotel. Cheshire was smiling away like a Cheshire cat; it was obvious he was well pleased with the take. I had never been to a place like it. There was a man in uniform just to open the door for you. We started with a drink in the bar. I noticed a cocktail menu, so when my turn came I asked for a champagne cocktail. Cheshire looked surprised and then laughed.

"You've got expensive tastes, young Rich," he said.

I wasn't sure if I liked the drink. The bubbles got up my nose and it was a bit sour, but if that's what the rich drink then I would have to learn to like it. It's funny what stands out on a night like that. It was the nuts that amazed me. The bowl on the table reminded me of Christmas at home, but better. They were the best nuts I'd ever seen. It didn't take me long to scoff the lot.

We moved on to the restaurant, where we were shown to a huge table, glittering with knives and forks and glasses. I had no idea which ones to use, but I guessed I'd be all right if I just watched Cheshire. We were given enormous menus the size of a newspaper. Before I'd had a chance to look, the waiter suggested the special, a steak and kidney pie.

"It's-a good," he said with a heavy Italian accent. "In fact, it is so good that if you do not like it, you do not have to pay."

Everyone round the table started to laugh.

"Wait, wait a moment!" the waiter said, cottoning on very quickly. "You eat it, you pay!"

I looked at the menu. It was all in French. I could understand the prices though. I pointed to the things I wanted, the most expensive. I thought at first that Cheshire might stop me having them, but in the end he just laughed.

As I lay in the hotel room that night, I realised just how good life could be. All you needed was the cash, and there was plenty at the exhibition for me to lift.

The National Stamp Exhibition was a great place to get to know who's who in stamps. It was here that I found out that Grey, that trade customer of

Cheshire's, really worked for Ray Mumford, who also had a stand. Mumford suggested that it would be in my interest to go round to see him one night when the exhibition closed. It wasn't really a good time for me, I didn't want to miss any of Cheshire's posh dinners, but business is business. I had to have an excuse so I made a big song and dance about a girl I'd pulled during the day. They were all jealous of my success with girls so I had to put up with all their dumb jokes for the rest of the day.

Ray Mumford was an unpleasant red-faced git. He was gross. He hadn't got much hair left, but what was left of it was black and slicked down. He wore a lot of gold; a chunky ring, an impressive watch, and his gold cufflinks were monogrammed 'RM'. His suit was flashy and he had Gucci shoes and belt. I liked his gear. It would look much better on me, I thought, after all, I hadn't got his vile hair and the fat body!

"Evening, Mr Mumford," I started cautiously.

"Hello, John," he said, putting his arm round my shoulders. "Call me Ray." He smiled unappealingly, showing his yellow teeth. "What'll you have to drink? I've got a particularly nice whisky."

"Yeah, I'll have one. Have you got any American dry?" I realised that the ginger might be a mistake, looking at his face. "Second thoughts, I'll take it straight!" I quickly added. I'd got a lot to learn about the good life – so many chances to get it all wrong.

I sat drinking the whisky, which to be honest I didn't really like, although I wasn't going to admit it.

"Well we've got a nice little number going with the mint postage stamps, you, me and Colin," started Ray.

"I'd like to become Cheshire's biggest supplier. If I do, we could work the same scheme with the first day covers and coins. All you've got to do is provide us with the stock, which shouldn't be difficult for a smooth operator like you." He smiled a knowing smile and sat back in the chair, sipping his drink and lighting up a large Churchillian cigar.

"I'm not so sure. Coins and covers are bulky, whereas mint stamps go into a briefcase." I'd have to work out an excuse. I was thinking on my feet, as they say, which was something I prided myself on being able to do well. "It might work if you started to buy from Cheshire as well as selling to him. If you became a big customer, I could deliver your orders and slip in the extras for you to sell back to him. Now that would make it possible. In fact, as they say, that will do very nicely."

By the end of the evening we'd worked out another promising scam. *Poor old trusting Cheshire,* I thought. *What a bloody mug! Him and his stupid ideas that there's good in everyone!*

*

The driving test was a doddle. I passed easily and went straight out to buy a car. I particularly liked a flashy Mini Cooper. I could easily afford something bigger with all my 'extra earnings'; I was still only nineteen years old and already I was coining it, but I didn't want to get anything too flashy and arouse suspicions back at the office. I knew enough about theft to know that I must not bring attention to myself.

The arrogant salesman thought I was a time-waster but he quickly changed his tune when I told him there would be no hire purchase. I could see that the idea of readies got him thinking about tax fiddles so I got the price down. Although I bought it for cash, I told everyone at Cheshire's it was on HP and the payments were crippling. The big problem was how to disguise my spending. I needed a good cover story.

Ironically, the cover story turned into a nice little cash earner. Wayne, the Ozzie guy, who'd turned into a friend of mine once I'd got over Sharon, was moaning about the room he rented.

"The council pay the rent. I reckon they pay seventy pounds per week so it's bloody disgusting that the place is filthy. It's always cold and the roof leaks. The bloke's on a right racket. God knows how much money he's making. If I could find somewhere else I'd be off in a flash."

That got me thinking. If I bought a place with a lot of bedrooms I could earn good money, live rent-free and everyone would know I was well off. I looked round and realised I could be on to the proverbial gold mine. I got a good reference from Cheshire. I'd explained to him that it would be much cheaper buying rather than renting. This went down well. He was very keen on home ownership and liked his young staff to do well. He told the mortgage company that I was likely to get an extra couple of thousand a year in bonuses and that I was going to get promotion in the annual review. That tipped the balance for me and I was able to buy a large terrace house in a not-too-pleasant area. It was cheap and had six bedrooms. I converted five into bed-sitting rooms and found out that if I gave the tenants breakfast, I got paid even more and it gave them no rights. I got five tenants easily, including Wayne. With very little effort I was very quickly earning three hundred and fifty pounds a week from the house. I didn't want the bother of running it myself, so I chatted Sharon up. I pointed out that she could have much more fun if she moved out from her parents' house. She was eighteen and could do as she liked. I said I'd give her a special rate for the room. Well, why not? She became sort of sleeping business partner, if you see what I mean. The breakfast was a good laugh – we used to put a little bottle of milk and a packet of cornflakes outside every room each day to cover us with the law.

Everyone at Cheshire's was jealous of my newfound wealth. After all, with the recent rise I was now officially earning around twenty-four thousand pounds a year. What they didn't know was that my tenants paid cash so I didn't bother to tell the tax man about my new business. I had a very cheap MIRAS mortgage spread over thirty years, so my unofficial earnings were about thirty-five thousand a year. I was feeling very prosperous.

With a really good excuse for my affluence now established, I started to enjoy myself. I swapped the Mini and bought an almost new red Toyota Celica; that was certainly more like it. I bought a gold signet ring, a gold medallion, and got myself some flash gear. I also used my newfound wealth to good effect with a variety of girls. With money and the technique taught to me by Mrs Radcliffe and perfected by Sharon, most of them were very easy. All I had to do was flash a little money and treat them right and Bob's your uncle.

I took to taking the girls to luxury hotels –

Gleneagles Lodge, The Imperial in Torquay, The Royal in Bournemouth and of course my particular favourite, the London Hilton. The girls all loved it; the thick towels, the monogrammed dressing gowns, the beauty parlours and of course the swimming pools. It was amazing what they would do in a suite in a five star hotel. I used to ensure that all the mirrors were positioned just right so I could watch me performing. Some of them even allowed me to take photographs of them jerking off. The best hotels were those that showed porno films late at night and I found that particularly interesting – watch the film then try to repeat it with the bird you were with. It was amazing how much they would do once I'd got them going. The nice ones ironically were the worst, or to be more precise, the best. I loved watching our own show in the mirror; it was better than the porno films any day. As I got more experienced I bought a video camera and made my own amateur films. In the evenings when I hadn't got a bird, I could relive memories and relieve myself at the same time.

Cheshire trusted me more and more. To celebrate another promotion I stepped up my thieving. I had even worked out an even better scam, which was so simple and easy to do it made me laugh. I credited Mumford's account with a thousand pounds and he paid me six hundred pounds in cash. I didn't even have to leave the shop to do it! Aren't computers wonderful?

Sharon was now quite important at Cheshire's, too. She ran the key accounts section, in other words, those with money, the sort of people that I liked. The combination of my selling skills and her being in charge of the accounts was a very attractive proposition. It had worried me that such a lot of my income was generated from Ray Mumford. Cheshire was always lecturing us on the importance of not being dependent on one customer and that we must diversify. It seemed only business-like to diversify into other areas. I began to cultivate the big spenders. If I found something nice round the exhibitions, I would buy it myself and offer to deliver it to the customers. Some of them put me up for the night in their posh houses. I always gave them a very good deal; softly, softly, catchee monkey!

On my twenty-first birthday Sharon had a special present for me. She told me the evening was to be a big surprise, and she certainly didn't disappoint me. She told me that my present was on my bed waiting to be unwrapped. When I went into the bedroom, lying on the bed was a very attractive friend of Sharon's dressed in a nurse's outfit with the skirt rucked up, showing blue stockings and looking very sexy.

"Hello John," she said. She smiled invitingly. "I'm part of your birthday present. Do you want to have your bed-bath now or later?"

"What do you mean 'part'?" I asked hungrily. "What's the rest of the present?"

With that Sharon came in, wearing a new outfit I'd never seen before – a gymslip and white blouse and long white socks. She was sucking her thumb. God she looked incredible! It was a scene from one of our favourite pornos.

"Well," she said, "you've always wanted make love to two in a bed. Tonight you can make your fantasies comes true. Let's see if you're up to it, shall we?"

Not only was I up to it but the girls themselves put on a special show for me which they allowed me to video. They also filmed me with each of them. I'd only seen myself in the mirror before and had never seen any live sex, so the pictures were very exciting. I don't know how many times I performed that night for as soon as I wilted they made me watch them, which got me going again. At the end the girls wanted to erase the tape. I pretended I had, but didn't really. I still enjoy watching it. It was a bloody good way to come of age.

Despite the attractions of having Sharon on hand with her particular skills, I decided it was time to get my own private pad. After all, I was making a lot of money, and as I always said: if you've got it, flaunt it. Once again I had to approach Cheshire for a financial reference.

"Are you sure you can manage two mortgages?" he asked. He always seemed to talk to me as if he was my dad. He thought he knew everything. Still, it didn't hurt me to humour the old git. "You realise that if you don't pay the instalments on time that you could lose both the properties?"

"No problems, honestly, Mark. The main house makes a profit of around three hundred and fifty pounds a week. Add that to my income, I could easily afford a seventy thousand pound mortgage. This flat's only sixty thousand and if I move out of number twelve I can get another lodger in and that'll give me another seventy pounds a week. And to be honest, Mark, I'd like to get away from Sharon, if you know what I mean."

"I thought you and Sharon were an item," said Cheshire with a puzzled expression on his face. "Sort of common-law thing." How old-fashioned can you get? He wasn't even that old, he just sounded it.

"Christ, no!" I said quickly. "It's just a business relationship. Trouble is, I think Sharon's beginning to believe it's more. That's why I want to move out if you know what I mean?"

"Don't forget that you will have to pay income tax on that. Have you taken it into account?"

"Of course!" I replied, thinking to myself, *Not likely! As far as the Income Tax Office is concerned, I still live with my mum.*

"All right, I'll help. But I won't lie. I'll only put down exactly what you earn."

Pompous git. "No, that's fine. That's all I need."

*

I moved into the flat the following month. It was at the top of an attractive Victorian building close to the seafront. It had the benefit of being in the right part of town, unlike my other dump. I was reviewing my situation, two properties, a newish flash car, twenty thousand in the bank – everything was going exactly according to plan. The big problem was I hadn't reckoned on nosy old Maitland, Cheshire's accountant, getting involved. He certainly needed seeing to, he was poking his bloody nose into things that didn't concern him.

PART V

MARK CHESHIRE

Chapter 10

"This tape's dynamite," said Reg Knight, with a cockney evangelical fervour. "Give this to the right person at the Post Office and we've got the lot! It's practically a full confession, I couldn't have asked for more. The entire phone call was taped without Len Hawkins or Colin Grey knowing a thing about it."

"How did you get away with it?"

"Oh, it was easy, I got one of Len Hawkins' Post Office colleagues to help. He was convinced something was wrong, so he put a bug in the phone. I got the bug incidentally from that friend of yours you put me in touch with, Peter Pike. He's been very helpful – seems to know a lot about these sort of things. What is he, a policeman or something? Mind you, he doesn't half pollute the atmosphere; what does he smoke, manure?"

"No I think he calls it tobacco, something Sir Walter Raleigh introduced him to! As for his job, I think something like policeman is about right."

I'd been helping Reg with his investigation because I, too, was convinced that Mumford and his crowd were forging large numbers of covers. Forging was good business if you could get away with it. One set of George V stamps fetched a few pounds if they were mint, but on envelopes dated by a postmark on the first day of issue, they would sell for nearly ten thousand pounds. I'd never seen a set before the previous year and yet at least ten had surfaced since then, which meant that somebody had made an illegal hundred thousand pounds. These were just one of the many different rarities hitting the market. Someone was making a small fortune out of it and I was sure that the someone was Mumford. How else had he suddenly been able to buy so much at auctions? One minute he was just a small stamp shop-keeper, the next he was an international buyer.

Needless to say, the Post Office was not happy. No big organisation likes to get involved in controversy, especially if it only refers to a very small part of their business, but under pressure from the top, the evidence was passed on to the Post Office investigation department. They in turn went straight to the Fraud Squad. I was summoned to the City of London police station by a Chief Inspector Sandy Neil. I was shown into an immaculate office. All the papers were neatly arranged on the desk, behind which was a wall of neatly labelled box files. There were two men in the room, one was a small brown-haired chap, wearing a once-smart suit. You didn't really notice him that much as the other man dominated the room. He glared at me with the most extraordinary piercingly green eyes I'd ever seen.

At first he was offensive, which made me angry.

"You should have brought this to us months ago!" he shouted. "Why did you wait? You've made our job much more difficult."

"Simple," I replied. "The Post Office said they wouldn't co-operate. I had to wait to get firm evidence so don't have a go at me. I've been trying to get something done for years." I realised I was shouting at him too.

His sergeant laughed and said, "Well, that's telling you, Gov!"

The inspector looked at me for a minute and then he too laughed. After that, Sandy and I formed a friendship that was to last for many years. He was an extraordinary man. He had a first-class brain and a degree in criminology that was higher than anyone else serving in the police force had achieved. He was very tall and imposing and his face was half-hidden by a bushy moustache. Like me, he did everything very quickly and our conversations were a bit like machine-gun fire. During the investigation he suffered a major blow with another case. He'd spent two years investigating a pair of rogues who'd been involved in millions of pounds worth of fraud. Just when he'd got everything in place, one had a heart attack and died, the other hung himself. Sandy was very upset by this.

"Two years wasted. I've got three rooms full of evidence and now there's no-one left to prosecute."

"Well, at least they've been tried by a higher judge and found guilty. You should be pleased."

"Yes, but I don't get the credit," he moaned. "Two years' graft – what the hell do I do with all the paperwork?"

Everything had been going well for Sandy in connection with our case. But he rang me up one day, sounding very upset.

"Len Hawkins is dead," he told me. "He's had a sudden heart attack. It's just my luck. The principal witness gone just before the trial opens again."

"Can't you use his statement?" I asked.

"No can do. It's dead as a dodo and with it my case against Ray Mumford collapses and I'll have to drop the charges against him. The only evidence we have against him was Hawkins' testimony. He's been too clever, all we'll get is the small fry. But at least it will stop any more forgeries coming onto the market. I'm sorry, I know it's important to you.

"It was a heart attack, I suppose?" I asked. "It's very convenient for Mumford, isn't it?"

"You cynical bastard! Yes, I asked the same question. A heart attack could possibly be induced, but who's going to prove it? It's as you say – very convenient for Mumford."

Just before the case came to court, there was a very unpleasant incident. I was a key witness and, as they say, I was leant on. One of the defendants was a repellent Irishman called Patrick Fahey, a small-time dealer, who sometimes used to do part-time work for Mumford. He turned up at my stand at Stampex late one evening. He'd been drinking and he stood grinning continuously, like drunks seem to do. He stared at me for some time without saying anything.

"Can I help you?" I asked. It was a silly thing to say, but I couldn't think of anything else.

He leered at me.

"I know where you live and I know it's very lonely up there at night. Very lonely indeed." He stated this in a slurred broad Irish. "Your wife is there all by herself." He continued to grin at me while everyone around the stand listened in a horrified silence.

"I've got friends back home who owe me favours. Good friends. They know what to do. It wouldn't be hard. Particularly when you're at Stampex." I was becoming more and more frightened.

"I wouldn't think of going to court if I were you. I don't think you'd like the consequences much." He grinned again and staggered off.

"Christ," said one of my customers, "that's an awful threat. What are you going to do about it?"

"I'll report it, but you can't really take seriously an idiot that threatens you in front of at least ten witnesses. He'd be in trouble if I was run over on the way home tonight or if anything happened to Beth. Forget it, he's drunk."

Although I said this confidently, inside I was very frightened; we did live in an isolated spot and Beth was very vulnerable. I phoned Sandy up at home and he reassured me.

"Don't worry. He's got no IRA connections. He's tried this one earlier and it didn't run. He wants to be careful though, they don't like people using their name in vain. He'll be getting a ten-pence coin through the post if he's not careful."

"Ten-pence coin. What does that mean?"

"I had a witness a while ago and he wouldn't testify as it involved the IRA. He got a ten-pence coin through the post and he rushed to us for police protection. You get the ten pence to make the phone call after you've had your kneecaps blasted." He laughed and continued his story. "The bloke spilt everything after he got it and his testimony helped to make our case water tight. I often wondered about it, who really sent the ten-pence piece.

"Anyway, Fahey is relatively harmless. I'll have him in and read him the riot act. He's rather stupid though. I'm picking up information that he's absconded from a stretch in Ireland. We won't tell them unless he gets off, otherwise he can do his porridge here and then we'll send him back to complete his Irish stretch."

Sandy was as good as his word and I had no more bother. The case duly opened at the temple of high justice, the Old Bailey.

I don't know what I expected; I was certainly not prepared for what happened. It started badly and then went from bad to worse. In the first place, I couldn't believe the way that the jury was chosen. I sat with Sandy while the defence and prosecution selected them. The first candidate was a man wearing a pinstripe suit, obviously a city type.

"They won't have him," said Sandy, "he's too intelligent."

Sure enough, he was rejected. Another man turned up with a Telegraph under his arm.

"They'll reject him. They won't like the Telegraph."

Again, Sandy was proved right. Gradually the jury was chosen and seemed to consist of the dimmest-looking people available on that day. I began to realise why my mother's cleaner, who couldn't even follow a half-an-hour programme on television, had been chosen twice for jury service and I'd never been asked at all. Not only did we have the dimmest jury available, it was also a condition that they knew absolutely nothing at all about stamps or coins, which meant they would have a very hard job following a complicated fraud case. There were six defendants and therefore six Defending Counsels and one Prosecutor. The Prosecutor was an exceptionally able man, but unfortunately he was ill during most of the case. While I was being interviewed for two days he was lying groaning most of the time while the defence had a field day. At the end of my first day in the box I was manipulated by a particularly unpleasant Defence Counsel into one of those horrible situations where you have to say yes or no. I could see it coming a mile off and kept trying to wriggle out of it, but whatever I did the man relentlessly ground me back to the final position of being able to tell me, "Mr Cheshire, you must answer yes or no."

The judge, who was not only deaf as a post but also senile, backed up the Defence Counsel.

"Mr Cheshire, you really must answer yes or no."

I was so angry that I went straight back to the

office, picked up a lot of exhibits and came back the following morning.

"Your honour, before we start this morning I thought I confused the jury yesterday. I wondered if I could just straighten out a few matters."

"Anything that would help the jury would be valuable, certainly."

I walked over to the jury and handed them each a first day cover. I explained why what had happened at the end of the previous day was wrong. None of the Defence Counsels could believe it. I felt a bit like Perry Mason. According to Sandy, there'd never been anything quite like it in court. The judge allowed me to be asked so many leading questions it just wasn't believable, but then my behaviour was absolutely fantastic, too. It certainly bore no resemblance to the normal court cases Sandy had attended.

I thought I'd been treated badly.

"It was almost as if I was a mass murderer and rapist, not an expert witness," I complained to Sandy afterwards.

"Don't worry," he said, "you watch what they do to me. Police brutality, planted evidence – you name it, they'll suggest it." He was quite correct, I couldn't believe how they treated him. You've certainly got to be desperate to go voluntarily to be a witness in a court case.

The case went from bad to worse. There were so many red herrings and smokescreens dragged up by the defence, that the jury were absolutely baffled. Day after day the case dragged on, at enormous cost to the taxpayer, until one morning the Prosecution Counsel didn't turn up.

"Where's the Prosecuting Counsel?" asked the judge.

"I'm afraid he's ill," said the clerk. "He can't come in this morning."

"What do you mean ill?" droned on the old fool. "How ill?"

"Well, ill," said the clerk.

"Who told you he was ill?"

"The chief clerk at the Chambers, Your Honour."

"Get him here at once, I want to talk to him."

"What?"

"I said, I want the chief clerk now."

The chief clerk was duly sent for.

"Swear him in," said the judge. The chief clerk to the chambers of the Prosecuting Counsel duly took the oath and took the stand.

"I gather Sir Michael is ill. How ill?"

"I don't know, your honour. I just took a phone call and was told he was ill."

"Who phoned you?"

"His wife, your honour."

"What time was this?"

"I'm afraid I don't know, I was eating my cornflakes." The chief clerk was trying not to laugh.

The whole court was absolutely horrified. Sandy told me afterwards that he'd never ever seen anything quite like it. To put the chief clerk of a Prosecuting

Counsel in the dock and interrogate him, now that was something unusual! Eventually after the judge had continued his questioning for about half an hour, he let the clerk go and the Court was abandoned for the day. The extraordinary thing was that anyone could see that Sir Michael, the Prosecutor, was very ill. It was amazing he'd managed to continue with the case for so long. The judge really must have been blind and deaf not to have realised it.

"What on earth is he doing up there?" I asked Sandy. "The man's unfit."

"Well, put it this way," he replied, "if you had the choice between sitting on a park bench and feeding the birds or sitting up there and earning seventy-five thousand pounds per year, which would you choose? There's no way you can retire a judge, they make the decision."

"So he'll go on for a number more years. I suppose they go on until they drop?"

"Too true," said Sandy. "You want to see some of them. They're even worse than this one. If you ever have the odd week or so I'd be glad to tell you all about them."

So this was British justice. Grey, one of the Post Office workers, and a couple of small shopkeepers who I thought were unlucky, were found guilty and given suspended sentences. Patrick Fahey was sent to prison for a year, with the recommendation that he should be deported to Ireland afterwards to complete his other sentence. In all, probably the taxpayer paid a million pounds for nothing. From my point of view, though, at least it stopped the forging racket. With my expert testimony in the dock about the older forgeries it meant that I'd cleaned up the problem. So at least that was good news. The bad news was, of course, that Mumford was still completely free. He had no criminal record and I had to continue dealing with him as he was a major customer. I must admit I found this rather distasteful.

Chapter 11

One of the sad parts of running a business was the coming and going of staff. In some cases, I have to admit, I was delighted when people went, but normally I was sad, as Cheshire's was just like my family. I knew I would eventually lose Charles, after all, he wasn't in the first flush of youth having retired once before when he had been a director of a bank. He certainly didn't need the money I paid him and only came in because he enjoyed helping me to build a successful business.

When he came into my office, I was not totally unprepared for what he was going to say.

"I am afraid I'm going to have to retire again," he said sadly. "Bea wants to go on a cruise to Australia so she can see her sister again. I've been given my marching orders."

I suspected at the time that Charles had not told me everything. I was worried that his health may have been the real reason for him going, but it was none of my business anyway.

"Do you remember when you came for your interview?" I asked him.

"Yes," he replied, "I was surprised at the time how big your firm was. I couldn't have imagined anyone making any money out of stamps. But I've thoroughly enjoyed watching you grow and go from strength to strength. I'll buy shares when you go public!"

Charles had applied for a job as a book-keeper. I interviewed him along with five other candidates, most of whom were young mothers returning to work. Although the standard of applicant was high, I was certainly not prepared for Charles. It's difficult to describe how I felt; it reminded me of when I was at school and had to visit the Headmaster's study. Charles had a presence and I instinctively knew that here was somebody of quality. He wasn't very tall and was dressed in a light grey suit. His immaculate silver-grey hair matched his small neat moustache, his shoes shone like glass and the creases on his trousers looked so sharp that you thought you could cut yourself on them. I was terribly embarrassed when he called me sir; it didn't seem right that I should be interviewing Charles at all. I couldn't offer him the job I'd advertised as it was beneath him, but I saw an excellent way of strengthening my accounts department. I asked him to come and reorganise the whole department. I would get one of the young ladies to do the day-to-day work. He was delighted and kept telling me that he was not as good as he used to be and that he'd do his best not to let me down. This he certainly didn't do.

Not only was he to reorganise the whole accounts department, but it was also reassuring to have such an experienced businessman in the office. In life you come across very few people of such high calibre and I was fortunate to have had the pleasure of knowing him for so long. The accounts systems that he'd set up ran well but were not quite as efficient without him and his experienced eye. He had the knack of putting his finger on a particular problem.

Just before he went he provided me with one last idea. Part of the business had been based on buying new issue stamps from all over the world and sending them off to thousands of customers; Charles was concerned that we didn't make any money out of this operation. When I checked, I realised that he was right. The turnover was probably over half a million a year but we made little or no profit on it. After double checking the figures I sold the business to Butlers, the new issue specialists, for fifty thousand pounds. They were delighted; it fitted in with their other activities and they thought they could make money out of it.

After that was settled I found to my horror we were overbuying stamps to the level of about fifty thousand pounds a year. By taking Charles' idea and getting rid of part of the business, we could redeploy staff to work on more profitable work, we saved an outlay of around fifty thousand pounds per annum and also realised fifty thousand pounds capital. I would certainly miss Charles very much. We didn't see much of him after he left to go on his world cruise. Tragically, he never saw his family in Australia. The cancer, which he had failed to mention, claimed him on the voyage.

After Charles' departure, Wendy, the young girl whom he had trained as his assistant, took over the day-to-day running of the accounts. Her job was getting more and more difficult though. Britain was in the middle of a recession which had caused massive unemployment. When people are short of money, they tend to spend it on essentials – food, heat, light.

The last thing they need is stamps or coins. Cheshire's produced special first day covers which were sold to shops all over the country. Wendy was finding it almost impossible to get the money in from our customers. In the North, the shops were closing at a frightening speed, many were going bankrupt and we normally got nothing back from the liquidator.

The only bright spot during this recession was the skill of John Rich. He was a real champion and I was very glad I had given him a chance. He had become like a son to me. He was always popping into my office with good news.

"I've just sold that PUC £1 cover for four thousand pounds," he'd say, or another day he would come in and tell me about a fantastic collection he had bought. Most days he reported success stories which helped to keep my morale up. He'd also taken my advice and learnt to work well with Ray Mumford. I still disliked the man and thought him a crook, but I had to admit that we would be in a completely different situation if we lost his business.

Rich was the exception, everywhere else around me was doom and gloom. Not long after Charles had left I got a phone call early one morning from Len Wyatt who was not only my bank manager but also a friend.

"Hello, young Mark," he started brightly on the phone. "You're going to have to get yourself a new daddy to look after you 'cos I'm off on a new adventure."

"What do you mean you're off?" I asked. "Have you been promoted? If you go to another bank, I'll move with you." I'd already moved twice to stay with him, as I knew him to be the best bank manager in Essex.

"No can do, young Mark, I'm off firefighting."

"Firefighting? I thought you were a banker not a fireman," I laughed.

"No, you dozy twit. That's the bank jargon for fraud. It won't take me more than a couple of months to sort out the problem, it's only a small branch and it can't be that big a fire. You'll be in good hands with Jim Turner. When I get back, well, if you want to move back to me you're very welcome. If not, you might find you prefer Jim Turner, he's a good bloke. There's only one difference between him and me; if you get into trouble he'd bankrupt you."

"So you wouldn't? Well, that's nice to know," I said.

"Of course I'd bankrupt you, but I'd laugh, that's the difference. I'll bring him over next Tuesday, if that's all right, and introduce you to him. Give you a lunch. Book the cheapest place in town, will you?" Same old Len. On the surface a song and dance man but underneath as hard as nails.

"Well, I won't make any secret about it, Len, I'm going to miss you. But I hope your fire goes well."

As it turned out his fire was a little bit larger than he anticipated and he got stuck in the branch for about two years. The new chap, Jim Turner, was all right but didn't know our business and hadn't got the same confidence in me that Len had. All this was not good news, particularly as my accountant, Phil Maitland, had been unwell for some time and had got behind with his regular auditing.

I prided myself on being a fairly good businessman. I trimmed our expenses as quickly as I could. I closed the Southwold shop and moved the stock to Clacton. For once I was pleased if any member of the staff left, as it represented another saving. I took on job after job in order to save money. God! Was I tired! I worked a ten-hour day in the office doing the work I no longer employed people to do, and then I would do my own work in the evening at home. As if I didn't need any more problems, the computer system developed gremlins and seemed to crash every day. It always seemed to misbehave if I tried to find one of our better customers. I was given a chance to buy a rare cover for seven thousand pounds, which I was sure we could sell for ten thousand pounds quickly, but I didn't want to spend so much money out on a gamble. I persuaded the owner to give me first option for a week so I could try to place it.

"John, who bought that PUC £1 cover?" I asked Rich that afternoon. Rich looked at me in amazement. It was unusual for me to get involved with his side of the business.

"Don't look so shocked," I laughed. "Remember, this is how I started. It's about time I got involved again." I thought he looked frightened. He probably thought that I was after his job. "Don't worry," I said reassuringly, "it'll only be an occasional thing but I enjoy playing with the expensive covers. Anyway, who was it who bought that cover?"

"I can't remember. It was a new customer. I'll see if I can find out for you."

"Never mind, I'll get the information from the

computer. You did sell it for four thousand, didn't you?"

I had hardly started searching when the system crashed. The computer was out of action for a week and by the time we were up and running again, the cover was no longer available. Normally I would be worried out of my skin about the business, but at the time I had more pressing worries. Beth and I had been trying for a family for a long time. Every time Beth became pregnant, she miscarried, which had left her a little weaker each time. I blamed myself as I was sure she had damaged herself while carrying all the heavy stock into the exhibitions with me in the early days. Eventually, things became so bad that our doctor told her that she had to give up work and rest for at least a year. The loss of Beth's skills in the business was enormous. It was like losing six people. It also, of course, increased my workload, but that didn't matter. I'd gone past the point of caring about me. All that mattered was Beth. At least the enforced rest was having some effect. Although she was bored, she already looked much less pale.

Try as I might, I couldn't keep up with everything and some things were drifting badly. I felt sorry for Wendy, my workaholic book-keeper. I was not surprised when she came to see me looking very worried.

"The overdraft's up again, I'm afraid. I just can't get it down. I'm trying. We're going to have to make some more economies."

"How bad is it?" I asked, hoping by some miracle it would only be slightly up.

"Well it's sixty-five thousand which is ten thousand more than last week. It just keeps growing. It's like a monster."

"All you can do is slow down some of the payments. I'll look at the production figures for the new issues again and see if I can reduce them further."

"Well that's all right, but the trouble is I've got to pay the Post Office next week and that's a big invoice and the VAT will be due in three weeks. We need something more than just reduction of figures," she said, scratching her ear violently as she always did when worried.

"I agree. The answer, as you know, is to reduce our costs, and that unfortunately includes staff." I'd never had to make anyone redundant, yet it was something I dreaded. I just hoped I could avoid taking that sort of action. I hated the idea of sacking anybody. It just wasn't Cheshire's style. I believed we were a family and families should stick together to solve their problems.

"I'll check the debts again and look at the stock. We could perhaps sell a chunk, which would help." I'd done it before and it could produce a short-term effect. Trouble was, the stock you sold was the very stock you should keep. But it was worth trying.

A couple of days later, Wendy came to my office again.

"Mark, could I speak to you off the record?" Wendy's face was white.

"Sounds serious, you're not going to leave me, are you?"

"Oh no, nothing like that. You know me, I'm here till you kick me out. No, it's about John Rich."

"Well, what about him?" I asked, knowing well it would be not good. John had never got on with the rest of the staff, who regarded him with great suspicion. His trouble was that he was too arrogant and wanted success too much. The others were jealous of his rapid rise through the company and hadn't liked him much before he got the rooming house and now he'd got money, their resentment had grown alarmingly. He was the best dealer I'd ever employed. He'd learned about covers and stamps very quickly and he had an excellent eye for a bargain when he bought.

Wendy was red with embarrassment. "Well, there are a lot of rumours going around about his money. Opinion from some is that he's on the fiddle. There's also talk of him being involved in selling drugs. I'm not saying any of these rumours are true, but you ought to know what's being said." Wendy had been with the company for a long time. I trusted her completely. I was sad that she didn't get on with John Rich, as they were both key figures in the business. She was a tall, impetuous girl who always told you what she was thinking, a practice that made her just as unpopular with some of the staff as Rich was. She was, however, a hundred percent loyal and I was glad that she could tell me things even when she knew I didn't really want to hear what she was saying.

"Well, thanks for telling me, Wendy. I'm sure there's nothing in it, but I'll keep my eyes open just in case."

I didn't really get much of a chance to think about

it because, as Phil Maitland was always telling me, things were either double good or double bad. You know the sort of thing, when you've had a bad year in the accounts and you try to look for extra profit, you can only find losses. If on the other hand you've had a good year and you're looking for any losses you've missed, so that you can reduce the tax liability, you only find profit. I used to think that money worries were perhaps the worst you can get in the business, but then I discovered there is something that can be ten times worse and that's if your computer system crashes.

We'd had computer problems before but suddenly they were becoming a nightmare. I didn't fully understand how computers worked, but the one thing I was sure of was that without a computer Cheshire's couldn't work. We'd started some years earlier with a massive mainframe computer which we bought second hand from our office supply merchant. They didn't tell us at the time that one of their secretaries had thrown a cup of hot chocolate over it so that it never really worked as well as it ought to have done. It was, I suppose, some compensation that the smell of hot chocolate wasn't that unpleasant when the machine overheated. The computer had been an expensive mistake in some ways but it had started us on the right road and we replaced it with a wonder machine which some brilliant engineers in America had invented, and which was light years ahead of its opposition. The only trouble was they forgot to go out and sell it. It's no good having the world's best of anything if you don't market or sell it, and in the end the firm went bankrupt.

We were in the process of replacing the system, it would be months before the new one was up and running, and the old system had no technicians to back it up. Although it was more reliable than the mainframe had been, it still crashed fairly frequently and no-one on the Cheshire staff, not even Beth, who had learnt a lot about computers since we started, could put it right. If it were to crash permanently, it could have meant the end of Cheshire's. We spent hours every night printing out all the records so as to have a hard copy of all transactions in case the worst should happen.

I found myself living on my nerves. I'd never known quite so many problems at the same time. Our modern offices were open-plan except for a glass partition round my office, which meant that I could see most of what was going on through the windows. It was summer and very hot. The south side of the office was all glass and the sun beat in, heating the room to tropical temperatures. We certainly could not afford to install air-conditioning and the ceiling fans stirred the air just enough to blow paper around and get everyone annoyed. Tempers were frayed. Every time I saw a group around a table or a computer my heart started beating faster.

"What's going on?" I asked Wendy, who was standing with a group looking, I thought, rather worriedly at a computer terminal.

"Oh sorry, Mark, we're just discussing Bill's love life."

"Bill's love life? That's got a lot to do with work hasn't it? Go on, get back to work, dogs, or I'll get the thumb screws out again! Anyway, nobody would be interested in those sort of details, would they? Come to think about it I don't think I even knew Bill had got a love life."

"I'll tell you about it over coffee," said Wendy mischievously as she went back to her desk.

It was nice, to have Wendy laughing. She'd just gone through the ending of a particularly messy affair. It always amazed me that the strong, determined girls could be absolutely destroyed by some bastard of a bloke. She was a very strong character, in fact I'd think three times before I'd take her on. But as far as love was concerned she was just a doormat. The chap dominated her and treated like the proverbial dirt. He'd taken her down and down until her confidence and self-esteem were at an all-time low. It was pretty traumatic when he left. Thank goodness now she was beginning to get back her confidence, and it was nice to see her giggle again.

As it happened Bill's romance was short-lived and he threw himself into his work, which was good for me but very sad for him.

Life continued at Cheshire's in the same predictable way; we kept losing customers, the computer continued to crash, people were not paying their bills, and staff numbers kept falling. I had known better times at the office.

PART VI

JOHN RICH

Chapter 12

"That bald-headed bastard is on to something," I was moaning to Sharon while we were relaxing after a particularly strenuous workout. I never understood where Sharon got her ideas from. If fornication became an Olympic sport she'd certainly be in the British team, probably as captain.

"Which particular bald-headed bastard are we talking about?" Sharon asked.

"That bastard Maitland. He's worked something out. I know it. I've been watching him carefully. I don't think it'll take him long to suss out what we've been doing."

"Oh Christ!" said Sharon. "It's not something I even want to think about. I told you to stop. After all, you're doing bloody well out of the tenants with all the money you've got, why take the risk? It's just asking for trouble."

"Yeah well, it's a bit late now, so the big question is – what do we do about Maitland?"

"How about a bribe?"

"Do you reckon he's bent?"

"He might be bent," giggled Sharon. "In fact, I'd say he certainly is. After all, he's not married and he lives with his old mother; but dishonest? Probably not. Perhaps you could try bribing him with your body. That's a bribe he might be interested in!"

"Sod off. I'm not that desperate! Well that just leaves frightening him. He doesn't look very brave, does he?"

"There is his crippled old mother. I reckon that if you threatened her you might get somewhere. Trouble is, it could go wrong and then he's got even more to get us with."

I could see only one solution and I wasn't about to tell Sharon about it. Safest way was to change the subject.

"Well, whatever we do, we've got to get a scapegoat. What about that little bleach-blond, druggy friend of yours? What's his name, Paul? Let's get him working for Cheshire and get ready to catch him stealing. He'd do anything for drugs. Perhaps I'll become his supplier," I added.

"What do you know about supplying drugs? It's not like cigarettes, you know."

"It's no different. All you gotta do is find a wholesaler. It only takes money and I've got plenty of that."

I left Sharon still worrying and purred off in my Celica.

As I drove along I got to thinking. I don't know why I hadn't thought about it before. Drugs – it could make me a lot of money. It was only another kind of dealing. You bought from the source as cheaply as possible and then sold to the suckers. Don't get me wrong, I didn't want get into starting kids off on a habit, but those who already had their little habit, why not help them? After all, I would be providing them a service. Particularly if they were already friends like Paul. I knew at least ten takers. I'd always laughed at them for being so stupid. Wasting all their money. Stands to reason – they could waste it with me.

The other idea that was buzzing round my head was that druggies would do anything for a fix. I'd heard that 'anything' included assault, robbery, and possible murder. I couldn't think of anything else that would stop Maitland. He was too honest to bribe and I didn't think that threatening either him or his mother would work. He was the sort to call the cops regardless. I had to get rid of him or I would lose my position at Cheshire's just when the going was so good. I needed a murder arranged. It could be that someone out there, some drug-crazed addict could be the answer to my problem.

The first problem, though, was to find a source. It was no use just finding a pusher. There wouldn't be any profit in that for me. However, a pusher could be the easy way of finding out the information that I needed. If I could find some vulnerable little git that I could lean on, so they could tell me what I want to know. I couldn't see any point of working locally as it would probably be more expensive and I could be known. No, London was the place, lots of room where you could easily lose yourself. I decided to try my luck in the big city.

In life some things are easier said than done. Del Boy is always going to be a millionaire, so he tells Rodney regularly. I personally remain to be convinced that any no-hoper like him could ever make any real money, let alone become a millionaire. Mind you, saying that, he'll probably find some priceless antique and make it anyway.

When I said to myself, find a drug dealer and get rid of Maitland quickly, it sounded easy. The problem was, first, how do you find your drug dealer? And more important, who murders Maitland? And how much would it all cost?

I took to going round the clubs, looking for a likely lad to lean on. Luckily I could fit in easily to such places and I was able to continue the admirable education Mrs Radcliffe had given me by adding some overseas variations. I found the Indian and Chinese girls particularly interesting, even though I had to admit that Sharon could teach them a thing or two. There is, however, a limit to the amount of ear-shattering noises and eye-bashing lights that I can take, not to mention the stupidity of spending a fortune on excessively priced drinks. Eventually I found what I was looking for, a weak-looking ponce who was a small-time pusher. His clothes were a joke. I expect he probably thought he looked real cool, but as far as I was concerned and, I suspected the majority of the ravers, he looked a complete nerd. Still, I have to admit modern fashion was not to my taste. I like my suits to be sharp, my ties silk, my shirts from Jermyn Street and my shoes from Jones. I had acquired a taste for the good life and it didn't fit in easily with the scene I found myself in. The druggy-nerd was called Charles – wouldn't you know it, a real Charlie! I played along at first, buying cannabis regularly, and established myself as a good cash-paying customer. I waited one evening till he was sitting alone.

"Hey Charles, you and I need to talk. Can we go somewhere quiet, if you know what I mean?"

He seemed very reluctant at first until I pulled out a wad of notes and flashed them in his face.

"I think it will be worth your time," I said, watching his greedy little face light up.

"All right," he said. I found it hard to keep my face straight. He sounded just like Kenneth Williams. "But not for long, I don't want to miss any trade."

"It will only take a few minutes," I reassured him, thinking at the same time I didn't want to be seen with an obvious poofter like him anyway. I didn't want to spoil my reputation, did I?

We walked down the street a bit till we came to a convenient alley which I had sussed out earlier. I pushed him down it.

"'Ere, wait a minute," he whined. "I don't mind talking, but why down here?"

"Shut up and just listen. What I want is easy. I need to talk to your boss, the one you get your supplies from. I want to set up in my own town. Don't worry, it's miles from here and I'll only supply people I know. Where do I go to meet him?"

"You must be joking!" he said. "I wouldn't last long if I told every addict in the world where to go, would I? Talk sense man. Who do you think you are, the Godfather?"

I grabbed him by the shirt and rammed him back against the wall. "Now look, tosser. I've wasted enough time with you. I told you it would be worth your while." With that I took out five twenty pound notes. See this hundred pounds? It's yours if you pass on the message. You will get half now and the rest I'll give to the Man, and I do mean the Man, when I see him. You don't have to tell me his name. Just get him to phone 0376 68241 and ask for Rich. I've written it down for you to make it easy. There, that isn't too hard, is it? Even you couldn't get it wrong." Just for the hell of it, I shoved him against the wall once more. I really did enjoy the thrill. "Don't let me down. You don't want a nice holiday in the local hospital." With that I walked off, not looking back. Hopefully this would mean that I wouldn't have to visit any more rubbish clubs.

As it happened, I didn't have long to wait. I got the call the next day.

"Rich speaking." I had taken to answering the phone like that since I heard Mark do so first day at Cheshire's.

"I think you want to meet me," said a cockney voice. "Be at the Leicester Square theatre ticket office at three o'clock this Saturday afternoon. Bring a large white handkerchief with you and blow your nose at three p.m. when the clock at the Swiss Centre strikes.

Got it?"

"I think so. You mean that cheap place next to the cinema where all the American tourists go to get half-price tickets."

"You got it. See you there." The phone clicked.

I punched the air. Yes! We're getting there!

It was certainly a lot quicker than I had expected. During the next few days I kept myself busy round the office, but everywhere I went, I seemed to find Maitland, checking papers, adding up figures or asking questions. I just hoped I could get things organised quickly enough.

I drove up to London early on the Saturday. There was a car park at the back of Leicester Square which was very convenient – mind you it was also bloody expensive. But what the hell? Cheshire could afford it! I paid using Cheshire's credit card. I'd told him I was on a buying trip so I didn't need to use my own cash. I walked round the corner to Leicester Square and got my handkerchief ready for the big blow. The man that came up to me was not what I'd expected. A short balding cockney, wearing a cheap leather coat and faded blue jeans. He certainly wasn't a good advert for drug dealing.

"You Rich?" he asked.

I thought this was a bit stupid. How many other people were blowing their noses on big white handkerchiefs?

"Who else would I be, Little Boy Blue?"

"All right, so it's a bit corny but it worked, didn't it? Would you have preferred a red rose? Right then, let's go and get a drink."

We walked round the corner and sat down in the seats outside the Hampshire Hotel. We ordered two cappuccinos and sat watching the world go by.

"Now, I've already done most of my checking, but I needed to see you. I can smell a copper a hundred yards away."

"Well you won't smell anything on me, unless I've just trodden on something! How come you reckon you're that good?"

"Cos I'm an ex-copper, that's why. I now do more lucrative work."

The penny dropped. This was not Mr Big, nor even Mr Small. He was just a cheap private detective, checking me out.

"Well, do I pass?"

"Yes, you'll do. Your father was a tea-leaf wasn't he? I suppose it's natural for a son to follow in the family tradition."

"Didn't take you long, did it?" I was quite horrified to find out how quickly an apparent jerk like him could find out so much so quickly. "What do I do now?"

He grinned at me. "You do nothing. I report back and you will probably be contacted. I gather you've got something for me."

"Not so fast. I told that wanker Charlie that I'd give him the parcel after I'd met the Man. With due respect, mate, you're not the Man."

He got up and left me to pay the bill. He

disappeared into the crowd of tourists, but he was as good as his word and I received a call the following Monday evening.

"Mr Rich, I understand you want to see me." The voice was very public school and not at all what I'd imagined. "Can you make eight o'clock tomorrow at the Green Jade on Wilton Street?"

As it happened, I did know Wilton Street. The Cheshire staff used to stay at the Eccleston Hotel for Stampex, and Wilton Street was close by.

"I'll be there. How will I know you?"

"I booked a table in your name as you will be paying. Just go to your table, I'll meet you there."

As I would probably be drinking, I took the train into Liverpool Street and the tube to Victoria. I was quite excited at the prospect of getting started on the road to solving my problem.

Wilton Street is a small back street filled mainly with restaurants. The Green Jade, as well as being expensive, was obviously popular as it was very full. After giving my name, I was shown to a table close by the window. I sat drinking a vodka and tonic and watching the other diners arrive, speculating on which one would be my drug dealer. A tall blondish chap arrived, sat down and sniffed. He introduced himself as James Robinson, though I doubt if that was his real name. It was obvious what his nickname was, and from the moment he sat down I thought of him as Sniffy.

"I understand you wish to make some transactions. I'm quite happy to help you with your new business venture. However, as you have no previous record with us, I have to insist on cash in advance. Perhaps when we have built up a relationship, we could talk about credit terms. I do hope this will be satisfactory."

"Yeah, I can live with that," I said. "Is there a minimum order?"

"One would expect wholesale quantities. After all, you'll be retailing. I don't deal with individuals and cut out the trader. Now, that would be unethical." The way he was talking, you would think we were discussing cars or furniture.

"Yes, but how much is the starting point? How much do I have to buy?"

"Well, the usual minimum would be a thousand pounds. Incidentally, I would recommend the Green Jade Seafood Delight as a starter. It's excellent."

Despite the fact that I was paying, he ordered pink champagne. I subsequently learnt that was all he drank. He then went on to ask for lobster, crayfish, goose, sizzling steak, Singapore noodles and rice. I wondered if I could knock the price of the meal off the thousand pounds, but thought he might not like it. I'd brought a lot of cash with me but not a thousand notes. As we crunched our way through the lobster, I said, "I'm happy with your terms of business. I'd like to start straight away. Trouble is, I've only brought six hundred notes. Will that do as a deposit and I'll pay the balance on collection?" Sniffy cracked a particularly difficult chunk of lobster and pulled out the delicious white flesh.

"Fine. Pass the money under the table and we'll call the deal done." He smiled and grabbed another lobster tail. I noticed he seemed to pick all the bits worth having whilst I worked extremely hard and didn't get anything. It didn't help that I spent so much time on the head.

I pulled the money from my back pocket and slipped it to Sniffy. He didn't bother to count it. He just put it in his pocket and continued to enjoy the excellent Chinese food.

"Well I sincerely hope that this will be the start of an excellent business relationship. After all, we are here to serve," he joked. I paid the bill, leastwise Cheshire did. Mark wouldn't have been too amused though, if he'd known just which 'customer' I'd been entertaining that night.

I was just about to leave when I remembered Charlie. "Oh, James, could you give this to your colleague? I promised him it." With that, I gave him the other fifty pounds, safely sealed in an envelope.

"Thank you," he said politely. "However, the man you refer to no longer works for me." The look on James' face was not nice. "I'll credit your account with the money, so that'll be three hundred pounds on completion. Goodnight, Mr Rich." He smiled and left. I would have liked to ask him what had happened to Charlie but I had a horrible idea that I wouldn't really want to know.

I was to meet Sniffy a number of times in the next two weeks. I had already decided to stockpile the powder if necessary, in order to create a good impression, but as it turned out, business was very good so I really did need to keep buying. We always met in restaurants and I'd always pay. Mind you, to be fair, he did give me some free samples which easily made up the difference. It was just as well because I thought Cheshire's card had been given a bashing lately and there was no point going to all this bother and end up losing your job just by being careless.

*

The next day, I was paying one of my regular visits to Ray's shop on The Strand when he told me about his new way of making me rich; leastwise, he came up with the idea, I understood the riches part.

"John, I'd like to buy the Cheshire mailing list," he said, thoughtfully sucking on his revolting, sodden cigar.

"I should think you would!" I said, grinning at him. "I would imagine everyone in the trade would want that one."

"Well? What about it?" he asked.

"Sod off! He'd know at once it was one of the staff, it's just not worth it. We've got a nice number going, why spoil it?"

"All right. But supposing I'd worked out a way where he wouldn't be able to prove who'd taken it?" said Mumford smugly.

"Go on then. How?" I challenged him, expecting it to be a non-starter.

"It's got to be done in three stages. All are important to my plan. The first involves you. Cheshire must have a large number of names and addresses on the computer who no longer buy from him."

"Yeah. Cheshire calls them the dead list. So what?"

"Do you reckon you could persuade him to sell the list? After all, he's short of cash and he would see it as money for old rope."

"I don't see that it would be a problem," I said. "But why?"

"Wait. You'll see. Now, the second part is again easy. Do you remember Greenbank?"

"Yeah. He was that cover dealer; Cheshire bought his stock and mailing list last year."

"Exactly. I've already persuaded Greenbank to sell me his old list. And for that matter, he's going to sell it to a few other dealers. He shouldn't, of course. It's very naughty. It's really Cheshire's property now. But what does he care? He's old and he knows Cheshire's too soft to do anything about it."

Mumford leant back in the chair, looking really pleased with himself. Mind you, he had good reason. Both of these sales would make it difficult for Cheshire to tell where the name and address had been obtained, if a customer complained about unwanted offers from other dealers. After all, they could have come from the dead list or Greenbank's list.

"You said three things?" I asked, getting more interested in his idea. "What's the third?"

"What's the security like at Cheshire's? Do they shred all computer print-outs?"

"No, they just go out with the rubbish," I said.

"Just as I thought! Right. You get some yobbo to steal the rubbish on a night when it's known that a lot of print-outs have been left out for the dustman."

"Nice one, Ray! Three different ways anyone could

have got at his lists!"

I had to give it to him. He wasn't a fool. The plan worked well. Greenbank sold his list several times and I persuaded Cheshire to sell his dead list. Stage one was accomplished.

A few weeks later, Mumford started up about mailing lists again.

"Now then, young Rich, what about this mailing list?"

"How much?" I asked, getting down to the important bit first.

"I'd see you right, of course. Five grand cash do you? Not bad for a bit of paper. Will you do it?"

"Yes," I said, and Mumford grinned. Well, he might. He thought he'd just stuffed me. But he'd have to get up earlier in the morning to catch me. "Yes, I'll do it – for fifty thousand notes."

"Fifty grand!" he squeaked, as if his trousers were suddenly too tight. "I can't pay that!"

"Take it or leave it! It's not worth the risk otherwise."

"I could go to, say, ten grand," said Mumford cautiously.

"Come on, Ray! You know it's worth a fortune. Don't try to con me. Fifty grand is cheap. You needn't pay all in one go. I'll take five thousand a week for ten weeks. I couldn't be fairer, could I?" I leant back on his shop counter. I knew he'd pay it. I could see it in his greedy, piggy eyes.

"All right. But I'm not happy," he begrudgingly

agreed.

"Poor old Ray! You thought I was as green as Cheshire! Come on, I'll buy you a meal to cheer you up."

I'd begun to work out what Mumford's game plan was. He hoped to weaken Cheshire's business so much that he could buy it cheaply. I wondered where I fitted into his plans. Probably nowhere. Still, wait and see. Softly, softly, catchee monkey.

Chapter 13

Knowing I was going to ask a different favour this time, I invited Sniffy to the International Club. I thought he'd enjoy it. I particularly asked for a secluded table where we would not only not be seen, but we could talk discreetly. Sniffy was impressed with the place and very much enjoyed the pink champagne which I gather was excellent. Mind you, so it ought to be at a hundred and twenty notes a bottle! I was a little nervous at first so I asked him about his life. "I don't want to be rude, but you don't sound like one of us."

"Thank you, I'm not. I'm the proverbial black sheep, expelled from Gordonstoun."

"Drugs?" I asked.

"Good Lord, no! Girls! I was caught three times too often. The last one was the Headmaster's daughter! Mind you, I was only fifteen at the time."

"What then?"

"Oh, expelled again. This time it was for drugs. I didn't fancy the family firm so I set up in business for myself. Now forgive me for being impertinent, but you haven't brought me here for a meal and some small-talk. What's the real reason?"

So it was that obvious. I thought I was being clever.

"Well, I've got a problem. My main line of business is good, but involves certain transactions that are, well, a bit dodgy."

"So you're a thief, that's what you're saying, isn't it?" said Sniffy with remarkable accuracy.

"All right. But there's this interfering, nosy accountant coming round the firm who's likely to ruin everything."

"So you'd like this obstacle removed and you wondered if nice old James could arrange a convenient disappearing act? Have I got the correct idea?" I nodded and he went on, "I thought so. I'm sure that could be arranged. We like to help our friends. I take it that this was the real reason you chose me in the first place. Did Charlie open his mouth a little wide to you too?"

"No. I just got lucky. I've got a good racket going and our deals have been sweet. But I thought to myself that someone like you would have the contacts to help me."

"Let's get down to business shall we? How do you want it done and what's the timetable?"

"Now, there's got to be some rules. I don't just want him dead – it's got to look good; you know what I mean? What d'you reckon?" I asked.

"An accident's is normally the best way. Fall off a ladder or a cliff, car trouble. Brakes failure – now that's a good one; drain the brake fluid and hope for a good result." Sniffy said all this extremely coldly, as if he was talking about Arsenal's prospects for a good win on the following Saturday.

"Yeah, what if it goes wrong?" I asked worriedly. "We only get one go at it."

"There's always a chance he'll only break a leg or something. You want to be certain, don't you, so that really leaves us just one method. It's got to be a robbery that goes wrong. You know, a vicious burglar gets caught in the act and then panics and kills him. Now that's good, very good indeed, but it will be very expensive I'm afraid to say." Sniffy grinned at me. "I hope you have a lot of money available for this transaction."

"How expensive?" I was dreading that it would be out of my price range.

"Well, there's all sorts of costs involved as I'm sure you appreciate. But it shouldn't cost more than, say, twenty thousand pounds at the most. And we charge no VAT on top," he joked, "we're not registered."

Twenty thousand was all I had in the bank but it was worth it to protect my operations.

"All right, provided it's understood that it's the maximum and that I have no part in it."

"I can give the Robinson guarantee of satisfaction. We only use the best operators and they take their work very seriously. In fact some even take the work home."

"It'd better be this week, I think he's close to telling the boss and that would be a disaster."

"Well, no time like the present. You organise the money, I'll see about the transaction. I take it you don't need an invoice for tax purposes?"

We parted outside the club. Sniffy apparently had

some business in the Dorchester Hotel next door. I walked slowly back to the car, relieved to have got that meeting over and done with.

There was no doubt about it, Sniffy was a cold-hearted bastard. It would be easy getting the twenty thousand pounds, but that would mean I was virtually broke. Cheshire would have to make it up to me. After all it was his fault – he employed Maitland. I went down to my local NatWest and presented a cheque for twenty thousand, cash. The girl behind the counter became excited. She asked me for identification so I produced my driving licence, and said, "Now don't say you don't remember me! That's an insult, that is!" But that didn't shut her up.

"That's almost all of the money in your account, Mr Rich. Are you sure you want it all? In cash? It's unusual, I'm sorry I have to ask, but we have to be careful."

"Yes, I need it," I said confidently. "I've got a chance to buy a good collection of stamps but the owners want cash."

"I'll just go and have to see about it." She went behind the counter and talked to a tall grey-haired man who was her superior. He came out to talk to me.

"Mr Rich, will you step through to my office for a moment?" We went through into the cubicle he called an office.

"You're not in any trouble are you, Mr Rich?" he asked.

"What do you mean – trouble?" I asked.

"Not being blackmailed or anything like that are you?"

I laughed. "Nah, just that I got a good stamp collection to buy and they don't trust me. They'll only take cash. Sorry to disappoint you. You're not going to be on News at Ten if that's what you're thinking."

"Well, it's your money. I hope it is a good buy." He gave me the withdrawal slip and I signed it.

I have to admit I shared his view. I too hoped it would be Good Bye to Phil Maitland.

I took the twenty thousand out in fifty pound notes, that way it fitted easily into my briefcase, the briefcase that Cheshire had given me so I would look a bit more professional. I had never seen so much money in my life. I had a thought for a moment that I could go back to the flat and make love to Sharon lying on the scattered money. I'd seen it done in the movies. I thought it looked really cool but then she didn't know I was organising Maitland's departure and might get a bit upset. And so I got the car and drove slowly back to London. I crossed the Thames using the Blackwall Tunnel, came in on the City Road and parked my car by St Katherine's dock on a scruffy old bomb site. I walked through the dock, lusting enviously after the expensive yachts and anticipating the day when I would own one.

Sniffy had arranged to meet me in a cafe overlooking the boats. It seemed to be strange place to be paying for a murder, but then it didn't really matter where you did it. He was the first to arrive. I walked over to his table and sat down.

"Want a coffee?" he asked. "I'm having one of

those orangey biscuits. D'you want one?" Sniffy had a posh voice. It was rather odd sitting in this beautiful place with a posho, about to discuss a murder.

"Why not? I'll have two sugars in mine, please."

We sat sipping the coffee looking at the boats, eating the chocolate and fiddling with the silver paper. Sniffy looked me in the eye.

"I've got the best for your job. I've used his services in the past and I've always found him to be a professional." At this point Sniffy became confidential. "In my particular line of business, we get a lot of amateurs. They seem to feel that this is the age of competition. Despite what this government may recommend, I don't like people who try to move in on my territory. This is why I can vouch for him. He has been extremely useful in the past. If he has a weakness, it's that he does tend to enjoy his work."

"You mean he's a psycho," I asked, wondering what the hell I was getting in to.

"No, I wouldn't say that; as I said, he's a professional. He works for hard cash. It's just…" He hesitated for a moment. "He does prefer to do the job with his hands. Is it all there?" asked Sniffy, changing the subject.

I nodded.

"Well, the job should be done this weekend. Make sure you're with someone the whole time, understood? Right, you've got the details I asked for – address, map, description?"

"Yes, I've written it all down, but get rid of it quickly. I don't want it traced back to me."

"What do you think I am, an amateur? Give me a little credit, please."

I gave him the briefcase and left him drinking a second cup of coffee. For all I knew he could be arranging yet another murder as I walked through St Katherine's Dock. It seemed as if it was all some sort of dream. Surely you couldn't have a human life ended so easily? But I knew it wasn't a dream and Maitland's innings was about to end.

When I got back to the car I found I'd got a bloody parking ticket stuck on the windscreen of my car. I'd forgotten to buy a ticket as I arrived. I pulled it off and threw it in a puddle. I wasn't paying that.

I thought about the meeting with Sniffy. Odd really, wasn't it? A bit like organising a summer holiday, one payment and it was all arranged.

Chapter 14

The car was stifling hot and I couldn't get any air into it to cool it down as there was a wait-wait driver holding up all the traffic turning onto the main road. Because of this dick-head, I'd had a long wait under a hoarding advertising new luxury apartments due to be built shortly on the car park. They would have excellent views over St Katharine's Dock. I thought, *If the man does the business with Maitland, perhaps I'll put my name down for one.* I liked the idea of a luxury Thames flat. Thinking about it made me wonder what was in Sniffy's mind. There was something about his smirk I didn't like. He seemed to be laughing at me. I wondered if the same man had been the one to deal with Charlie. I had a horrible feeling that I'd been responsible for that particular no-hoper's death. Still, best not to think about it. He was nothing to me. Why was Sniffy so happy? Had I paid over the odds? I bet that was it. Still, why not? I'd have done the same in his position. I was excited, yet terrified at the thought of murder. I didn't like Maitland. He was a nosey old queen. Besides, he'd left me no alternative. It was his own fault. No, what worried me was if anything went wrong.

What I needed now was some easy money and a woman to take my mind off things. But money first. It was still reasonably early, I could always pay a call on one of Cheshire's suppliers. I'd buy a lot of stock and sell it to Mumford. Thinking about it, I knew just the bloke. I stopped the car at the next phone box. Surprise, surprise! It was actually working. I looked up the number in my Filofax and called him up.

"Hello, Robbie, it's John, yeah, John Rich. Look, I'm passing your place and I'd like to buy some stamps. Will you be there about seven thirty?" I'd never known Robbie turn down a chance of some money.

"Yes, all right, but you'll have to be prompt. I've got to be out before nine and I can't be late."

I took the M25 round to Hatfield, picked up the A1 and headed north. Robbie Jacobson lived in Letchworth in one of those mock-Tudor houses. He had a fantastic stock, yet he rarely advertised. He was too mean. The whole set-up was ideal because his prices were always reasonable and I should easily be able pick up enough to make five grand and still have time to go on to a club after.

As I left the streets of London behind and started passing through the parklands of Knebworth, I found myself thinking of Robbie's wife, Eve. I'd always fancied her and I reckoned she quite fancied me. She reminded me a bit of Mrs Radcliffe. The Jacobsons hadn't been married for long and had a young child. Come to think of it, if he was going out at nine, perhaps Eve would be staying at home. Now that would save me the expense of going to a club.

Seeing the factories of Stevenage flash by, my thoughts turned again to the road and soon I was heading up the old A1 and into the garden city. I'd made excellent time and I was at Robbie's front door by quarter past seven. Even though it was evening, the heat was almost unbearable. It was just a matter of time before the storm broke. It couldn't come quickly enough for me. I rang the doorbell which had one of those annoying jingles. Robbie opened the door. He was already dressed for his evening out in a penguin suit. It was obvious that my sexual fantasies about Eve were not going to be fulfilled tonight. She was wearing a gorgeous gold, low-cut evening dress which shimmered in the low sunlight. I felt myself hardening just looking at her. Perhaps it was the heat, but she seemed to be looking at me in the same way. I think Robbie could sense the atmosphere as he quickly ushered me through to the back of the house where he ran his stamp business. The room was long and thin with filing cabinets on one side. Stock lay everywhere. Robbie pulled out a drawer.

"I think you'll find these interesting. Some of the signatures on the covers are fantastic. I've just bought a collection and you're the first person to see them. You can have twenty-five percent discount on the prices and remember, that includes VAT, so they are very cheap. Don't even think about asking for any extra discount!"

He wasn't wrong! I'd do well with this lot. Mumford would pay the full price so I would have made money even if I'd bought them myself, not Cheshire. Not that I would though. What's the point? I needed all the money I could get.

"I'll have the Elvis Presley, Bing Crosby, Frank Sinatra and the Rolling Stones autographed covers," I started.

"Knew you would," grinned Robbie. "What about the Beatles? It's a good price."

"Yeah, OK. I'll have these World Cup team signed covers too. Have you got any Royalty covers?"

Robbie put that drawer back and gave me another to look at. It contained the best selection of signed Royalty covers I'd ever seen. I bought a Prince Charles, Duke of Edinburgh, Princess Anne and lots of others. After about an hour, I reckoned I had taken about ten thousand pounds' worth of stock and Cheshire wouldn't want me to spend any more. I sorted the covers into two piles, his and mine.

"Look, Robbie. I know you're in a hurry. Just give me an invoice 'signed covers as selected'. That will do me this time."

Robbie looked surprised. "Won't Mark want to see all the prices himself?" he asked.

"'Course he will. I'll go through them all with him. After all, they're all priced."

He was just organising the invoice when Eve came into the room. The light caught her blonde hair and the gold dress glittered like something from a Hollywood movie. She looked like a film star and totally wrong for Robbie. I wondered what the attraction was: father figure, money, security? It certainly couldn't be his looks.

"The babysitter's going to be late," she said.

"I've got to get there on time, you know that. I just can't be late!" Robbie thundered.

"You go on, I'll wait for her and catch you up. I'll be there before the dinner starts. Everyone will understand." She said this slowly and calmly, but I felt she was talking to me at the same time.

Robbie finished the invoice and I wrote out Cheshire's cheque for seven thousand five hundred pounds. Robbie carefully checked that everything matched and then locked it away in his desk.

"Nice to have done business again, John. I'm sorry I've got to rush. I'm being inaugurated as president of the Rotary tonight. Eve'll give you a cold drink before you go, I'm sure you could do with one. Hope to see you soon." He left, obviously worried about the evening, but not so concerned that he'd pass up some quick money. I thought he was extremely careless leaving a desirable woman like Eve alone with me in his house, after all, he must have heard of my reputation. I was sure Eve had, judging by the way she looked at me. Perhaps he trusted her; if so, he was a bloody fool.

We listened as the noise of the car engine dwindled in the distance and Eve smiled at me suggestively.

"Are you as good as people say you are?" She asked in a way that made it obvious that she wasn't talking about my stamp dealing.

"There's only one way to find out," I replied, knowing that I had no reason to make any effort to seduce her. She was more than ready.

"Let's go upstairs. The girl won't be here for an hour so you will have plenty of time to impress me."

To give her her due, we used the spare room. She said it wasn't right to do it in Robbie's own bedroom. Eve was very practical. She removed her expensive dress and carefully hung it up. She took off her beautiful lacy underwear so that nothing would give her away when she returned to the function. I stripped off too and watched the show with great interest. It amazed me the various ways women prepared for sex. I'd thought earlier that Eve reminded me of Mrs Radcliffe and the picture was even clearer as she clinically removed her clothes. What we were about to do was just simple sex; no complications, no pretence, just getting the maximum pleasure from two bodies. I could sense her excitement under the surface and I was determined that I would live up to all she had heard about me. Afterwards she thanked me as if I was some gigolo, unpaid at that, and took a quick shower to wash the smell of sex away. After she had restored herself to her previous perfection, she came and sat with me in the lounge on their expensive leather sofa.

"Don't get me wrong, John. I love Robbie. He's a good, kind man. It's just that he's never been very good at that sort of thing. It nice to have some satisfying ·sex sometimes with no complications. I knew you'd be just what I needed. You know when Robbie's away at auctions, perhaps you'd like to come again sometime?" I don't know if she intended the pun, but it amused me all the same.

"Why not give us a buzz when you're free and I'll try to get something organised."

"Can you do me a small favour? I must get off to Robbie's do. Will you wait for the babysitter?"

"No sweat. I've got nothing else to do. You get off. How long is she likely to be?" I had a good reason to ask that particular question.

"Not more than fifteen minutes. I arranged it with her earlier. Thanks." She gave me a quick peck, picked up her handbag and went off.

I couldn't have wished for a better evening. No, not the sex. That was a bit disappointing. I quickly made my way out to Robbie's office. She'd never admit to leaving me alone in the house after what we'd just done and I reckoned it was only my fair due to be paid for the services I'd rendered. I knew I'd got to be quick as I didn't want to be caught in the act. I only took items where he had a number in stock and nothing too expensive, nothing over two hundred pounds. It was like being in the market again: don't steal any big notes, only coins. It was still good advice.

After about ten minutes I'd collected together another ten thousand pounds' worth of covers. It hardly even showed with the massive stock he'd got. God knows what it was worth all together, at least half a million I'd reckon. He kept it in such a mess that I don't think he'd any idea what he'd got. I'd pay Eve another visit just for the chance of getting in here by myself again.

As I said, not a bad evening's work. I could show Cheshire these and then steal them back again in a couple of weeks' time, meanwhile I'd sell Mumford the first lot for around ten thousand. That would pay for half of Sniffy's fee. I went and put all the stuff in the car. As I went back in, I saw an attractive young girl heading towards the house. If she was the babysitter, I might just be prepared to keep her company. The doorbell rang with that irritating jingle. I opened the door and there she was, a picture of young innocence.

"I'm Becky, I've come to babysit."

"Yes, I know. I'm John. Eve asked me to wait for you and give you a drink." I lied easily, particularly as I saw from her face that she liked what she saw and I saw what I liked, which made it mutual. I had no problems with her looks. *What the hell?* I thought. As I'd said to Eve, I'd got nothing else to do. It'd be better than a club. It was just too bloody hot.

As I drove back later that evening, I reflected that the babysitter was by far the best. She might not have had Eve's figure, but at least she showed some enthusiasm. She reminded me a bit of Gail.

Next morning I showed Mark the signed covers I'd stolen from Robbie and he was pleased with the lot. I then took the others up to Mumford, on the pretence that he'd phoned me with an urgent order. For some reason, he was not as excited about my signed covers as I thought he'd be.

"I think these could well be forgeries," he said.

"No! No chance! They come from a very reliable source. Lots of them were personally signed for the owner," I told him, exaggerating just a bit. He still seemed doubtful. Perhaps he'd been caught by somebody before.

"I only want ten thousand for the lot. You'll easily be able to sell them for double that."

"I'm not sure, John," said Mumford, who really was sweating like a pig. This heat really got to fat people. "They'll be difficult to sell without any provenance," he said. "I could perhaps go to five thousand."

So that was his game! Trying to weasel on me!

"Don't be such a mean bastard, Ray," I said. "I need the money and you know they're good." In the end, we settled on what Cheshire had paid for them, seven and a half grand. Even then he couldn't give me the money straight away like he used to. He said he'd sort it out for me in cash in two or three weeks' time. I thought he'd done well, but he still looked worried as I left. I couldn't understand the bloke; I'd just given him as good as money in the bank!

PART VII

PHILIP MAITLAND

Chapter 15

Sunnyside Lodge was probably one of the worst named houses in the area. The house was set in a dip, which meant that whatever the time of the year, the sun found it difficult to penetrate the ever-encroaching vegetation. When it was built, about 250 years ago, with no trees surrounding it, it was probably in a delightful situation when the sun really did shine on it. But today it was damp, dreary, and as Estate Agents so aptly put it – ripe for improvement. The indigo sky helped to give it a sinister appearance, but all the heat achieved was to bring out swarms of mosquitos and flying ants.

Philip Maitland, Mark Cheshire's friend and accountant, lived in this remote cottage with his mother.

Phil's life had not been easy. His brother Harold had left home as soon as possible, leaving Phil to look after his crippled mother. Although she was a delightful woman she was also a considerable burden, both in time and money. She hated being left alone so Phil had given up most of his friends and rarely left the house except to go to clients' offices. Other than that, he did all his work sitting silently in the same room as his mother. He was a very able accountant. If he'd have wanted to he could have got a far better job, but he wasn't ambitious and as he got older he became rather shy. He was happy doing accounts for his dwindling bunch of old clients. He didn't really need much money. The house was paid for, although there was a lot of work that needed to be done on it, and his expenses were few. In all, though, it was a very lonely existence.

The more Maitland looked at the Cheshire accounts, the more certain he was that Rich was stealing considerable amounts of money. The obvious fraud was in the postal accounts. As far as he could see, Rich was removing thousands of pounds of everyday stamps. They would be easy to sell, after all, all businesses needed stamps and everybody liked a bargain. Maitland was not looking forward to telling his friend Cheshire. They went back a long way and Maitland knew that Mark looked on Rich as a son. He sat fiddling with his watch, a present from Mark some years ago. Mark had even had a message engraved inside it. The heat was getting to him and he went out to get some fresh air. Before he went out, however, he carefully sprayed himself with insect repellent.

He walked round the overgrown garden wondering whether he ought to get in a garden contractor to hack back the worst of the jungle. He even found it difficult driving his Humber Sceptre down the long drive to the decaying wooden garage. It really needed work doing on it, or even better, knocking down and rebuilding. He looked back at the house. It was a builder's dream. The roof needed doing. He'd had it patched every year for more years than he cared to remember and it looked very dilapidated. Phil was depressed. There was so much to do and so little money to do it with. He'd better get back and do some work. He trudged slowly back up the slippery moss-covered path and let himself back in through the narrow front door.

At about six o'clock he stopped for a break. He went out into the kitchen and prepared their evening meal. After they had eaten, he cleared up and they settled down to watch Inspector Morse on the box.

The story was getting complicated as usual when he thought he heard a noise out by his car. He listened carefully and there, sure enough was the same sound.

"I'm going outside for a minute, Mother," he said as he pulled himself out of the armchair. "I'll be back in a minute." Phil shuffled along the corridor in the darkness. He almost fell down the three steps to the front door, thinking to himself not for the first time that he must do something about those as they were very dangerous. Perhaps he would get a man in next week. One of his builder clients owed him a favour and he could knock the cost off his bill, after all, the blighter never paid anyway. Phil grabbed the torch and walked down the drive to the garage expecting to see deer. They'd been plagued with them recently. In fact, one had eaten all his mother's tulips in the spring. He got to the garage and looked around. There was no sign of any animal. He was sure he heard something. There it was again, a cracking sound. He turned round. To his horror, a large, bearded, unpleasant-looking man was standing between him and the house, brandishing a nasty-looking stick. The man grinned at him and moved slowly towards him.

"You're Mr Maitland, aren't you?" he said coldly.

"Yes, I'm Maitland. What do you want at this time of night?"

He saw the stick coming and felt the pain as it struck his head. His head felt like it was exploding. Everything went black.

His mother continued to enjoy Inspector Morse until the second advertising break.

"Phil? Phil, where are you? Phil, are you working again?"

The house was still.

What on earth is he doing? "Phil! Phil!" she shouted, but all was silent. *I bet he's playing with that car of his,* she thought, and once again settled down to enjoy the concluding part of Morse.

It wasn't until the final credits were shown on the screen that she began to get concerned. It wasn't like Phil to leave her alone, particularly with Morse, a programme he always enjoyed. She tried to pretend everything was all right but in her heart she knew something was wrong. Eventually she levered herself up, got the Zimmer frame from beside her chair, and pushed herself slowly towards the front door. To her amazement it was open.

"Phil! Are you out there?" she called as loudly as she could.

Nothing. Just the rustling of the wind in the trees.

She moved again slowly forward and like Phil before her, misjudged the steps. Those very steps that Phil had wanted to get rid of. He had always worried that they were likely to be dangerous to her. She fell badly, smashing her head on the edge of the open front door. As she lay there, a trickle of blood ran out of the cut and down onto the concrete.

***

"It's raining cats and dogs," I miserably complained to Beth late on Friday evening. "I'm not going to watch my game of cricket tomorrow, am I?"

"Never mind," replied Beth, "there's always a silver lining. You can decorate the spare bedroom. You know you promised to do it when you had time."

It was certainly true. I had, in a weak moment, agreed to sort out our dingy back bedroom. We were a bit ashamed of it when guests came. The problem was, I was the world's worst decorator. I couldn't cut straight which let me out of wallpapering, and when painting I always ended up the same colour as the room. I tried a tactical diversion.

"Funny old expression, raining cats and dogs, isn't it? Where does it originate from?"

Beth laughed. She knew only too well what my game was. "It goes back to the middle ages when heavy rain flooded what little drainage systems the towns had. The result was that everything, all the rubbish, floated up from the streets. It wasn't of course just cats and dogs, there must have been rats, mice, excreta – in fact anything that went down, came up. Simple, really. As you must think I am – trying to change the subject like that! I'll give you a hand. We can get it done over the weekend."

I listened anxiously to the weather forecast on the ten o'clock news. It didn't make good listening to a frustrated cricketer. Heavy rain was predicted for the whole weekend extending into the week. Flood warnings were being issued for low-lying areas – particularly those near rivers. At least that wasn't a problem for us, living as we did on top of a hill.

As it happened, we did get the room decorated. I didn't see any cricket and as I drove off to work on Monday morning through the torrential rain, I still had the evidence of the weekend on my hands. It was amazing how long it took to get rid of paint.

***

"I hate bloody rain," moaned Sharon late on Saturday afternoon, "I don't think I've ever seen it so wet. I wish it would just stop, it's so bloody depressing."

We'd finished shopping and had gone back to my flat for a bit of peace and privacy. The lodgers were getting restless, not that I could blame them. Their rooms were small and they had nowhere else to go. I certainly didn't want to be anywhere near them in this sort of weather. As I hadn't got anything better to do, I thought I'd be nice to Sharon; there was no need to be bored whilst I was getting myself an alibi.

We were warming ourselves in front of the electric fire when Sharon produced a book.

"Believe it or not, I bought this in WH Smith's." She laughed. "You wouldn't have thought it, would you?"

She passed over the book. I had to admit it wasn't the usual sort of Smith's book.

"The Art of Love." I read the title aloud and then began to dip into it. "What's this? A do it yourself fucking manual?"

"I thought as we'd got nothing better to do we could study together. I like the look of page forty-one."

I turned to page forty-one quickly. "Is that possible?" I asked incredulously. I don't know why I'd bothered. By the end of Sunday evening we'd mastered that and many of the other interesting positions even Mrs Radcliffe hadn't shown me. I felt completely knackered. Sharon was a bit like a suction pump pulling the very life out of me. I could hardly get up on Monday morning but Sharon gave me a hand. Afterwards we dressed quickly, grabbed some cornflakes and faced the rain again.

"I reckon it's worse now than it was on Saturday," moaned Sharon, shaking the drips all over the inside of my car. "It's going to be depressing at work today."

I felt a bit better by the late afternoon and invited Sharon back for the evening. The rain continued to pour down and according to the news twenty-one people had died during the weekend. Bridges had been brushed aside, rivers changed courses and virtually demolished houses in their paths. God knows how many road accidents had been caused by the floods.

"Look at those poor animals," commented Sharon. It was typical of Sharon. Having been told of death, maimings, people being ruined, all she was worried about were some stupid animals. "Come on," she urged, "let's get back to our research. Page forty-one needs some more practice."

*

Most people would agree George Partridge was normally a cheerful sort of chap. Ask anyone. His co-workers at the Post Office where he'd worked over twenty years, his drinking cronies at the Rose and Crown, his County Councillor colleagues, in fact anyone who knew George would say he was a happy man. However, he was not happy about the Saturday delivery.

"Bloody double glazing leaflets again! I'm a postman, not a household delivery service! I hate the sodding things. They're not even in an envelope. Cheap and nasty, that's what they are, and what's more, nobody wants any double bloody glazing!"

His mate, Bill Parsons, listened patiently. He'd heard it all before. George did not like the household delivery service.

"See you in the Crown for a drink at lunchtime?" asked Bill hopefully.

"I suppose so. That's if I don't drown. Look at that sodding rain. It's pissing down out there."

George thought for a moment and started again as if he'd only just come up with a new idea.

"I know one thing. I'm not going out to Sunnyside

Lodge just to deliver a double glazing leaflet; nor to Rook's Cottage that's for sure. They can wait till Monday."

It was still pouring down on Monday. George noticed a gas bill for Sunnyside Cottage. He carefully hid it so he could avoid a long, wet journey. Sunnyside Lodge was towards the end of his round. He never liked going out there unless it was a hot sunny day. It wasn't until Tuesday that he headed out in that direction. The entrance was always damp and dreary and today dropped water all over him, which made it seem as if it was still raining. The cottage itself was more like a ruin set in a damp depressing dell. It was more than likely flooded after such a deluge. The wettest weekend of the century, they'd said on the news.

As George cycled in through the open gate he heard an enormous noise of screeching and fluttering of wings, as if of a massive horde of birds. He cycled down the badly surfaced drive down towards the ramshackle garage. As he turned the corner, giving him his first sight of the house, he almost fell off his bike. A flutter of large black birds flew up noisily. The sight he was to see was to haunt him for the rest of his life. Floating by the garage was the body of a man, at least he thought it was a man, after the rooks had finished pecking it. The water round the body was a reddish brown colour. George got off his bike and was violently sick.

When he had finished retching he got back on his bike and peddled frantically back up the lane. The first house he reached was Walnut Cottage. He rushed up the crazy paved path and bashed the brass knocker hard.

"Whatever is it?" asked Mrs Wilson as she opened the door. "You look like you've seen a ghost, George!"

"Well, I have in a matter of speaking," said George. "I must phone the police."

*

The first I knew about the tragedy at Sunnyside Lodge was on the Tuesday's two o'clock news. I didn't realise it was Phil at that point. It was just reported that the police were investigating two deaths in suspicious circumstances and that more details would be forthcoming during the afternoon. At the time I was discussing the sales figures with Alice, who'd brought me the latest details.

"Are you sure you've got these right?" I asked hopefully. "It seems amazing that we could lose so many orders in one week."

"I'm afraid they are, Mickey. I've checked and double checked them. It's not one big customer, it's everyone reducing their orders almost daily."

It was worrying. The excitement of the rapid climb had long since been replaced by the depression of the spiral decline which seemed to be irreversible. Alice went back to do some more typing and I sat looking at the figures over and over again, trying not to accept that I'd already made a decision that some of our product range would have to go. I could only guess what effect it would have on the market, but it was pointless continuing to produce at a loss when there was no prospect ever of returning to profit again.

I was in this state of depression when Detective

Constable Sutton arrived. Alice brought him through and I assumed it was the usual crime prevention visit.

"Good morning, Officer, and what brings you here today?"

It's a rather unpleasant duty I'm afraid, sir. I understand you are a friend of Mr Maitland from Sunnyside Cottage, and also his mother."

"Yes, Philip Maitland is our accountant and also a very close friend. What's this all about?"

"I'm sorry to have to tell you that they are both dead. You may well have heard on the news about two deaths in suspicious circumstances. Mr Maitland was murdered and his mother fell trying to get out of the door to find out what had happened. This is very much a routine visit, sir. We have to contact everybody that knew them in case they have any information that might help. You wouldn't for instance know if the Maitlands had any enemies, or if in the course of Mr Maitland's work he might have upset somebody?"

"Certainly not. He had very few clients and all of us have been with him for years. I can't imagine many people knew them very well. They kept very much to themselves. It couldn't be anything like that, I'm sure." He asked me all the routine questions about where I was on the day Phil and his mother died which I answered to the best of my ability, though I was in a daze of shock. Finally, as he got up to leave I said, "Sorry I can't be of more help."

He thanked me and left.

After Sutton's visit I just couldn't stay in the office any longer. I told Alice I was going out to value a collection and drove slowly back to Beth and Clare.

Beth was in the hall as I arrived.

"What's wrong?" she asked. "You look awful."

"I've heard some terrible news, and I'm finding it very it very difficult to come to terms with it."

"Come and sit down, I'll get you a cup of tea."

I went into our sitting room and sat on one of my parents' old chairs which I'd known since I was a child, looking at an awful monstrosity of a fireplace. When Beth and I agreed on buying the house we said we couldn't live with it more than a few weeks – that was many years ago. We still promised ourselves we would do something about it as soon as possible but it still sat there, grinning at us as if to say, 'Leave me much longer and I'll become an antique.'

Beth arrived back with the tray with some of her delicious oatmeal biscuits and sat looking at me, waiting for me to tell her what had happened.

"Phil Maitland's been murdered," I started, "battered to death sometime last week. He lay out in that dreadful rain until he was found this morning."

"God, that's awful!" said Beth. "No wonder you feel bad. Do you want something stronger?"

"But that's not all. By the sound of it, his mother came out to find out what had happened and must have fallen down those old steps, you know the ones that Phil was always meaning to do something about. She smashed her head on the door and she's dead, too."

"Oh no! It's like something from some horrible book or film." Beth's face was crumpled with distress.

"Who on earth would want to murder Phil?"

"It looks, although the police don't know yet, like it was a robbery that went wrong. Poor old Phil. He always thought there was something better for him around the corner. He could never have imagined this was how it was going to end. Funny thing is, I didn't realise how much I liked him. He was a bit of an old fuddy-duddy but his heart was in the right place. I'm really going to miss him. I've also got the job of finding another accountant very quickly and the accounts aren't going to be very good this year. In fact we're heading for quite a large loss."

Beth came across and hugged me. As we sat there in the growing gloom, I reflected. How quickly things changed. It seemed only yesterday that everything we touched turned to gold.

*

Sharon burst into the shop, flushed, very excited. It was obvious that she had heard the news about Maitland. I made a mental note to keep very cool and pretend I knew nothing at all about it.

"Have you heard the news?" she almost screamed.

"No. What news?"

"Maitland's dead."

"Dead? What, he's had a heart attack or something?"

"No! Both he and his mother have been murdered by some maniac killer. It was on the news a few minutes ago."

"Have they caught the murderer?" I asked innocently.

"I don't know. I shouldn't think so. There's a big police investigation going on. They're appealing for anyone that was in the area of Rookery Lane last Friday evening."

"Well, that lets us out then. We were rather busy on Friday night, weren't we?"

I could have kicked myself for saying that, it was so stupid.

"What are you saying? You don't think the police could think we could be involved, do you?" asked Sharon incredulously.

"Well, he was digging his nose rather deeply into our affairs, wasn't he? From our point of view it's very convenient, isn't it?"

"I suppose it is," said Sharon. "I'd never thought of it that way."

If I'd have kept my bloody mouth shut she would never had either. She was looking at me in a very strange way. I had a nasty feeling she was beginning to put two and two together. She wasn't making five. I did hope she wasn't going to be silly because that would be rather a pity.

"Come on, let's go and have a cup of coffee."

PART VIII

JOHN RICH

Chapter 16

They say it's the final straw that breaks the camel's back. In my case the straw was Emma, who finally made me realise I wanted something a little bit more permanent. Sure, Sharon was always there, but would you want to get stuck with a nymphomaniac with lesbian tendencies? Great for one night stands or long wet weekends but not for life. And anyway, Sharon had no class; I wanted a girl with style. I was going all the way, I didn't want to be stuck with a slut.

I met Emma at a really boring stamp dinner. It was one of those stamp affairs that was trying to show that dealers weren't all nerds. All it did was to confirm to me what I'd already suspected – that they were. The hotel was cheap and unpleasant, the dinner poor, the group was dismal and the company boring. Other than that it was a great evening. I hadn't even noticed

Emma sitting across the table. She looked a dowdy little thing but on closer inspection I could see that she had a pretty face and nice breasts pushing through her business suit. Half of me thought an early night might be a good idea, the other half considered giving Emma the night of her life. I started to chat her up over the pudding and by coffee I knew she would be putty in my hands.

By now I had a certain reputation. It didn't take me long to sort out girls into two classes: those who wanted to find out if I was as good as rumour had it, and those who didn't want to know. Emma was very much of the 'let's find out' brigade. I suggested a goodnight drink and took her back to my place. No, not the pathetic little room that I shared with Bill, that was all that Mark Cheshire would allow us – no, give me a little bit more credit. I always rented a small serviced flat in Bank Chambers in Jermyn Street. It was run by an eccentric Irish lady and her assistants. They didn't provide food but they'd go out in the morning and fetch you an excellent fried breakfast if you were in the mood to have one. Jermyn Street suited me well. It was central, adequately furnished, discreet, and the beds were large and comfortable.

As soon as we entered the flat Emma spotted the bedroom and refused a drink when I asked her.

"Let's go straight to bed," she said, and started a rather pleasant striptease.

I had to say she didn't seem quite so dowdy without her suit on. Her underclothes were certainly different from those I would have expected. Her performance was also a revelation. Emma was no innocent virgin. She seemed to have an appetite that was never satisfied. I lost count of the number of times I performed but it seemed like it went on all night. After a final performance in the morning I was well and truly knackered. Perhaps I was getting too old for all this physical exercise? Needless to say I was the butt of all the jokes on the stand that day. One of our customers gave me his card and told me he would do me a special deal. When I looked at his card later I found out he was an undertaker – very funny. One thing I was sure of: I wasn't picking up anyone tonight, nor was I going out with Emma. She could work her skills with some other bloke.

I left the stand officially to go buying but really to get away from the stupid jokes. It was while I was wandering round that I saw her. Sheer perfection. A beautiful, sophisticated, gorgeous, dark-haired goddess. She was working on one of the snob stands. You know the sort, they charge a thousand pounds just for their company. The stand was always arranged to be so frightening that the collectors tended to run past, leaving it available for those with the large enough wallets to purchase the stamps, and by 'large' they meant people with tens of thousands of pounds to spend. Mark Cheshire was always winding them up by asking them if they found their stamps in waste paper baskets or dustbins. I must admit it did look like they did. But the prices were outrageous, seventeen and a half thousand for a few dirty bits of paper. I knew they'd have nothing for me but for such a girl it was worth a put down.

"Excuse me, can I see your Great Britain covers?"

She smiled. She passed over the wooden tray. "You're John Rich aren't you?" she asked.

"Yes, have we met before?"

"No, but you're quite famous. Everyone knows of John Rich's adventures." She looked earnestly at me and I noticed she had brilliant blue eyes.

"You don't want to take any notice of that rubbish," I said. "It's mainly put round by Cheshire's staff as a joke."

"Oh, what a shame," she laughed, "I thought you sounded very interesting."

At that point the owner, who, as I was to discover later was also her lover, turned up.

"Can I help you, Lisa?" he asked, realising I wasn't a serious customer. "Look, I'll take over. You go and get a couple of gin and tonics, all right?"

I followed her with my eyes as she walked off. She had an attractive wiggle. I was well and truly hooked.

Giles Haverford was a short, pompous, overweight public-school twit, who was already losing his hair. On the other hand he was a millionaire wearing a Savile Row suit. "I wouldn't have thought there was anything here for you, Rich. We only deal in quality." I didn't like the way he emphasised the word 'quality' as if I was just trash. I watched him take his wooden box containing the covers and stack it neatly with the others.

"Well, it was worth a look. You see, I'm thinking about collecting myself." I walked off and completed my buying on the firm's behalf.

As it happened I headed in the direction of the bar, thinking, *Lisa, now that's a pretty name.* As luck would have it there was a long queue for drinks and she was still waiting. I got the bloke behind her in the queue to let me in, so I could go on chatting her up.

"Hello, Lisa. Coincidence seeing you here."

"Coincidence my foot," she laughed. "You knew I was going to get some drinks."

"How about coming out for a drink with me this evening?" I asked.

"I don't think Giles would like that," she replied.

"I didn't ask Giles. After all, three's a crowd."

"That's exactly what Giles would say. But thanks for asking anyway. Flattering for an old married woman with a child to be asked out by the infamous John Rich." At that moment she reached the counter, bought her gin and tonics and left, smiling at me as she took her tray and disappeared back to the elegant Mr Haverford.

I needed some more information on Lisa so I dropped in at the stand of Bobby Bliss, one of the biggest gossips in the stamp trade.

"Lisa Potter," he said, "yes, I know her. Beautiful girl but far too nice for Giles. What do you want to know?"

"Well, she's married isn't she?"

"Yes, she married a right one – she's divorcing him, or so I've heard on the grapevine. He beat her, you know. Got a little boy, nice little chap, I think he's about two. She's living with Giles at the moment. But the word has it that she likes nice things. She's a bit rich for you Rich, if you pardon the pun."

According to Bobby Bliss, Lisa had a passion for

pigs, she even collected stamps depicting pigs. Don't ask me why, I'm not a girl. It would appear her preference in men was for multi-millionaires but she would, in certain circumstances, if pushed, settle for just an ordinary millionaire. Bobby gave me this gem of information to confirm that she also had very expensive tastes. At least now I knew the ground rules. Either I had to play the game according to the rules or not bother.

Armed with this new information, I was determined to make it my business to take Lisa away from Giles. In order to do it I would have to appear to be very well off.

With all my fiddles at Cheshire's, my drug money and my rent money, I was on my way to being seriously rich, so why not go for it?

I started my campaign delivering an enormous bunch of flowers together with a small cuddly pig. I took them personally around to her apartment block, rang the bell and waited.

"Yes, who is it?"

"It's a personal delivery for Lisa Potter," I called through the intercom system.

"Right. Come in."

I entered the building and took the lift up to her apartment. She opened the door and gaped in amazement as she recognised me.

"What's this? Moonlighting?" she asked.

"Only if moonlight becomes you," I joked. "These flowers and the beautiful pig are for an old married lady with a small son. The pig is for your son, of course."

"Why thank you, kind sir. But why? With all the girls in the world at your feet, why bother with me?"

"Simple. You're the one I want. The others are unimportant. When I first saw you I realised everything else was worthless."

"Wow! I almost believe you," she giggled.

"I don't blame you, but give me a chance. I'll prove that I'm different."

"I still don't think Giles would like me to go out with you. But thanks for boosting my ego."

My second attempt was with a very expensive brooch in the shape of a pig. I know it sounds ugly but this one wasn't. She agreed, after the brooch, to have a quick drink with me. Things were looking up, I felt. Finally, I bought a large cuddly pink pig and covered it with jewels, rings, brooches, necklaces and earrings. It looked stunning and it finally did the trick, she came out for a meal with me. I took her to the International Club. She was very impressed, particularly as all the staff knew my name. I might have slightly exaggerated my position with Cheshire's. I told her I was a director and that I really only worked there as a hobby as I had a private income.

From then onwards it was a case of softly, softly, catchee monkey. It was expensive but what the hell, Cheshire could afford it.

Courting Lisa brought with it two different problems. The first was that I needed a lot more money every week. The drugs were useful but they were never going to be more than a sideshow. Luckily

I had the answer already planned. I'd been cultivating quite a number of Cheshire's rich clients and it was just a matter of explaining to them our new system.

I started with one of Cheshire's best customers, an accountant at Coopers and Lybrand. I dropped into the palace by Charing Cross that they called an office. I called him up from reception and they showed me up to his room. He gave me a cup of freshly brewed coffee from a jug on his desk and we sat down in the two easy chairs by the window.

"Now," he said, "what can I do for you?"

"I've got some good news for you. Mark's come up with a scheme to save you VAT on most of your covers. If his plan works, you'll save between ten and fifteen percent every time you buy a cover."

"Well that certainly sounds good. What do I have to do?"

"Virtually nothing. We've set up a new company called Rarc Covers. We are going to make sure that the turnover of this company is always below the limit for registering for VAT. All you have to do is pay Rare Covers, not Cheshire's, and we won't have to charge you the tax. Oh yes, and there's another thing. Mark's only going to allow a few selected customers to use this service, so please don't talk to anybody about it."

"Mum's the word," said Brian, touching his nose to indicate secrecy. "Your secret's safe with me."

His reaction and that of all the others was exactly as I would have expected. They were all so pleased with their savings they never thought to question the scheme. After all, the only loser was the tax man or, to be more correct, the VAT man, and nobody likes them. My rare cover business was very successful and I was soon averaging a thousand pounds a week. Of course it was all pure profit; the stock was provided by Mark.

After solving the first problem I turned my thoughts to the second and the potentially more serious one, how to make Lisa think that I was rich without giving the game away to Cheshire and the rest of the staff.

I toyed with various ideas. Most of them I discarded very quickly – winning the pools seemed to be the answer but on reflection, the fact that I'd never ever been known to fill in a coupon, plus the fact that it could probably be checked if anyone suspected me, ruled that one out. I could have had a distant rich relation die and leave me a fortune, but as I'd always moaned so much about my family this would be exceedingly unlikely. Betting on the horses was out as I had no knowledge, I'd give myself away if any of the other staff asked me for tips. Anyway, this wouldn't provide me with the sort of cash I needed. There seemed to be no easy way to make me rich without raising eyebrows and therefore suspicion. The answer when it came to me was blindingly simple. If I couldn't become rich, then as far as the nosey gits at Cheshire's were concerned, Lisa would have to be. The question was, how to build the right background. The story had to be good.

The one thing that was certain, Lisa looked like a million dollars, so it would be easy to convince people that she came from a rich family. It also occurred to me that if I eventually married her, which was what I wanted, there needed to be a jolly good reason why I didn't want to work for her father. Perhaps he should be involved in a particularly nasty business, which would give me a reason not to want to join him and so I could stay on at Cheshire's.

Lisa's fictitious father was therefore reborn as a crooked wholesale newsagent. He was to be very rich but at the same time a bit iffy, a sort of minor Ronnie Kray. He wouldn't like me for the obvious reason that he could see a fortune hunter a mile away. Obviously he would be against the wedding, and I would need help from my friendly advisor, Mark Cheshire.

I developed the story, adding nice little touches. As Cheshire was providing all the goodies, I thought it was appropriate that my new father-in-law should be called Mark. It made me snigger every time I used his name. I was amazed how easy the whole exercise was. Lisa's divorce was due to become final on the twentieth of July. I worked out a strategy that would happen on about that date. Lisa, I discovered, was really a big kid at heart. In chatting to her I found out that she'd never been to Disneyland. The pompous Giles had by that time become history. It wasn't hard to get rid of him; after all I was incredibly handsome, very rich and what's more, good in bed, which was more than could be said about Giles, who was apparently not particularly well endowed. He also worked too hard making money to have energy for Lisa's personal entertainment. Even better, her first husband was a drunkard who'd suffered from Brewer's Droop, although in his case Distiller's Wilt would be nearer the point. Most of her sexual experience had been either hurried gropes by schoolboys, drunken attempts by her husband, or unsatisfactory couplings with Giles. I was able to bring a new dimension to her life and once she had experienced real satisfaction, I knew she would be unable to go backwards.

Boosted by my new confidence, I booked a holiday for two to Florida in July. I was determined to propose to her as soon as she was free. The sooner I had her safely installed in the flat the better. Even Cheshire was finding it expensive to keep Lisa happy. I was finding it harder and harder to find covers that Cheshire owned to sell to finance my expensive lifestyle. I'd also become increasingly worried about Sharon who, ever since Maitland's timely exit, had been acting very strangely. She thought the death was in some way to do with me.

From my point of view everything went very well indeed. The police seemed baffled and the new accountants didn't know squat. Sharon was a possible risk so I diffused it by giving her free samples. It didn't take long to get her hooked. After that she was too preoccupied to worry about irrelevant things such as what had happened to a pathetic accountant. I also had to ensure she didn't visit my flat anymore. I couldn't imagine Lisa would appreciate my relationship with Sharon. I didn't want to stop seeing her as she had a lot still to offer and she increasingly enjoyed introducing me to her special friends. These threesomes were very interesting and if possible, I didn't want to lose them, but I also didn't want to lose Lisa. Sharon wasn't too excited about my news, but after I explained that eventually, once I'd settled into married life she and I could probably carry on as before, she seemed much happier. One big problem was her work had started to suffer. She was always a bit moody but with her new habit she became very unpredictable. I was somewhat embarrassed when Mark brought up the subject.

"Is Sharon all right?" he asked over a coffee meeting one Friday morning.

"Why do you ask?" I replied, stalling to see how much he knew or guessed.

"Well she doesn't seem to be herself. I've had one or two complaints about her work. I've even had a customer complain to me that she'd been very rude to them on the phone."

"I think she's got family problems. I know she's been very low but I didn't realise she was bringing her problems into work. I'll have a word, Mark. All right?"

"I'd be grateful if you would. As you know I've been reducing the staffing levels quite considerably due to our reduced circumstances. I wouldn't like to have to let Sharon go."

Christ, nor would I! The thought of someone else doing her job was not one that I would relish.

"I'll make sure she gets back to normal. Leave it to me," I said.

"Oh, and while I'm on the subject. I'm not too pleased with that chap you recommended, Paul. He's another one who needs a sharp kick up the backside. Chase him, will you? He's bright enough but lazy. He also looks very ill. Does he eat? He's as thin as a pin."

"Yeah, I've been a bit pissed off with Paul's work

myself. I reckon if he doesn't improve you'll have to sack him but I'll give him one last chance."

I left his office reflecting that Cheshire was really making a cock-up of the business. It had been going down rapidly for the last two years or so. He seemed to be losing his grip. Everyone was saying it, both inside the firm and in the collecting world. He also looked a mess. I couldn't understand why a man in his position didn't buy himself some new clothes. He used to be so smart. It was the same with his car. When I first joined the company he used to drive a new Supra – you know the one, faster than a bullet. Well, that was until the advertising standards people made them remove the slogan, saying it encouraged speeding. His present car is a second-hand BMW. He bought it cheap from some firm in Glasgow of all places, the ones that advertise cheap deals in The Times. I don't think that's the right image for the company. Me, I'd upgraded to a Porsche 911 already. Now that was a car! No, all Cheshire did was to moan on about money. What a bloody bore.

*

"I've got a thief," I said to Beth after a particularly pleasant shepherd's pie. I'd never liked shepherd's pie before I married, but Beth's was magic. She put it down to the meat – top quality topside combined with plenty of onions, soft mashed potato and finally baked to make the potato crisp on top, but whatever the reason, it was great. As usual I'd eaten far too much but even the addition of a pleasant glass of Fleurie didn't alter the fact that something was very wrong.

"What makes you say that?" asked Beth, taken aback by my bluntness.

"It's staring me in the face. I've reduced all my costs incredibly, the turnover is down but not by that much. Either I'm a complete idiot or we're being robbed and if we are, my guess is by very large amounts."

"Any idea who could be the thief?" asked Beth, who by now was concentrating on every word I said.

"I'm not sure. My guess is Paul or Sharon but I could easily be wrong. What I need is a good dream again."

"You only have a dream once you've worked out what is happening, so get your brain into top gear and solve the problem, then you can have your dream."

I thought about it and my head ached. As it was the answer dropped onto my lap. Of all people, Ray Mumford supplied me with the answer.

He arrived early one morning just as I was opening the office. This was most unusual. We usually did all our business on the phone. Anyway, I had more or less given his account over to John Rich to run.

"Mark, I need a private chat. Can we go up to your office?"

I ushered him into my room and told Alice no calls.

"Mark, I bought a large stock on Saturday and as I worked through it I realised it was stolen, and stolen from you."

"How on earth did you spot it?" I said.

"Well, it was easy really. I sold you a complete collection of covers last week individually addressed to Major Read care of Buckingham Palace. I phoned

Major Read and he confirmed he'd sold no other covers and that some were unique. You couldn't have sold them on that quickly, and anyway if this chap had bought them legitimately, he'd have wanted a lot more money for them. I didn't need to be Sherlock Holmes to work that one out. I stopped the cheque and I've brought the covers back to you."

"Well, I don't know what to say! You really are the Good Samaritan. Thanks a million. What did the person look like who brought you the covers?" I asked.

"Ordinary sort of chap, shortish, balding with a mole on his cheek. But the really interesting thing was I had to go out to the bank a bit later on and I thought I saw him talking to one of your staff."

"Which one?" I snapped.

"I don't know his name. He's a very thin fellow, young, with dyed blond hair. He works with Rich. I hope you get the bastard."

"I will and I'll be in your debt for a long time. Thanks again."

"Oh don't even think about it. Us dealers ought to stick together. You'd do the same for me. Anyway, I gotta go. Glad to be able to help."

Once Mumford had gone I thought how much I'd misjudged him. The covers were worth thousands and thousands of pounds and he'd only paid peanuts. He was far more honest than I'd ever have given him credit for.

I interviewed all the young men on the staff to be fair but I was very sure it was Paul. The description fitted perfectly. After hours of interrogation I'd hadn't got anywhere. Paul was sticking to his story of being in Clacton all day Saturday and he said he didn't know anything about selling covers at The Strand. I wanted action and decided to gamble. I put it round that if the guilty person confessed by ten o'clock the next morning I would just sack them, but I wouldn't involve the police. After that the police would be involved and it would be out of my control.

Just before ten the next morning Paul came sheepishly into my office. He confessed to Saturday's theft, but said it was the only time he'd ever stolen anything. He sobbed like a baby and begged me not to take it any further. As I'd already said I wouldn't involve the police I dismissed him on the spot and congratulated myself on finding the thief so quickly. I was in a very cheerful mood when I returned that evening to Beth.

After we'd consumed a delicious bottle of Fleurie we sat on the veranda chatting about this and that. I got onto the subject of John's romance.

"The guy's gone all gooey. You wouldn't believe it! He's always buying her gifts, soft cuddly pigs, of all things. He's going to take her to Disneyland next week. Funny thing is, she's much older than he is and she's got a child. Mind you, she's very rich. Leastwise her father is and she's the only child so I suppose it makes sense. I never thought he'd become a toy-boy though."

"That's not really fair," said Beth, "he could well love her. You know what the songs always say – love is strange."

"Don Everley sang that and look what happened to his marriage," I replied, joking. "Apparently her divorce will come through while they're away. Nothing would surprise me to find they're married when they get back."

"I suppose you can get Micky Mouse to perform the ceremony with Donald Duck as best man and Minnie as maid of honour. At least it'd be a different wedding!" said Beth.

The sun had slowly disappeared while we were talking and the dew was beginning to fall, which I always thought was the worst part of our English summer evenings. I'd always meant to put up a canopy so we could sit out longer, but like so many other things I'd only thought about it and not done it. Beth looked particularly beautiful in the half-light, just like a teenager.

"I'd like to go to bed," said Beth.

"Are you feeling all right?" I asked worriedly.

"No, stupid. I'm not sleepy or ill."

"Oh, you mean bed!"

We retired early.

PART IX

JOHN RICH

Chapter 17

The flight to Orlando was lengthy and boring. It had all the atmosphere of a cheap coach trip to Blackpool. I thought I'd definitely travel first class next time. The travel agent should've warned me. Orlando airport was loud and noisy. Lisa and I quickly got a taxi to our hotel which was on Buena Vista Drive just outside Disneyland. It didn't take me long to realise that I had made a mistake; I should have booked us into the actual Disneyland compound. But then, like everything in life, you only learn the hard way.

The hotel was all right – nothing special. It was strange being there late in the afternoon when my body was telling me it was time for bed. We walked out to a nearby lake where there was a large Disney shop, where Lisa managed to spend several hundred dollars on assorted rubbish. We ate on a paddle steamer moored on the lake. The food wasn't bad. It amused me to eat a Mississippi Mud Pie.

Disneyland itself was magic. Lisa loved every bit of it, the stupid tiny dolls ride, spinning in the giant teacups and being terrified on Space Mountain. Personally I preferred the haunted house, particularly the bit where you come out and they plant a hitch-hiker ghost in the car with you. We quite enjoyed Epcot centre, the rides were good and the firework display in the evening was magnificent. I couldn't believe the French restaurant though. The head waiter tried to be rude to us. I soon put him in his place. But to be honest four days in Disneyland was more than enough for two adults and the rest of Orlando was not exactly the place to have a really good holiday. We went down to the old part, near by the old train station, but it was all rather tacky and when we wandered away from the main part, it was a little bit frightening. Lisa was not terribly impressed by it all and it didn't seem to me the place to pop the question.

I got to thinking it might be better to move on and I remembered Cheshire talking about a hotel in Barbados called Sandy Lane. He seemed to think this was pretty good and so I did a bit of checking and found I could get a direct flight from Orlando to Barbados the next day, and that Sandy Lane had rooms available. Lisa loved the idea so we packed up, left Micky Mouse and Co. and flew off to the Caribbean.

Sandy Lane was much more like it. We had a luxury room looking straight over a white beach and turquoise sea. The food was excellent and it was good news that as it was the summer everything was much cheaper. We hired a little Moke and drove round the sugar plantations and over to the other side of the island to Bathsheba, where we found an old colonial building called the Kingsley Club and we stopped for a cool drink and sat looking at the breakers smashing their way up the large sandy beach. It was here, with the salt spray of the Atlantic in our lungs, that I proposed to Lisa. To my surprise she accepted and we decided to get married there and then while we were in Barbados. We found out that we could get married at Sandy Lane, all we needed was to give them a few days' notice. So we decided to get married on the beach.

I arranged for the wedding to be videoed as a souvenir for us, and quicker than I would have believed it was possible, Lisa became Mrs Rich. To celebrate we went to a Bajan evening which was being held at the Hilton hotel, which was on the other side of Bridgetown. There was an old fort in the grounds and this was where the evening was held. It was a very romantic setting and Lisa loved it. Her eyes were bright and she had a slight flush to her cheeks. She was so beautiful that I thought I would never want to mess around with other women any more. She was the one I had been waiting for. We enjoyed the limbo dancing, the flame eating and the colour and excitement but not the food, which was a bit of a disappointment. It was all like a little bit of paradise, but like all good things it came to an end far too soon. It was annoying having to fly the wrong way back to catch the plane back to Orlando so we could rejoin our original flight back to London Heathrow.

Once we got back to England Lisa, her son Crispin and I moved into my flat. I wanted to give Lisa something really nice for a wedding present so I bought her an MG, which I knew she'd always wanted. It was also something that Beth, Cheshire's wife, had wanted so it was rather nice flaunting it, knowing that Beth would be extremely narked.

We weren't in the flat long before it was obvious that it was not going to work. It wasn't big enough for the three of us and to be honest it wasn't also quite what Lisa was used to. We talked it over and decided the best thing to do would be find a house and so I put the lodging house on the market as well as the flat which would give me enough for a decent deposit on the next house. I'd have to lie about my income. I knew Cheshire wouldn't help me; I couldn't tell him the kind of mortgage I'd got in mind anyway, so I decided to use Mumford, it wouldn't hurt him to lie for me. Luckily we were in a housing boom and it didn't take me long to sell the flat and the lodging house. Lisa found us a beautiful detached house with its own paddock just outside Chelmsford. Trouble was, it cost a little bit more than I'd intended to spend. I ended up with a two hundred and fifty thousand pound mortgage, but then Cheshire had always told me to buy the best I could afford. It had always worked for him in the long run so I was only taking his advice, which was good because he was going to have to stump up the repayments, even if he didn't know it.

I was particularly pleased to get Lisa away from Cheshire's as she wasn't aware of how rich her father was supposed to be and that he loved her to death, and would give her everything she wanted, but didn't think much of me. Nor did she know I'd told everyone that her father's name was Mark. I liked that joke. When I said to Cheshire, "Mark gave us that," little did he realise which Mark I really meant! All of these small things were unknown to her and so she might drop me in it at any time.

With one small exception everything was going very well. The exception was that it was getting more and more difficult to raise the sort of money I needed every week. It seemed to me that I was the only person working hard at Cheshire's; nobody else seemed to be pulling their weight properly. I suppose that was to be expected as Cheshire seemed to think we could run the firm on a tiny staff. The number of people working for Cheshire had dropped to twenty, which was amazing, bearing in mind that he used to have a staff of over fifty. I reckoned that was half the problem. If we'd had enough staff, we'd soon have been able to generate the sort of profits which would keep both Cheshire and me happy. It was worrying that my drug customers were getting difficult and I knew some were buying from elsewhere.

Chapter 18

"It's very convenient for us." These awful words kept coming back into Sharon's brain.

John was right. It was very convenient. Too convenient. There'd always been something about John that worried her. If she was honest with herself she knew he was an evil bastard He didn't care for anybody. Sure, he liked sex – no getting away from it and Sharon knew she was good in bed. Sex, yes, but that was as far as it went. She always knew he would drop her without any compunction if he needed to. She was, as he always jokingly described her, just a sleeping partner. She couldn't think of a single person that liked him. John Rich was always out for just one thing, and that was himself.

It's very convenient, very convenient.

He couldn't be involved in Maitland's death, surely? No, she was just being stupid. John wouldn't get involved in something like that, would he? However, the more she thought about it, the more the timing had her worried. It was a godsend to them. But surely such good luck was extremely unlikely? The more she thought the more she became convinced that he had had some part in the murder. Where did that leave her? Accessory? Did it matter that she didn't know or had no part in it? Would people even believe her? What about Rich? Where would he stop? Or for that matter, where could he stop?

That wet weekend they had spent together had been very strange. He didn't want to leave her at all, not even for a moment. He'd never spent the entire weekend with her before. At the time she thought it was odd but secretly hoped he was becoming fond of her. It might just be sex as far as he was concerned, but she had dreamed for some time that it was for real and that they would eventually get married. She saw in her dreams two or three kids, a nice house, a wood fire burning in an open fireplace, John in slippers wearing an old pullover and looking lovingly at her across the room. The house would be in the country with a large garden, possibly a paddock for their children's pony. She knew in her heart she was just being stupid. He only really wanted one thing and he was even getting tired of that.

That weekend though, had been different. He had shown more interest in her, more kindness, more love than he had done for many years. It was hurtful when he switched it off so quickly afterwards. At the time she thought it was perhaps just the weather. A wet weekend romance. Now she was inclined to believe it was something far more sinister.

She was finding it much more difficult to concentrate since he'd introduced her to cocaine. She had to admit the exhilaration at first was fantastic. She'd never, ever, felt better. The problem was the feeling only lasted twenty minutes or so and it was expensive to keep buying the bloody powder. She'd also found it very difficult to relax since she started and she had an awful tummy bug which was probably nothing to do with the drugs anyway.

John had become more and more distant, particularly since he started going out with that rich bitch-cow from hell. He had told her that once they were married he would make more time for her. She couldn't really see what he saw in the bitch, she was so old and she had a kid. Sharon had also noticed that John had started looking at her in a funny way, although funny wasn't the right word. Frightening was more like it. The final straw was Paul's dismissal. She was convinced Paul had told Cheshire all he knew. How long would it be before the police were involved? If John had had Maitland murdered, would she be arrested? What would happen to her? The more she thought about it the more frightened she became. It seemed to her she faced two horrors – either the police arrested her and she went to prison or she became too dangerous to Rich and she would end up the same way as Maitland. Death or prison was all she could see and neither appealed. If only she could sleep properly.

She'd tried to stop sniffing the powder and get back to normal. It wasn't easy and she found herself losing her temper frequently. Concentrating at work became more and more difficult. Ironically, it was her bad temper that allowed her to escape. After Paul left suddenly, Cheshire came out of his glass palace to help with the orders. She should have been grateful; after all, how many managing directors would bother with the manual work? The funny thing was, she was convinced he was spying on her.

"How's it all going?" he said one Friday afternoon in his usual cheerful manner. "Can I help you in any way, Sharon?"

It was said kindly, but all it did was make her feel more guilty. He and Beth had always been good to her. She remembered his face as she slagged him off and gave him her notice. He'd looked so hurt and shocked that she'd almost apologised. However, she'd realised quickly that it was the answer to her problems. Rich was not in the office and he probably wouldn't find out until Monday. With luck she'd be long gone and difficult to trace by then. She'd have liked to send Cheshire a letter telling him she was so sorry and she'd always be grateful for his kindness to her over the years, but was too scared that Rich would find out and trace her.

An old school friend had gone to live in Yarmouth and was always saying Sharon should look her up. As it happened, old friendship just wasn't enough, they had both changed so much in the last couple of years. It was obvious after a few days that living in the same house wasn't going to work and that Sharon was not wanted. She saw an advertisement in the Yarmouth Advertiser for a general helper to live-in and look after an old lady in a rural location near Bressingham. She phoned and was taken on at once. She guessed correctly that she was the only applicant and that the advertisement had run for many weeks.

The old lady was extremely rude, incontinent, and very fat. The work was not at all pleasant, but at least Sharon thought that she was virtually untraceable. The only consolation was the old lady's son, a kindly old man; at least he had seemed old to Sharon, but as it turned out he was still in his thirties. Sharon thought she'd be able to put up with the old lady's temper tantrums for a few months. That would give her a breathing space and then, if she found she just couldn't stick it, she could move on to something better. At least neither Rich, nor the police, would find her there.

The one good thing about the old lady's temper was that it gave Sharon justification for being irritable and nobody associated it with her fighting against her drug habit.

PART X

MARK CHESHIRE

Chapter 19

"Could I have a word?" Rich asked me on his return from Florida.

"Of course. Did you have a good holiday?"

"Brilliant! That's what I want to tell you about. I'm married! We flew out to Barbados and did the deed at Sandy Lane. I'll show you the video one day."

"Congratulations," I said.

"You don't sound surprised."

"No, probably not. But then you see, I'd already guessed that you might do it. Anyway, I'm very pleased for you."

"It means I'm going to have to move. The flat's not really suitable for a two-year-old boy and we're not moving into the other place."

"What are you going to do?"

"Mark, well that's her father, the miserable bastard, he hates me. He seems to think I'm a fortune hunter. He dotes on her. He's given her a lot of money to help and an MG for a wedding present. He'll give her anything but he'll give me nothing," Rich said.

"He'll come round. It's just a matter of time then I suppose you'll go off working for him."

"Christ no, he's a horrible man. I don't see myself in wholesale paper, and anyway, I wouldn't work for him. The way he feels I'm more likely to end up as a concrete pillar supporting the M4. No, I'm staying with you. I like my job. That is, of course, if you still want me."

"Of course I want you. You know you're a key man within the company. Where are you going to live – locally?"

"No, Lisa wants to be nearer her family so we're going to go up near Chelmsford. I'll make sure it's an easy drive for me in the morning but I do need your help though. I want to rent a house for a month or so until we can find a place. I'll need a letter from you."

"How much is the rent for this house?" I asked cautiously.

"Nine hundred quid a month, but her old man, Mark, will be paying it, not me."

"Your income won't justify that sort of rent. Supposing he stops paying?"

"No problem. We'll just move out."

"All right. I'll say you're a very sensible employee and would not enter a commitment you were not confident of being able to meet. Will that do?"

"Great," replied Rich.

"The one thing I'd like to say," I added pompously, "is that you need to be careful. You're getting rid of all your assets and if anything goes wrong, you'll be left with nothing. That rental income made you very well off, but without it you're going to feel the pinch. If you just rely on Lisa's father's money you'll almost be a toy-boy."

I realised I'd gone a little bit too far, for Rich looked very angry. But then he laughed.

"Yeah, thanks for the advice, Mark, but I'm a big boy, I'll take my chances. I'd better get back to work. Thanks for the chat."

After Rich left I sat reflecting on how little I knew of him. He liked spending money. Sandy Lane! I remembered sitting on a terrace drinking gin and tonics and eating the best club sandwiches ever. Beth and I were staying at the Hilton – a great location provided you liked petrol. The oil refinery next door was not ideal. We'd have loved to have stayed at Sandy Lane, but it wasn't in our price range. The same could be said for the car – Beth had always wanted an MG. I'd never really been able to give her her dream and here was Rich's wife staying at the Sandy Lane and driving an MG. The way things were going Beth would never have either.

It had been funny while Rich was away. For one thing Ray Mumford kept turning up. He apparently had an elderly relation living locally who was not very well and so Ray had come down to help. He'd found it a bit boring and kept coming over for a chat. He was a bit of a nuisance really. I was trying to do Rich's work as well as my own and I was finding it very difficult. Mumford had even had the cheek to offer to buy the business for three hundred and fifty thousand. I told him I wouldn't sell twenty-five percent of the business for that figure. I was very annoyed at his cheek. Probably more annoyed because I knew that if our turnover and profit kept falling, it wouldn't be long before I'd be lucky to get this much. Ironically, I could have sold the business for over three million two years earlier. Hindsight is a marvellous thing. If only I'd known, I'd have sold then.

I still couldn't work out why the business was doing so badly. We'd caught the thief so things should have improved, but the reverse was nearer the truth. Things kept getting worse. I'd been going over the figures trying to spot where the problems were. There seemed to be two areas of concern. Our stock purchases seemed exceptionally high in relation to sales and yet I couldn't see any evidence of large quantities of valuable covers in the drawers. Postage was the other worry. We bought enormous quantities of stamps for postage but I couldn't believe we needed quite that number. I started doing some rough calculations based on our mailshots and the invoices we'd issued. My figures were less than fifty percent of the purchases. I checked the stamps in stock and added that back. I was still thirty-five to forty percent out. I rechecked again and again and whichever way I looked at it seemed to be out by about seventy-five thousand pounds per year. It was very difficult to work out an exact figure as we bought stamps at between a twenty percent discount and full price. I was also concerned that the stock showed a similar discrepancy. Every time I seemed to get my teeth into checking, the computer seemed to go wrong or there'd be staff problems. On one occasion I talked to my book-keeper about the postage problem.

"It's a funny thing you should ask that," said Wendy. "Poor old Phil Maitland was asking me the same question just before he died. He was very excited about the whole postage position. He'd got stacks of paper, graphs, bar charts – he wanted to know mailshot figures and the figures of the invoices we'd issued – just like you do."

The significance of Wendy's words were to haunt me in the time to come.

As with many things in my life the answer to my problem was to come from an unlikely source. It was now nearly a year since Rich's romantic wedding on Saint James' beach. I'd hardly seen Lisa during that time, but of course I'd seen the video of the wedding. It did look very romantic. A bit better than our weekend in a country hotel. Rich was getting more and more arrogant about his newfound wealth. He looked more like a Christmas tree literally covered in gold. Lisa apparently had tired of the MG and Daddy had ordered her a Mercedes Sports for the first of August so she could have the new number plate. Rich was becoming increasingly unpopular with the few remaining staff, too. I was getting complaints about him on a regular basis. He'd also lately been very odd when dealing with me. We'd just spent a few days at a major exhibition. He seemed obsessed with his father-in-law and how badly he was treated. He also kept telling me a bizarre story.

"Here, Mark, have I told you about the burglary?" asked Rich during a quiet patch on the stand.

"No, what burglary?"

"Well apparently Lisa's father and mother went away for a romantic weekend at the Savoy and while they were there they got burgled. They got back and found that all of Lisa's mother's jewellery was stolen. But Lisa's dad wouldn't phone the police. He said it wouldn't do any good. The police would never find who'd done it. He said he'd just put the word round, that'd be enough. Within a few days all the jewels were back with an apology."

"What, you mean the thieves were so frightened of him they just returned everything?"

"Yeah, I told you he was a bit dodgy. He's quite a big man in the underworld. I wouldn't want to cross him."

He told me this story about three times. It wasn't always the same story but vaguely the same. I reckoned he was losing his marbles. I told Beth when we got back I didn't think I wanted to go with him any more to exhibitions. He'd become really odd.

I went to the office on a Monday morning and found Bill, the post-clerk waiting to speak to me.

"I need to talk to you, Mark. It's important."

Bill was a shy man and very nice. It was very unlike him to ask to speak to me about anything, so I knew it was going to be something very important.

"Come in, Bill. Sit down. Now what's the problem?"

"I don't really know how to start," said Bill. "It's about thieving really. I think someone's stealing stamps." He sat twisting his hands in his lap. His face was red and he didn't look me in the eye.

"Well take your time, Bill. Just tell me in your own words."

"Well, I've been a bit worried about the stamps for some time. It seems we're losing a very large amount regularly and I couldn't work out where they were going to. Even worse, it seemed they were going overnight. At first I thought it was me being stupid so I started playing a few tricks. I put the safe key at an angle and marked it. When I came in the following morning, the key had been moved. I've done the test six times now and each time the key has been put in a different position than I'd left it in the night before, and each time I'm sure stamps have been stolen."

I sat there horrified, taking in what Bill was telling me. "You're sure, Bill, that it was definitely at night when the safe key was being moved?"

"Yes, Mark, definitely. There was no way it could be done at any other time. I made sure everyone had gone and I was the last person out. In fact, I even locked up and set the burglar alarm on four of the occasions. The stamps were definitely taken overnight. I have also done a rough estimate of what's missing. In two weeks, it's £2,000 worth, Mark."

"You do realise what you're saying, don't you Bill, and how few people it means could possibly be the thief?"

"Yes, yes I do. That's why I've been so long coming to you. I've been worried sick about it. I'm very sorry, but I had to tell you, didn't I?" He looked at me anxiously. I could see how much courage it had taken for this shy man to face the unpleasant truth and come to me. I hoped that he realised that his ordeal had not ended there. If he was right, then there was every chance that he would have to be a witness in a court case.

"Of course you did right," I said, "you had no alternative. Are you prepared to repeat this to the police and make a statement?"

"Yes, I am." He seemed quite firm.

"Right. I think you'd better leave me and let me think about what I've got to do but I'm very grateful to you. Well done, and thank you again."

After Bill left I leant back in my chair and stared at the wall in front of me. If the theft was at night there were only three people that could be guilty, other than Bill himself. I was one of them, the second was John Rich, and the third was Richard Gough, my office manager, who'd been sitting in my office not two days earlier asking for a pay rise as he was finding it difficult to exist on his salary now that he had a mortgage and would shortly have a wife or as near to one as today's youth manage. To back up his request, he'd worked out his weekly expenditure even down to the last can of baked beans. It was highly unlikely that a man who was worried about the price of a tin of baked beans would be stealing thousands of pounds from me every month. On the other hand John Rich, who was covered in gold and who was driving a Porsche 911, and whose wife drove an MG, which was shortly to be replaced by a Mercedes Sports, was a more likely subject. If Rich was guilty then the amount of money we were talking about was considerably more than I had ever imagined possible. In his position of trust he had access to every possible way of stealing from Cheshire's. I thought I'd just check up a bit on John's wife's background. I remembered that when John had first met her she had been living with Giles Haverford. I picked up the phone and dialled his number.

"Hello Giles. It's Mark Cheshire here. Can I ask you some apparently very weird questions?"

"Fire away, dear boy. How can I help?"

"Well it's about Lisa Potts. What do you know about her father?"

"Oh, him. He's a right bastard. Lives in Brent I think."

"I gather he's very rich."

"Rich? Good God no! He hasn't even got a job as far as I know. Lives in a council flat. Awful man. Lisa hates him. I think there's even some question of him making advances to her. Where on earth did you get the idea that he was wealthy?"

"Well, Lisa, for a start. She hardly looks like a council worker's daughter."

"No, she wouldn't, would she? I mean the amount of goodies she's got out of various men. She took me pretty well. I honestly don't know how your John Rich can cope with her. She must have changed a lot. The only things Lisa likes are presents and then she likes them every day at least. I was very grateful to young Rich. He did me a real favour taking her off my hands."

"Well thanks, Giles. You've been a great help."

"I've hardly done anything. Glad to be of assistance anyway."

Oh my God! I thought. *I'm the Mark. I'm the Mark who is the father-in-law that gives her everything; the Mark John is always saying has given them presents! What a nice sense of humour. He must have been laughing his socks off. I'm the stupid idiot that's been paying for everything. No wonder the business has been doing badly. I should have known, it was so obvious! What a stupid fool I've been. Still, at least I can do something about it now.*

My emotions were a strange mixture – both horrified and excited. I was appalled that the person I trusted had let me down so badly, but excited that I now could see a way out of it all. If Rich's lifestyle was based on the theft then all I needed to do was to get rid of him and the business should be able to regenerate itself within a couple of years.

I left the office and went over to the police station to find out what was the best thing to do. There I met a most depressing policeman. As far as he was concerned everything I had to say was hearsay and it wouldn't stand up in a court of law. The only thing we could do would be to put a camera into the office, wait a month or so until the dust died down, and then with luck we might get the evidence we needed. This was all very well, but I was due to go on holiday within the next ten days and the thought of leaving Rich unsupervised in the office really didn't appeal to me. I was also worried about staff morale. There had been already worries about theft and it wouldn't take long before the story of the stolen stamps would become common knowledge. If I wasn't careful, I'd start losing good staff which was something I couldn't afford to do. I talked to my solicitor who told me off the record, that it might be worth frightening Rich, getting him to resign on the grounds of ill health. At least this would solve the problem in the short term and I'd be able to sleep at night.

The more I checked, the more the evidence against Rich grew. I can't explain why, but I still didn't really want to believe that he could have been quite as nasty as he appeared to be. Half of me hoped that it was all a mistake. It was with this sort of mixed emotion that I tackled him in my office. I gave him my ultimatum; he read it, looked at me, grinned at me in a most alarming way, signed it and left. I could hardly believe it. Everything was true – he really was the thief. At one time I had thought of him as a son. I had put all my trust in him, only to have it thrown in my face. I should really have seen him off the premises, but I was so upset I just sat there, staring at the wall. I know it was silly. I was really quite relieved to get rid of him, but I just felt numb. The tension had triggered off one of my blinding headaches, which stayed with me, on and off, for the next few weeks. It took me a while before I could cope with the pain and pull myself back into action.

I phoned the burglar alarm company and got the code of the burglar alarm changed and then phoned the locksmith, who unfortunately couldn't come for a few days. That meant the keys posed a risk as they could well have been copied, but at least the alarm had been changed. I phoned and faxed the credit card company and cancelled his company credit card. I then went down to check the safe and found to my horror that Rich had stolen the key. I also realised then that we didn't even know where he lived; he'd never given me his new address. However, we did have his car phone number and we phoned to ask him to return the key immediately. He was most apologetic and said he'd drop it in on Monday and like a fool I didn't insist, as having changed the burglar alarm combination I assumed we were pretty secure.

I got the police call at about eleven o'clock on Saturday evening. The burglar alarm at the office had gone off. I went in and checked, but nothing appeared to be missing. I reset the alarm and locked up and thought nothing about it until later. Rich phoned on Monday to say he'd lost the safe key, apparently it had fallen out of his pocket as he got out of the car and unfortunately he was just above a drain and it disappeared into the sewer. He was very apologetic and said that he hoped we'd got another. We had no duplicate key, as he well knew, and so we had to arrange for a professional to come and open the safe. I had to admit I found it slightly amusing after watching films where the baddy opens the safe in a matter of minutes, to watch professionals take five hours to get into ours. It made me realise how misleading the films were. The staff were delighted that Rich had gone; he was very unpopular and no-one missed him at all. I took over his job for a while and only then did I start to find out just how serious my problems were.

It didn't take me long to realise that almost all of the rare covers we had were not ours. We apparently owed tens of thousands of pounds to suppliers who'd provided covers on sale or return, and some of my old friends had not been paid for some considerable time. Within a month I'd probably spent the best part of a hundred thousand pounds to pay off all the people we owed money to, which left me free to spend most of my time rebuilding that part of the business. As one would expect, our turnover started to increase quite rapidly, as did our profitability. Even within the first month it was obvious just how much of a drain Rich had been on the business. Ray Mumford was very supportive during those first few weeks. He told me that he'd never trusted Rich but had put his feelings down to the fact that he didn't like him rather than anything more concrete. He offered me any assistance I needed, even to the level of offering to loan me money. I assured him that it wasn't necessary and that we would soon pull ourselves out of trouble.

Chapter 20

I wasn't really prepared for the next bombshell that was to hit me. One of our customers sent me an auction catalogue and price list for a firm called Rare Covers. The list was full of treasures and the proprietor appeared to be John Rich. Within days, hundreds of my customers were complaining that they'd already received the list without having asked for it, which meant that Rich had also stolen my mailing list. Looking at the quality of covers on offer it was also obvious that he had plundered virtually all our decent stock before he left. I realised then why he'd kept the safe key and why the alarm went off on that Saturday evening. He wouldn't have needed long. We had changed the alarm, but we hadn't been able to change the locks immediately.

All he needed was a copied set of door keys and he could have been in and out within a few minutes. He would not have been able to get a copy of the safe key and that is why he had kept it. He'd been in and removed anything worth having from the safe as a final bonus. I hadn't wanted to prosecute him, but things now looked completely different. I started to build up a case against him and for once luck started to move my way. I got a phone call from Peter Pike, my British Intelligence Officer friend.

"Hello, Peter. I haven't heard from you for a

while. Where have you been?"

"Oh I've been a doorman at the British Embassy in East Berlin," said Peter with a chuckle.

With Peter you never knew if he was joking or not.

"Look, Peter, I've got a very serious problem. I really could do with your help. Can we meet as soon as possible?"

"Of course, I can come round to your house tonight, about seven o'clock."

"Great," I said. "Come to dinner; and bring your thinking cap. I've got a real stinker for you to help me with."

"Sounds just what I like, the more complicated the better," said Peter. "I'll look forward to it."

The more I thought about John Rich and his thieving, the more concerned I became about Phil Maitland. I remembered my book-keeper's words: *Funny you should ask that. Poor old Phil Maitland was asking me the same questions just before he died. He seemed very excited about the whole postage position and had stacks of paper, graphs, bar charts. He wanted to know how many letters and parcels we sent out and the number of invoices we'd issued.*

If Phil had been getting suspicious, then his death was remarkably convenient for Rich. The police had said there was no apparent motive for the death. If Maitland had been about to expose Rich, then that would have given Rich a very good reason to kill him.

Oh no, it's silly! I thought. I couldn't imagine Rich as a murderer. But then who can imagine anyone as a murderer? The more I thought about it the more concerned I became.

When Peter arrived at seven o'clock I told him the whole story, holding nothing back, not even my concern about Philip Maitland. Peter puffed on his trademark pipe and consumed several glasses of my best malt. He made quite a few notes while I was talking.

"I don't think you're being silly, Mark. I'd have said it was too much of a coincidence that Maitland died at that particular moment. I think you should seriously consider the possibility that Rich is not just a thief but also a murderer. How far do you want to go with this? I've got a few friends who could help but these things cost money."

"What sort of thing can you do?" I asked.

"Well, for example, it would be nice to see Rich's bank accounts, wouldn't it?"

"Yes, but isn't that illegal?"

"Yes," said Peter, "but it still can be arranged. As I say, it just costs money. It's amazing what can be done with computers these days. I also think it would be useful to stake him out a bit to find out who he's seeing. He won't be in it alone. You need to know who else to be concerned about. Again, I'm afraid this will cost money. Are you prepared to finance it?"

"Yes, of course. What sort of money are we talking about?"

"Well, a few thousand pounds to start with. But it could escalate. It all depends on how much they find out. Let's limit it to say ten thousand pounds to start with and you can make a decision if and when that runs out."

"Yes, all right. That seems fair."

"Now as for the murder – if it is a murder – we really need to get something else going. Haven't you got a friend high up in the police force somewhere?"

"Well, yes, I do know someone, I've been an expert witness for him a number of times. It's Chief Inspector Sandy Neil."

"Well I suggest you have a meeting with him and get his advice. He'd know exactly what to do from the police point of view. You need this case reactivated bearing in mind the new circumstances."

We went over everything again very slowly and carefully. The more I looked at it the more likely it seemed that poor Philip had been murdered by Rich or someone he had hired to protect himself. If that was the case then I wanted Rich brought to justice. I wanted it very badly.

I phoned Sandy, but he'd moved from the City of London Fraud Squad into a new set-up at Elm House investigating serious fraud. I was eventually given his number after I had convinced the police that I wasn't a vindictive criminal, released from prison and wanting to get even. He seemed genuinely pleased to hear my voice.

"Now then, Mark, how's life in the world of stamps? Any more good frauds lately?"

"Yes, I'm afraid there are and one of them is at my expense this time."

"Oh I'm sorry to hear that – I'll cut out the joking. Is there anything I can do to help?"

"Well, yes there is. Can I come and see you for

some advice?"

"Advice doesn't come cheap from the likes of me you know. It'll cost you."

"How much?" I asked.

"A good lunch. I mean a really good one. No mucking about. None of your fish and chips in the bag. Something we can really take some time over so I can put my mind to your problem."

"All right," I laughed, "you book the restaurant, I'll provide the credit card."

I arranged to meet him at his office in Elm House the following Thursday. Meanwhile, I started to do whatever I could to get more information myself. Now I knew of the existence of this company, Rare Covers, it seemed sensible to try to find out anything I could about it. I put out a notice to my customers asking any of them who had had dealings with Rare Covers over the last year to let me know. I also thought it was about time I looked at the computer records of the customers that Rich would have been interested in. Our system at that time had been having some problems and Rich had been on a separate system until about a month ago.

I started looking through the customer accounts which had been transferred from his system and found, to my amazement, that none of them had any record of previous transactions. They all started with a nil balance. I asked Wendy to use the old system and print off the records for me. It wasn't long before she came back looking rather white-faced.

"I'm sorry Mark, there's nothing on the system. It's been wiped totally clean. Rich must have done it before he left."

"Oh God. Can you see if you can find a backup tape anywhere? He may not have been that clever, and we might just be able to restore it all."

Wendy scuttled off and I thought how once again I'd underestimated Rich. He might not have any qualifications but he was very fly when it came to covering up his tracks. I didn't expect that Wendy would find any backup tapes, so I wasn't disappointed when she came back to inform me that it appeared that all the tapes for his system had disappeared. That meant that there was no way we could restore the original records or get any print-out or any information about his previous transactions. I phoned up my computer people to find out if there was anything they could do to help. The man who did our programming work was apparently in America at that time, creating a programme, of all things, for the American army, but his partner told me he would phone him as soon the time difference was acceptable, to see if there was anything he could do to help.

There's nothing worse than waiting when you desperately want information, but you've just got to be patient. I found it difficult to settle down to any work. My mind kept coming back to poor old Phil, beaten to death and his mother lying there, dying, probably all because he was trying to help me.

The weekend was unbearable. I watched cricket on the Sunday, but Surrey, the team I supported, lost, so it didn't do much to help cheer me up. It would probably have been more sensible not to open the second bottle of Julianas with the delicious roast chicken that Beth had served up for our evening meal, but as it had two sorts of stuffing as well as bread sauce, roast parsnips and the first of the broad beans of the season, I'm afraid I made a bit of a pig of myself. On the Monday morning I really was feeling a little bit hungover and very depressed, but my mood changed dramatically when I got the phone call from my computer company.

"I've got some good news, Mark," said Max, the Managing Director.

"Well I could do with some good news. I feel absolutely awful," I said. "What's is it?"

"Barry did the work for Rich, transferring all his records onto the new computer system and you know what Barry's like, two belts, two pairs of braces and an extra bit of string."

"Yes, so?"

"Well, he hid a copy of the backup tape, just in case it was ever needed."

"He did what?"

"He hid a copy of the backup tape. He was very worried when Rich told him that he didn't want any backup and just wanted the names and addresses transferred over with nil balances. He thought you might need to know the clients' history with the company at some time so, you know what he's like, he made an extra copy and squirreled it away. I've got it here now. Do you want me to send it over to you?"

"Yes. No, wait. Can you copy it first? I'd hate to lose it after all his trouble."

"Sure, no problem. I'll get someone on it straight away."

"And take a printout just in case anything goes wrong. This tape could be crucial evidence."

"Understood. I'll get the copy done straight away. In fact I'll do two copies and get one over to you by courier."

"Max, you're marvellous! When you next speak to Barry, tell him I owe him and with any luck, I'll owe him more than I can possibly pay back."

That was the best bit of news I'd had for a long time. If Rich had gone to such lengths to destroy all the records then those records ought to be very interesting. It's funny how you get good days and bad days. Over the last few years I'd experienced some awful days but this one was turning into one of the most interesting ones of my life.

The computer information was fascinating, but there was more to come. At around one o'clock I got a phone call from one of our fanatic customers. He'd been a bit of a favourite with Sharon before she'd left in such a huff. Although I hadn't had much to do with him, there was no doubt he was one of our better customers. Most of his dealings had been with Rich.

"Hello, is that Mark?" The accent was definitely Birmingham.

"Yes, it's Mark Cheshire speaking. How can I help?"

"It's not how you can help me, it's how I can help you," continued the voice. "It's about time you knew exactly what's been going on. You seem to be blundering around like a complete idiot."

"Is this about Rich?" I said.

"Of course it's about Rich and Mumford, and all the others."

"What do you mean Mumford and the others?"

"Rich has been working for Mumford for some time, didn't you know? You want to have a really good look at Mumford's account. Both what you sell to him and what he sells to you. I bet you'd find it interesting. Do a check over the last three or four years. I've got a friend on Mumford's staff. He tells me most of the postage you buy is the same postage you've bought over and over again for the last two or three years. It just comes in, gets stolen, goes back, comes in again. Nice work if you can get it."

"Can you prove this?" I asked.

"No, not easily. But I think my mate who works for Mumford might be prepared to come forward. I'm putting it all down on paper for you. Everything I know. I'll send it to you in the next couple of days, but I thought you ought to be aware that Mumford is not in any way your friend."

As soon as he rang off, I started work analysing the Mumford account. He was quite right: it did make fascinating reading. I'd always been led to believe that Mumford was our best customer, but once you put all the records together it was obvious something was seriously wrong. Mumford had sold to us over two hundred thousand pounds' worth of stock more than he'd bought from us, and the credit notes looked very strange. It was important we got hold of this chap who worked at Mumford's as quickly as possible. I phoned Peter and told him about the two things I'd learned that morning. He agreed that it was essential that he got on to it straight away, and went off to Birmingham to interview Rob Bailey, my helpful customer, then on to find the person at Mumford's shop and get a statement from him. It was all looking much more hopeful and I remembered that evening not to open even the first bottle of wine. I needed to keep my head clear to deal with the computer records that would be with me the next morning.

I hardly got any sleep on that night. My brain felt like bursting. When I did drop off, my dreams were horrific, Phil being beaten to death by monsters, Mumford screaming at me that three hundred and fifty thousand pounds was the best offer I was likely to get – take it or leave it – and there was Rich in the background killing himself laughing. This was mixed up with various members of staff telling me, "I told you so, I told you so," over and over and over again. It was absolutely horrific. As soon as I woke up my mind switched straight back into all my problems and what to do about them next.

I got up early and went into the office, waiting impatiently for the delivery of the backup tape which was due to arrive by Datapost early that morning. It arrived at about ten o'clock. Wendy loaded it onto the machine for me and we ran a printout of all the information. I was convinced that it would be the evidence to finish Rich for good; it was just a matter of wading through and finding it.

I picked on five customers to start with, those with the most transactions. The first thing I did was to check the credit card records. It didn't take long for me to find out that we'd never received any of the money that was apparently paid by them with their credit cards. I phoned the credit card company and got a very pleasant, but luckily for me inexperienced, young lady. She was more than helpful, giving me information that I should never have been given. She looked up the records for me and found out there'd been some form of mistake. All of the payments had gone to a firm called Rare Covers.

I left Wendy with the task of going through the entire list to work out which payments we'd never received and how much money we were talking about. While she was doing that, I double checked the customer list with our own customer list and found there were something like forty customers whose names had never been transferred from Rich's old computer onto the main computer system. I isolated those customers and started looking at them very carefully. On paper they all looked good customers, but why were they not transferred over? There had to be a reason. It may have been that they were Rich's personal customers and on a long shot I wrote a letter to each one of them saying that we seemed to have left them off our system, and apologising, I sent them a voucher worth twenty-five pounds if they spent a hundred pounds with us – which would have been small beer according to their previous transactions. I also sent them our latest lists. I don't know what I expected but I thought it was worth a go.

Peter popped in briefly on Wednesday to update me on his progress.

"I've just got back from Birmingham," he said. "I got a statement from Rob Bailey about what he knows. Most of it's hearsay, so it's no good to you as far as a court of law is concerned. It does point us in various directions though. He's given me the name of his contact in Mumford's firm and I'm going to see if I can get hold of him tomorrow. Anything else you want me to do?"

"Well I had all sorts of nightmares last night and I got to thinking about the whole situation. The one thing that stood out was that we had a thief a little while ago. It was Paul. We caught him through some information supplied by Ray Mumford. Knowing what we now know, then it might be worth talking to him. Can you see if you can track him down?"

"Shouldn't be a problem. Just get Wendy to give me his National Insurance number. I should be able to track him down reasonably quickly. I should have some of Rich's bank statements come through in the next couple of days. I don't know what they're going to tell us, but it might prove interesting. I think also it's about time we went to the police with what we know, particularly as it's more than likely that Rich was involved in Maitland's murder."

"I'm seeing the Chief Inspector tomorrow. I'll put it all together and then go to the police after that. Do you want to come with me?"

"No, I think you should go by yourself. Don't mention me at all. I don't think they'd approve of some of the things I'm doing."

Elm House was the headquarters of the Serious Fraud Squad, an elite band of policemen, accountants, and lawyers, specially selected for their exceptional abilities. It was a grim building made of grey brick, large and faceless; a depressing place to come if you were under investigation by the staff here. We sat in Sandy's small cubicle of an office while I went through the whole saga. He listened, took notes and asked the occasional pertinent question. When I eventually finished he said, "Right, let's go and have some lunch. I'll give you my advice afterwards."

We went to a small Italian restaurant not far from Elm House. Sandy banned me from talking about my problem over lunch and we chatted about various things.

Afterwards, we went back to Elm House.

"Right, let's get down to business," said Sandy. "The most important thing is that I agree with you. I have no doubt that Maitland was murdered. I have never believed in co-incidences. The timing of his death was just too convenient. It is obvious that Rich had guessed that Maitland was on to him, which meant that he had to either leave quickly and lose his source of income or get rid of Maitland."

"What should I do now?" I asked.

"Go to your local police tomorrow and tell them everything you've told me. But Mark, tell them slowly. I can keep up with you, but I doubt if they will."

"Should I tell them I've been to see you?"

Sandy shook his head.

"I wouldn't. We don't like other people involved, particularly if the other people are from a different force. Anyway, you've got plenty to interest them without my input. Push the idea that they should raid both Mumford's and Rich's places. With any luck, they'll get all they need to connect the two. Don't expect miracles though, Mark. And be nice to them, you need them more than they need you."

I was quite pleased that he had agreed with my suspicions and I was about to leave when Sandy picked up the phone.

"Jim, come in please," he said. Sandy indicated that I should keep my mouth closed.

The Detective Sergeant came in.

"What's up, Guv?" he asked.

"I need some information about a Philip Maitland. He's an accountant who was murdered in Essex. I've written a few things down here for you. I think he might fit into something I'm working on. Can you put out a general call nationwide, for any information please?"

Glover looked at him with a puzzled expression, but, being a good copper, obeyed orders and left immediately to get on with it.

"Thanks," I said, "I really appreciate it."

"I shouldn't have done it, you know. It was very unprofessional." He grinned. "But what are friends for?"

I started to leave and was already at the door when Sandy called me back.

"Mark, don't expect the police to think for you. All they'll be interested in is a result. A conviction of any sort will please them." He hesitated. "What I'm trying to say is to look out for yourself; things could get messy."

The next morning I went to the local police station

and presented all I had, and also told them of my suspicions concerning the murder of Philip Maitland. I suggested it might be prudent to raid Mumford's premises at the same time as raiding Rich's. They seemed reluctant at first, but eventually saw the logic that it was highly likely that the news would get out and that the two of them would have time to cover their tracks. They even asked me to be present at the raid on Mumford's premises to help them identify our property.

PART XI

JOHN RICH

Chapter 21

I had hoped that by marrying Lisa my expenses would be reduced. This was to prove a hopeless miscalculation. The mortgage repayments were horrendous. I gambled that interest rates would fall and so I didn't take a fixed rate mortgage, which seemed a good idea at the time. How was I to know the pound was going to fall so far and so often? It seemed to me that the mortgage rates went up every Friday and within a year I was paying five percent more interest than when I'd started. Five percent doesn't sound much if you say it quickly, but I can assure you, five percent of two hundred and fifty thousand is painful. It meant I had to steal an extra two hundred and fifty pounds a week from Cheshire just to stay the same. It was the same with the house. I naively thought we could move in and keep it as it was. When we bought the house we acquired the carpets and the curtains. As it had been recently

235

decorated I thought my idea was quite reasonable. My view and Lisa's were not even vaguely similar.

"You couldn't expect me to live with that awful carpet could you, darling? We'll have to sort it out. Don't worry about it, though. I'll organise it all."

Organise it she did. Interior designers, decorators, carpet fitters, curtain makers, furniture salesmen, double glazing merchants – in fact anyone wanting Cheshire's money turned up. I could hardly believe the bills. Admittedly the house looked fantastic, but I was beginning to wonder if Bobby Bliss's original appraisal was correct, that Lisa was a bit rich even for me.

I didn't begrudge her the new clothes, though. Whenever we went out I was fantastically proud of her. She really looked the part of a millionaire's daughter. Unfortunately, the credit card bills were mounting – I had the usual American Express, Diners Club, three different Visas and a couple of MasterCards and Lisa had a complete set of every card that was issued too. You couldn't believe the amount of credit they allowed us. I was managing to pay the minimum payments off each month but the debts were rising faster than a space rocket from Cape Canaveral. I did a rough total of the damage one day, and could hardly believe it. We owed over sixty thousand pounds on plastic alone and that wasn't including the builders and the decorators, and as for the various overdrafts, I didn't dare look.

The drug money was reducing as well. I had lost a couple of very good cash generators and some of the others were not loyal; as far as they were concerned any supplier would do.

Cheshire wasn't much help – he'd lost his grip on the business and I was finding it more and more difficult to steal what I needed. I started getting in stocks on sale or return as he clamped down on my buying. It could only work in the short term as the other dealers would expect to be paid eventually. My most lucrative scam was my Rare Cover operation. More and more of Cheshire's money was being siphoned off, but I was beginning to be frightened. I was finding it much harder stealing the covers to sell, and my customers wanted only the best. It was obvious to me that unless Cheshire sorted out his difficulties, I'd have to start my own business. My particular problem was more simple. How did I tell Lisa that I wasn't as rich as she thought I was?

In spite of it all, I loved my new life. I enjoyed spending time with Crispin and I got a real kick when he called me Daddy. Lisa was a great cook. She was good at producing delicious meals and fairly soon she had organised a dinner party circuit. I was moving in amazing company – stockbrokers, lawyers, accountants – and I really enjoyed the fact that they envied me my beautiful wife and my youth, even if they did think we were common.

In reality I was on the slippery slopes, just waiting for the disaster to happen. When it did happen, I couldn't believe it. Of all the people to bring me down, I would never have bet on it being Bill, who I'd always thought of as being thick and only interested in beer. I'd got a feeling that Cheshire knew about my game and I wouldn't have been surprised about that. But Bill? That, I never expected.

When Cheshire sent for me to talk about the

irregularities in the stamp stock, I knew he was aware that I was the guilty one. What I didn't know was how much proof he had. It didn't seem as though he had much. He came up with the idea that I should resign because of my bad health. I didn't take long to decide that this was a good idea. He gave me a letter to sign and I did it with a flourish. He seemed very upset. I just grinned at him. Stupid git! He let me get away with all I'd done!

As I left his office I realised that I'd left some valuable covers in the safe and even worse, a packet of drugs. I quickly grabbed the safe key and put it in my pocket. As I drove back to Lisa I tried to work out what I was going to tell her. She already knew I was considering going it alone so at least that wouldn't come as a complete surprise. She'd have to stop spending quite so much; that wasn't going to go down very well. I switched on the radio and listened to the news and surprise, surprise – I could have guessed it already – the bank rate was up half a percent. Great, I thought the fucking mortgage would go up again, just what I needed! The radio then went on to talk about the problems of falling house prices. By the sound of it I'd bought my house at the absolute peak and people like me could expect a large fall in the valuation of their house. In all, it was turning out to be not one of my better days.

Lisa was surprised to see me coming in at the front door.

"What brings you home early?" she asked.

Rather than get into a long conversation I pulled her to me and kissed her roughly, caressing her fabulous breasts lightly through the silk dress.

"Mmmmm," she whispered, "this is a nice way to start the weekend."

Crispin was at a friend's house so there was no reason to be cautious.

"Let's go upstairs," begged Lisa, but I had other ideas. I pushed her through into the dining room and onto the large Victorian table. I pushed up the silk dress and despite her protests about the cold I pushed her panties to one side and entered her standing up. It felt good, being in total control. As I shuddered to my climax I thought it was the only good thing that had happened to me that day. Lisa thought I'd come home just for her as I'd often left the office during the summer for a quick visit to the flat followed by a cold shower. I knew she found it romantic and reassuring, so I was pleased with my quick inspirational entrance.

Later that evening I drove slowly back to the shop so I could retrieve my property from the safe. The weather had turned wet and nasty and the drive was not a pleasant one. I parked the car well away from the shop in a particularly dark part of Harbour Way, hoping that nobody would notice it. I opened the door and keyed in the code of the burglar alarm. To my horror it wouldn't work.

Oh sod it, I thought, *the bastard's changed the code!* I rushed to the safe and opened it. The alarm rang out in my ears. I knew it would have already have registered in the police station which wasn't far away. I felt the cold sweat running down my back. I only hoped that the police car was not in the immediate vicinity. I grabbed my package and what covers I could that were easily available, relocked the safe and left quickly, locking the door behind me. Luck was with me and no police car appeared. As I drove slowly back home I reflected just how lucky I had been. Cheshire had to have moved very quickly and I suppose I should count myself lucky that he hadn't changed the locks as well.

As the lights of the oncoming cars flickered in my eyes I started to work out my strategy for Monday. I'd go and see Mumford and get him to give me a job. That was the least he could do for me under the circumstances. I couldn't be bothered to drive the car in the garage so I just left it outside the front door. Lisa had already gone to bed. When I got into bed I snuggled up to her. I started caressing her.

"Well, twice in one day. My, this is my lucky day!"

Chapter 22

As I drove across the Thames over the Waterloo Bridge to visit Mumford the next day, I wondered how the red-faced git would react to my dismissal. There wasn't much he could do, but knowing Mumford, I knew that he would certainly not give in without a fight. I walked into his office at the back of the shop.

Mumford was filing a particularly nasty-looking debt-collection letter in the waste-paper basket. I recognised it at once; Cheshire used the same organisation. *So Mumford's got cash problems*, I thought. *That's not good news*. He didn't want to see me but attempted a smile.

"I wasn't expecting you today, John. Why the unexpected pleasure?"

"We've got problems," I replied slowly. "Cheshire's found out about the stamps and I've been given the elbow."

"Oh God, that's all I need!" he shouted. "Does he know about my involvement?"

"Not yet," I said. "There's no reason why he ever should. I need a job. I thought you'd want to help an old friend."

"In other words, if I don't help you, you'll tell Cheshire. That's bloody blackmail."

"I wouldn't call it blackmail, just common sense. Besides I'm good – you know that – I'll be very useful to you." I could see him working out the various options in his head.

"All right, all right, but you can't work here and I can't employ you officially. It would be too risky. I'll give you work to do at home. I suppose you'll be running your own show as well?"

"I've got to, haven't I? Lisa's got expensive tastes. I reckon that with all my contacts I'm worth over a thousand pounds a week to you." I thought I was being reasonable but Mumford went even redder in the face and looked like he was going to explode.

"Don't talk bloody crap, even I'm not worth that much. I'll pay you four hundred pounds and that's top whack."

"No, that won't work. I wouldn't get out of bed for that, make it eight hundred pounds and I'll consider it."

Eventually we compromised on six hundred pounds which was far less than I really needed. Still, there was plenty of time to squeeze more money out of him. I knew just how well he'd done out of me.

Lisa had taken my leaving Cheshire's very well; in fact I think she was delighted. I'd made sure that she'd benefited by me being around more and I had to admit our sex life was good. I took Crispin to his playschool some mornings and picked him up later on if I was about. I got out in the garden and found I enjoyed digging the rose beds. Who'd have thought it? It was hard work but it meant I switched off my worries for at least an hour or so. Mumford's six hundred pounds a week barely scratched the surface of the money I needed. The mortgage alone was nine hundred pounds a week and I had to take on board the simple fact that stock was no longer free. Even worse, as I was no longer part of Cheshire's company, people wanted to be paid in advance. Sure, there were some fantastic bargains to be found, but not that many. If I'd bought badly in the past it was Cheshire's problem, but now it was mine alone. It really pissed me off when I got back a cover from some snotty collector saying it was damaged or the condition wasn't quite what they expected. The stupid bastards also asked for their money back. Fat chance – I'd already spent it.

In the end the answer to my short-term problems was very simple. I started an auction – it was like the old days again, free stock. I used the extensive connections I had built up when working for Cheshire and within a few weeks had tens of thousands of pounds of new stock and much more to come. People just sent the stuff in! I didn't have to pay them anything. I sold the better covers quickly, which helped me with my cash flow. Obviously it was only a short-term solution as eventually the owners were going to cause a fuss. It would take about six months before the first vendors became concerned and I was content to put the problem off till then. If I got lucky I could hope to pay them off. If not, perhaps I could tell them their collections were destroyed in a fire or stolen or something and ask them if their insurance would cover it. Otherwise I'd give them a small compensation. I quite liked that idea. It would show me off in a good light and I could pay them next to nothing.

In my travels I also came across some excellent buying opportunities. You'd be amazed how many widows don't know anything about their husband's collecting habits. It all comes from the fact that most people are basically dishonest; it is just that some of us recognise the fact and use it. The husbands dare not tell their wives how much they're spending on their collections and this made it very easy for me because the widows just wanted to sell and get rid of the past without any knowledge of what the collection was really worth. It was very satisfying, buying collections worth thousands of pounds for a hundred pounds or so. It was also much better for me, as I didn't have to worry about the problem of settling up in six months. I'd kept lists of all Cheshire's best customers and I wrote to all of them offering my personal services to help build their collections, or saying that if at any time they wanted to sell, I would act as their advisor. The letter worked very well and in a few months I was just about getting to the point where I could see daylight.

As I was sorting out a particularly valuable collection of gold coins donated by an old lady, I noticed, to my horror, a policeman getting out of a large and flashy-looking police car, you know the sort, the ones you crawl by on the motorway. He strode up towards the front door. I felt a tightening of my guts. This was the moment I'd dreaded ever since I'd started. Was it the drugs, Cheshire, or – even worse – Maitland? I considered my options. I rejected my first impulse of just running, after all, where would I go? Besides, how were they going to prove anything? No, the best way was simply to bluff it out. All this went through my mind in the few seconds it took me to ensure it was me that opened the door rather than Lisa.

I opened the door and awaited my fate.

"Good morning, sir. Are you Mr John Rich?"

I nodded.

"I'm afraid I've got some bad news for you, sir, particularly on such a nice day."

I just wished he would get on with it. Was he going to take me to the station? Would I be home tonight? I just stared at him.

"Yes, sir. I'm afraid I've got to serve you this warrant. It's not a nice job, but it's got to be done." He handed me the envelope and left.

What on earth was he on about? I ripped it open and tried to make sense of it; and then the penny dropped. It was that bloody parking ticket I got at St Katherine's Dock! Christ, all that panic for a few pounds! It was all very stupid. I ought to have known that Cheshire would do nothing, he hadn't the bottle. No, I was in the clear. I don't know why I even worried.

*

Start the day with a different position was my new motto. In all the best marriage books it tells couples to put a bit of excitement into their sex lives – try something different, it suggests, and with all the experience I had had from Mrs Radcliffe, Sharon, and dozens of other girls, I was in the ideal position to give Lisa exactly what the text books suggested. She enjoyed these early morning sessions and joined in with great enthusiasm. That particular morning we were both about to reach a superb mutual climax when all hell broke loose.

Bang! Bang! Bang went the front door knocker – the front door bell rang and so did the bell at the backdoor.

"Oh sod it!" I cried. "What the hell's going on? Jesus Christ, it's not even seven o'clock!" I pulled myself out of Lisa and quickly threw on the bathrobe I'd nicked from my first trip to the Savoy. As I walked down the stairs I could see the silhouettes of a number of people through the frosted front door panel. I opened the door cautiously.

"Police! Open up, we've got a search warrant!" said a bulky policeman standing in front of the door. I opened it – what else could I do? He waved a bit a paper in my face and the rest of the waiting crew burst in. One went straight through the house and let in another lot from the rear.

"What's this all about?" I was sick to my stomach. I knew.

"Are you John Rich?"

I nodded.

"Then we need all your books, personal papers, accounts, stock, records. Can you show me where you keep them, sir?"

I didn't like the way he said 'sir', nor did I like him.

"Also I'd like you to come down to the station for some further questions. Can you please get dressed?"

It was like a horrible dream. I stood and gaped. The sound of Lisa screaming brought me back to reality. I ran upstairs and found Lisa holding her dressing gown over her nakedness. She hadn't realised anyone would come upstairs so when the police entered our bedroom she was completely naked. The two coppers were leering at her, enjoying their early morning treat.

"For Christ's sake get out and let my wife dress in peace!" I screamed at them. They grinned knowingly at me, then left the room.

"What for Christ's sake is going on?" screamed Lisa, shocked. "How can they just walk in like that? The filthy scum."

"They've got a search warrant. God knows what they think they're going to find. It's some sort of dreadful mistake. I've got to go down to the police station to answer some questions. I'll be back as soon as possible." I tried to reassure her as best as I could, but it wasn't easy.

"What have you done?" She stared at me accusingly.

"Nothing," I reassured her. "It's probably Cheshire being vindictive. We did have a big row. He might have trumped something up. Whatever it is, I'll soon sort it out, I promise."

She didn't look very convinced, but I thought, *Deal with that later.* Crispin had started screaming and she glared at me as if it was my fault and ran off to see to him.

I went down to rejoin the police. They wouldn't let me take my own car; I had to go in the back of a bloody panda car. I noticed a number of our neighbours watching as I was driving away, nosy sods. Lisa would be pleased, I don't think.

Once we arrived at the station I was taken to a small cubicle which contained a very old, heavily stained wooden table and two chairs.

I was told to wait and that someone would be along as soon as possible. I sat alone in that soulless room for what seemed hours. Occasionally I heard voices outside. Eventually I recognised one of the voices. At first I couldn't place it, but then it clicked – it was Ray Mumford! Christ, if they'd got him as well, they must know a lot more than I'd thought.

Chapter 23

Until I heard Mumford's voice I felt fairly confident. I couldn't believe Cheshire could possibly have anything on me. I'd been very careful. I knew there were no computer records as I'd destroyed all copies and removed any traces from my computer. Almost all of the covers I had stolen were not unusual which made positive identification impossible. The burden of proof, I knew, lay with the prosecution and there was no way they were going to prove anything against me.

Mumford's voice did, I admit, change my mood. But what the hell! What proof could they have? I sat waiting in that dismal room, looking at the stained table and wondering what was going to happen next. I found myself thinking about my old dad. At least he'd never been in this position.

Eventually a sharp-faced cockney policeman came in, accompanied by the fat sergeant. The interview followed the usual pattern I'd seen on the box, starting the tape, informing me of my rights. I'd already decided to take advantage of one of those rights from the start – the right of silence. I happily answered all questions with 'no comment', 'you tell me', 'no, sorry, no idea'. The cockney interrogator was getting annoyed which I thought was good news. However, as the interview progressed some of the questions started getting slightly more worrying.

I didn't like to be asked why Mumford had paid me over two hundred thousand pounds over the last eighteen months. What on earth was Mumford saying in the other rooms? They produced a printout of my computer records and asked me if I recognised it. I answered, "No comment," but I knew I must look shaken. I hadn't thought there was any way they could possibly have that. I began to worry what else they had.

At last, the interview was just about over and I began to relax. At least I could go home and sort Lisa out now. The police were tidying their papers and both stood up as if go. I was just starting to move when they dropped a bombshell.

"Oh, by the way, where were you the night of May 12th?"

I gulped. Suddenly I felt faint and light-headed. My voice seemed to come from a long way away.

"How should I know? It was a long time ago." I was surprised that I sounded so normal.

"Perhaps you could give it some thought so when I see you next time you'll know the answer. Well, thank you for your co-operation, sir. You can go now."

I walked out of the police station into the bright glare of the midday sun. It was very hot and I had no means of getting home. I walked down towards the station and luckily grabbed the last taxi.

As I sat in the back of the taxi, I started worrying about the implications of the last question. They were trying to link me with Maitland's death. I couldn't see how they could as it was done at third hand, but it was worrying that they had their suspicions. I'd thought I'd got away with it. It had been so long ago and nothing had happened – until now, that is. Suddenly I felt cold. Murder meant a very long stay in prison and I wasn't sure I could cope with that. Even though I was cold, my hands were wet with sweat. For the first time I felt very frightened. As for the rest, I realised I was now in Ray Mumford's hands. I just hoped he was being sensible, but he knew he had more to lose than me.

As the cab neared my house, I started thinking about what I was going to say to Lisa. It would have to be good. After all, police raids were not the usual event in our part of expensive suburbia.

"So you're back," was her cold welcome greeting. "Everything sorted out?"

"Yeah, it won't be much," I replied. "As I suspected, it's all that bloody Cheshire making things up."

"He was here this morning. Did you know?"

"What! That bastard here in my house? What did he want?"

"He came with the police. He looked all through your personal papers. He spent a long time looking at them. As he was so interested in them, I thought I'd have a look too." I'd never seen her look at me that way before. I felt as though we were strangers and I was really seeing her for the first time. Her face was hard and accusing. "I've learnt quite a lot."

"What do you mean?" I said. But I knew. She had only ever really wanted me for the money.

"Well for one thing I heard him say to the policeman that we're going bankrupt. When I looked at our debts, he's right, isn't he? I thought you were well off but you're not. You're just a pathetic little crook."

She looked at me with an almost expressionless face. I recognised the look. It was contempt. The same as when Mum used to look at my father.

"No! No! You've got it all wrong. It's Cheshire – he's done everything he could to hurt us. He's jealous of me and..."

"Save your lies for the court. You're going to need them, you little creep."

She swept out of the room and disappeared upstairs. She would have left that afternoon with Crispin and her nice new Mercedes sports car. I say she would have done, but unfortunately for her the finance company got in first and repossessed it, just before she left. I don't think she found it very funny having to shift her luggage out again before they took it. The last thing I saw of Lisa and Crispin was them getting into a taxi and disappearing down the drive and out of my life forever.

At first I was convinced she would come back. After all, she loved me and would think more clearly away from home and realise her mistake. Every car that slowed in the road got me rushing to the window, expecting to see her return. With each disappointment I became more depressed and found myself drinking far too much whisky, gin, vodka, or rum. It was all the same to me as I steadily worked my way through the large stock of booze we kept for our guests. In the end I had to accept that she was not coming back. I don't think I have ever been so unhappy in my life as I was then. She had been the one thing I had really loved and now that was spoiled. I don't remember crying before, but now I just bawled and bawled until I hurt deep inside. I had no idea how long this lasted – was it hours, days, or even weeks? But like all illnesses it eventually passed. I found myself looking for reasons for my pain and feeling ever more bitter about Cheshire. If he had had more control I would not have been tempted to steal in the first place. And he shouldn't have gone to the police. God, I hated that man! I also had to face the fact that my Lisa was a slut who only cared about money. Thinking about it, I was glad she and her whining son had gone. Good riddance, I thought. I also hated that bastard Mumford. He always got away with it. I now realised how badly Grey and the others had been treated by him. Well, he wouldn't find me so easy.

The next few weeks were pure hell. My car was taken away, the bailiffs arrived and removed most of our furniture, and finally the house was repossessed. During those awful days I was invited regularly to come to the police station. The cockney inspector continued his barrage of questions. By now I had a solicitor, provided free by the state, and he advised me to continue not to answer any questions. Eventually I was charged with six specimen cases; the mortgage company had also pressed fraud charges relating to my mortgage. I was released on police bail and told to report to the police station every week, as the case would not be heard for at least a year.

Ray Mumford continued to pay the six hundred pounds a week, I made sure of that, but insisted I came nowhere near his shops. We met either at my new flat which he'd helped me to find. It was close to Tower Bridge, well that's how I described it – it was nearer Rotherhithe village, not a particularly attractive address but it had one advantage, it was free. Leastwise the landlord didn't know it was free, but he'd find out! We'd stroll round to the Angel, a riverside pub which served reasonable food and was normally very quiet. Not that it made any difference, but the views were probably the best in London.

"Now look," Mumford said one dark evening in early October. "We've got a real problem with the bank. You're going to have to plead guilty to the mortgage fraud, otherwise you're going to drag me back into it." Mumford, as usual, had wriggled out of any charges. He was the innocent businessman who simply bought from me without any idea that I'd stolen anything. He was even more shocked than Cheshire, naturally. The police had recruited him as a prosecution witness; not that he'd be any good to them. I could hurt him as much as I wanted.

"I doubt if they'll be able to make the other charges stick. Even if they could, you've got no previous form. You'll probably get off with a suspended."

He was probably right, but I was still worried. He didn't know anything about Maitland. The police hadn't given up. They still kept asking questions about my movements during that weekend. All my reasoned arguments told me they were on a loser, but still I worried. I had to make sure that he didn't rock any boats.

I told him, I said, "All right, Ray, I don't mind going down to protect you but I'll expect you to reward me. I hope we understand each other."

"Of course, John. We're friends, I'll see you right."

I reckon he trusted me as much as I trusted him, which didn't say much. I didn't trust him as far as I could throw him and he was a big, fat slob.

It was particularly galling to watch Cheshire's business becoming more and more successful. I kept seeing their coloured advertisements in the glossy supplements and I knew Cheshire wouldn't be advertising unless he was getting orders by the sackful. I, on the other hand, was finding reality much harder to take. A number of my previous so-called friends wouldn't even speak to me. They'd decided that Cheshire's business was too good to lose and wouldn't risk upsetting him. Not everyone liked Cheshire, but to be honest the group of no-hopers that befriended me didn't encourage me.

Then, just before Christmas, I got a phone call from Sniffy.

"Rich, we need to talk. Meet me at the Swiss Centre, the downstairs cafe at six o'clock today. It's important, so be there."

I was apprehensive. I couldn't really believe Sniffy just wanted the pleasure of my company, so it was likely to be unwelcome news. The only good thing was that it got me out of my disgusting flat. I walked down to the river, along the Thames path. As I went across Tower Bridge, I got the feeling I was being followed. I was probably being stupid, but I didn't want some copper seeing me with Sniffy, so I nipped down the tube at Tower Hill. I don't know why all those cheerful tourists milling about the bridge and getting in my way made me so bloody annoyed – at least they provided some cover. As usual the tube was packed out – I just don't know how they get so many into a compartment; if it was animals there'd be protest groups but it doesn't seem to matter for us humans. Just to make sure, I changed trains a couple of times, and I was pretty confident that by the time I got to the Swiss Centre, no-one was following me. I'd never been a fan of the food at the Swiss Centre, nor for that matter the dull wooden decor, but it was not the food I was interested in at that moment, nor the menu.

We ordered quickly. The waiter was a queer in a red waistcoat, whose ability with English matched the quality of the food, in other words they were both bloody poor. It didn't take Sniffy long to broach the subject that caused him to get me to come to see him so quickly.

PART XII

MARK CHESHIRE

Chapter 24

Things were on the up. Without Rich robbing the business, we were starting to do very well. As usual, the Royal family had come to my rescue. The nation's favourite lady was ninety and had been honoured with special stamps. We couldn't go wrong. Orders piled in, I had to recruit dozens of temporary staff. Just before that it was the fiftieth anniversary of the Battle of Britain and we'd done exceptionally well, both for Cheshire's and for the RAF charities. At home Clare was doing well at school and had grown into the perfect child. Beth had rejoined the company and was enjoying being an adult once again.

Peter was continuing to dig into Rich's affairs and had come up with some interesting information. He was concentrating on the Maitland angle which was something the police seemed to get nowhere with. He turned up one evening, looking very pleased with himself.

"I've traced Paul," said Peter as he supped yet another glass of my best malt whisky. "You'll never guess where he went after you dismissed him?"

"Well as I'll never guess I shan't bother," I teased. "Come on then, tell me."

"Piss off and fill the glass up, you miserable bugger. I've a good mind to charge you the full rate for my services, now that would wipe the smile off your face. That's right, grovel, but careful with my shoes, Cheshire, they're suede. Well, all right. He got a job at Templar Barracks, Ashford, Kent. Means nothing to you, I suppose? Not surprised, most people don't know it. Joke is it's part of British Intelligence. Highly classified work. Gives you great faith in the selection procedure, doesn't it?"

"You're not telling me that British Intelligence employed my thief to work on classified documents. Who did the checking, Comrade Donald Duck?"

"More like Micky Mouse! Fair enough, he wasn't involved with really sensitive documents but he was very close to them. I've sent a memo to an old friend pointing out they could improve their procedures."

"Well, what did Paul say?"

"Oh he's left there. He's in Luton now working for a magazine. I'm seeing him on Thursday. I'll be back late, but I'll call round for a whisky and keep you up to date. Incidentally, I've got the statement from Mrs Bishop, Mumford's employee you put me on to. She told me a lot about John Rich and Ray Mumford. Some very good stuff in it, particularly about the mortgage fraud. There's absolutely no doubt that

Mumford gave him a reference so that charge should stick. It also opens up the Mumford connection, with a lot of information about the thefts and the bogus credit notes. Rich was working for him. All round it makes the case against Rich much stronger. Wish it was that easy with the murder. We'll have him though. That I promise, one way or the other."

He was back the following Thursday with the follow-up saga of Paul.

"I'm afraid it's not good news. I reckon someone got there first. He looked like he'd done six rounds with Frank Bruno. He seems very frightened and insists he was doing it all alone with no help. I'll get someone else to see him again in a few weeks. I don't think we'll get any joy from him. But at least I have got some good news."

"Come on, Mark, get the whisky out. If I'm going to tell you what I know, I'm going to have to have a bit of lubrication."

I gave him the bottle and a glass. He poured himself a large measure, sat down, sipped it, smiled, and took out his pipe. I shook my head; he put it away again and then started with his story.

"I've been going through Rich's bank statements and I've come across a figure which looks interesting. Can you think of any reason why Rich would want twenty thousand pounds in cash?"

I thought about it. "Well it wouldn't be to buy stamps or coins as he'd use my money and then steal them afterwards. Blackmail? Had somebody been blackmailing him for what he was doing? Payment for some services? Buying a car? I don't know," I admitted.

"He withdrew twenty thousand pounds six days before Maitland died," Peter said triumphantly.

"So you reckon he paid someone twenty thousand pounds to have Phil murdered?"

"That's how it looks to me but, proving it's another matter altogether. Still, it is interesting. I'll pass it on to the police. They'll have to get the information officially so it'll take them a while, but as soon as they've got it, it will be interesting to know his explanation of why he drew twenty thousand pounds."

"I'll bet you anything what happened to that money. What a complete shit."

"But that's not all my news. Yesterday he suddenly went up to the West End and met a man in the Swiss Centre in Leicester Square. He didn't want anyone to see him as he was very cautious. He thinks he's very good, but he's out of his depth with some of my friends. They're all like me – properly trained."

"Who did he meet?"

"A very unpleasant drugs dealer – a certain James Robinson, but known to everyone as Sniffy due to his unfortunate nose problem. This bloke's an A1 bastard. He'd send his nine-year-old sister into prostitution if he could make money out of it."

"God, is he buying drugs as well? Perhaps that's what the twenty thousand was for."

"I think that's too much of a coincidence just before Phil was so conveniently knocked off. It could have been the payment for the job, couldn't it? Anyway, they spoke very conspiratorially in a corner so my man couldn't get close enough. Rich looked very worried though. They didn't stay long in the cafe, Rich then walked all the way back to his new flat in Rotherhithe, that's about three or four miles. He's never been known to do something like that before. I reckon he had a hell of a shock."

"Well let's hope the twenty thousand gets us somewhere. I don't know about Sniffy – he fits in somewhere in the plot."

Peter stayed on to eat with me that night, for as usual, his wife was out of the country, this time at a trade fair in Poland. As we sat eating a takeaway curry, Peter told us the rest.

"Incidentally Rich is not the only one with unpleasant friends. Mumford seems very friendly with a rather strange Colombian called Carlos. Seems an unlikely relationship." He laughed. "I always thought working with stamps was supposed to be relaxing and quiet."

"You'd be surprised. Like Miss Marple says, look in a village you see all forms of crime – look at the stamp and coin world and everything you could possibly imagine goes on there. I imagine that the relationship between this Colombian and Mumford's to do with hot money. It's always been the same in our industry, a great way of laundering. They buy stamps for cash over a long period and then sell the collection to make the money respectable. I've probably dealt with all sorts of dreadful crooks without knowing it.

"Do you know, just after the war the Post Office issued a pound stamp for the Silver Wedding.

Exchange controls were rather strict in those days and rich people used to take thousands of pounds in the form of these pound stamps in their suitcases out to Switzerland. They then sold them for fifteen shillings to get money out of the country. The Swiss then sold them back to England and they were used for postage. You don't think of stamps as currency but I could put into my wallet three or four million pounds in negotiable currency. I could cash them anywhere in the world and no-one would even spot it. Obviously you haven't seen the film Charade. There may be something sinister in it but I wouldn't bet on it."

"Pity," said Peter, "I was hoping to link him into it."

"But it could be to do with drugs, I suppose. Could it tie in with the Sniffy character, perhaps?"

"It would be nice but it's probably just a coincidence and, who knows, it's probably like a game of Cluedo – you won't know until the final envelope's opened."

Beth arrived back from her musical evening and immediately made some coffee.

"You might have done something about the smell. I thought I'd arrived at the Royal Bengal restaurant." It was very cold after she opened all the windows.

After coffee and port Peter made tracks and Beth and I sat shamelessly drinking our second, or was it third, large port.

"Do you think that Rich did have Phil murdered?" Beth asked.

"Yes, I do. I'm sure that twenty thousand paid for it. And it will have been all for nothing as Rich is now exactly where he tried not to be – facing charges and a prison sentence. What a waste of a life."

*

The next day. I got a phone call from Sandy Neil.

"Mark, I've got some interesting news. I took it upon myself to put out a notice asking for any information about Philip Maitland and I got lucky."

"What have you got?" I asked excitedly.

"His watch, leastwise I hope it's his watch. Have you ever seen his watch or know anything about it?"

"Is it inscribed with a date?" I asked.

"Yes, it's got his name and..."

"Don't tell me, 'From M and B.'"

"That's it! So it definitely is his. Good."

"How did you get hold of it?"

"The police in Shoreditch arrested a drug addict called Peter Gossop and when they searched him he had it on him. Incidentally, he's been arrested for murder. It's not Maitland's but another vicious killing. He beat someone to death in a very similar way to how Maitland was killed. It's highly probable he did kill Maitland. The problem will be to connect him to Rich. At the moment, we only know his supplier is a foul bit of work called Robinson."

"Wait a minute!" I shouted. "He's not known as Sniffy, is he?"

"Yes, why do you ask? How do you know him?"

"Rich met him yesterday afternoon at the Swiss Centre, late in the afternoon, and after they'd talked

Rich looked very worried. When did the police arrest Gossop?"

"Yesterday morning, so it all adds up," said Sandy, sounding pleased. "I suppose your mate Peter supplied you with that sort of information."

"Yes, and it's not all. I've got better to come. Rich withdrew twenty thousand pounds from his bank six days before Maitland's death," I said.

"So it looked fairly straightforward, Rich paid Sniffy and Sniffy provided Gossop. That's the easy bit – the hard bit's to prove it."

"Do you reckon you'll do it?"

"Well it's getting more likely, but we'll need help from Gossop. Hopefully as he comes off the drugs he'll be more co-operative. Let's keep our fingers crossed, shall we?"

PART XIII

MARK CHESHIRE

Chapter 25

The only problem about being invited to be present at the police raid on Ray Mumford's two shops was that I had to get up at four o'clock in the morning. Nevertheless, I wouldn't have missed it for the world. It was with a feeling of mounting excitement that I drove up to London to ensure I was in The Strand by seven a.m. I knew the police were not confident of finding much – if it had been up to them they probably wouldn't have organised the raid at all. As I pointed out, the longer they left it, the less chance there'd be they would find anything.

I parked my car at Spring Lane, an underground concrete monstrosity at the back of Trafalgar Square, and walked back along The Strand. Mumford's shop was virtually next door to the shrine of stamp collecting, the Stanley Gibbons shop. I waited outside, peering into Gibbons' window. It was so very different from the first time I had visited the world famous shop. I was then barely a teenager and had travelled fifty miles to see the world's biggest stamp shop. I could remember still the excitement of buying my first grown up stamp album.

As I watched I became aware of a build-up of burly men close to Mumford's shop. I assumed that they were not stamp collectors. At about twenty minutes past seven a police car drove up and a dishevelled Mumford got out. He'd obviously been in bed when he received the invitation to come out, as he hadn't shaved nor, by the look of it, combed his hair – he was even wearing yesterday's clothes. It made quite a contrast to his usual dapper self. He wouldn't have looked out of place sleeping rough in his own shop doorway. Mumford opened up the shop and all of the non-stamp collectors gathered round and went in, presumably to search it. A few minutes later, a thin man dressed more smartly than the others, came across to me.

"Mr Cheshire?" he asked.

I nodded.

"I'm Detective Inspector Richardson. Would you come with me please, sir? " He had a cockney accent. "We would like you to take a look round and see if there is anything that you can identify as definitely coming from your firm."

What I was particularly interested in was proof that Mumford and Rich were in cahoots.

"Have you found his bank statements or old cheque books?" I asked him.

"Yes, we've found some. You could have a look at

them, if you like."

He indicated towards a desk so I sat down and started looking. It was the old cheque stubs that made the most interesting reading. J. Rich, eight hundred pounds. J. Rich, two thousand pounds. J. Rich, three thousand pounds. J. Rich, two thousand pounds. J. Rich, fifteen hundred pounds, and so it went on, cheque stub after cheque stub. I quickly did a rough count and came up with over two hundred thousand pounds spread over the last eighteen months.

"Inspector Richardson, I think you'll find these interesting," I said, pointing out the cheque stubs and explaining their connection. "I've already worked out they come to over two hundred thousand pounds and that's just over the last eighteen months."

I looked through the rest of the papers. I found to my horror a complete print-out of my own customers. Again, I made the inspector aware of the fact.

"Valuable is it, sir?" he enquired.

"Well, let's put it this way, if I was offered this list honestly I'd expect to pay at least a million, but nobody would sell it – after all, it is the key part of a mail-order business."

By now Mumford had been taken away to the police station for further questioning. As I looked round the shop and in the back stores, I was horrified to find so much of my own stock there. Mumford had the best part of a million pounds retail value of my stock alone. The effect on the market, if he sold it cheaply, would be catastrophic. It could wreck Cheshire's, as all confidence in our product would have gone. It would be like a run on a bank. The thought was so horrific, I resolved to buy it all back, if possible, to protect all the collectors who had faith in me.

D.I. Richardson asked if I would go and have a look at Rich's place and see if I could help there. I agreed readily and said I needed to make a quick phone call.

"Is it an expensive one?" asked Richardson.

"No, only a quickie to my office."

"Well use this one," he said, indicating Mumford's phone.

I'd suddenly realised that Mumford owed us over six and a half thousand pounds. He'd allowed us to charge his credit card on a monthly basis. Well, it wasn't the end of the month but I had a feeling that after today Mumford wouldn't be paying us the six and a half thousand pounds. I phoned Wendy and told her to charge the balance now and at the same time to cancel all his standing orders. I wasn't going to supply the thieving bastard any more. It was slightly irregular to charge his card a little early, but then under the circumstances I thought it prudent. It quite amused me that Mumford should pay for the call.

Rich's place was a real eye-opener. He had led me to believe that he lived in a cheap semi-detached house I called Ersanmine in Chelmsford. I was not prepared for the house he lived in. Estate agents would describe it as a small gentleman's estate. It had extensive grounds; the drive up to the house was impressive enough. The imposing detached Tudor-style house had the unmistakable look of money. Knowing as I now did that Lisa's father was an unemployed labourer from Brent, it was hard for me to appreciate that I was the generous Mark, the father-in-law who had provided all of this.

As I walked through the open front door, I saw Lisa standing at the far window, gazing into the garden. She sensed me. She turned and stared at me, a look of pure hatred. She then moved quickly towards me.

"What have you done to John? You bastard!" she screamed. She lashed out at me with her hands, scratching my face badly. One of the policemen pulled her away.

"This is a police matter, not mine," I said. "I'm just helping." I was very shaken. I wiped my face and turned away.

"You'll find the financial stuff in there," said D.I. Richardson, "and the stock in the adjacent room. Take your own time."

I looked through Rich's personal papers. It didn't take a financial genius to work out he was going bankrupt. The house alone was a disaster. He'd apparently borrowed two hundred and fifty thousand pounds from the Essex Building Society, however, he now owed well over three hundred thousand pounds. With the housing market as it was, they'd be lucky if they got half their money back. He owed money everywhere. I couldn't believe how much credit everyone had given him. In the months since I'd got rid of him, his problems had escalated and completely spun out of control. It was easy to see that he'd been stealing over two thousand a week at his peak. Without that tax-free money he was unable to live. The pile of threatening letters from various finance houses made grim reading. Both the cars were soon to be repossessed and it couldn't be long before the bailiffs were in. I wouldn't get any of my money back, that was for sure.

I wandered into the room he kept his stock in. There wasn't much of any value in there, and again, I found a complete Cheshire's customer listing. I wondered how many other dealers had been allowed access to it.

D.I. Richardson came in and leant on the doorframe.

"Anything for us?" he asked.

"Well, I'd dearly like to know why the sensible people at the Essex Building Society should feel they could give Rich a two hundred and fifty thousand pound mortgage. I didn't give him any reference, so someone did. I expect you'll find it's Mumford but I could be wrong. He's also pinched my customer list – here's the evidence."

I pointed to the document.

"I checked on that with the Fraud Squad," said Richardson. "Unfortunately, the law doesn't recognise computer crime at the moment. It is only a civil case. We could charge him with stealing the paper. At least I suppose that would get it into court so the judge would be aware of it. You could sue him, if you like, but we can't do a thing about it."

I always thought it ridiculous that an old lady stealing a loaf of bread in a supermarket committed a crime the police could charge her with, and yet a clever operator could rob shops of tens of thousands of pounds by just not paying for goods received and be outside the law as far as the police were concerned.

The shops had to take action at their own expense through the civil courts. To me it was a mockery, particularly as in the cases I'd taken to court it always ended in disaster. Even if you won, they didn't pay, and to my amazement I found the only thing I could do was to take them back to court again at my expense. Some chap once owed me two thousand eight hundred pounds and the courts awarded me a pound a week. It meant it would take him over fifty years to repay me. Not that it really mattered as he stopped paying after six payments.

PART XIV

JOHN RICH

Chapter 26

It wasn't difficult to find Sniffy in the Swiss Centre. I just went to the darkest corner and there he was.

"I'm afraid that we've got problems," he started in a confidential whisper. "Goss has been arrested."

"Who the fucking hell's Goss?" I asked.

"Yes, of course, you didn't know, did you? Goss was the chap you employed to do a little job for you. His arrest could be quite unfortunate given the circumstances."

I felt sick. It seemed that everything was falling apart for me.

"They can't link him to me, can they?" I thought frantically for any connection.

"I shouldn't have thought so, but he's in a mess. He did a bit of unpaid work, very naughty really, he's really messed it all up. It's not normally good business to beat someone to death in front of twenty or so witnesses. I'd have thought he'd have known better but then that's the drugs isn't it?"

He paused for a while, toying with his food. "You have got a good alibi for the night, haven't you?"

"Course I have, do you think I'm stupid? I made sure I was with someone for the complete weekend. Just as you told me to."

"Then there shouldn't be a problem hopefully. What about the twenty thousand pounds? Could that be traced? Where did you get it?"

"I drew it from my bank, I had to. It was the only money I had," I replied.

"Well, that could be a little tricky, you'd better think up a good reason why you wanted the money because if anything does happen they'll pick that up for sure and they'll want a good answer."

This was getting frightening. It never occurred to me that the twenty thousand pounds was dangerous. Stupid really, I should have thought it was rather obvious.

"Thanks, I'll come up with something. What do we do now?"

"Wait. That's all we can do. I'll keep my ears open. If anything turns up I'll phone you. At the moment though my advice is to keep a very low profile." He got up quickly and left, leaving me with the bill, as usual. I thought it was bloody charming that I still had to pay, in my circumstances. I wandered out of the Swiss Centre and walked aimlessly through Leicester

Square, and on into the Covent Garden lanes.

I was furious with myself for not realising how dangerous the money was. I was also worried about Sharon. Since she'd walked out of Cheshire's I hadn't seen her. I didn't know where she was. She'd got the idea that Cheshire knew everything and panicked. I did have a postcard from her from Yarmouth but whether she was living there or just on holiday, I didn't know. I suppose the logical thing was to go and see her old mother. It wasn't a prospect that I relished. She was a disgusting old tart with a bad drink problem. She'd probably know where Sharon was if anyone would, though. I supposed I could buy her a bottle of whisky and pay her a visit. I hadn't really got much else to do. As it was a pleasant afternoon and as I didn't fancy getting back to the flat too quickly, I decided to walk back.

I crossed the Thames along the Charing Cross footbridge and kicked a beggar crouched at the south end. It was the only fun I had all day. I walked along by the ugly South Bank complex and looked at the happy faces of the tourists enjoying the surprisingly hot October day. As I passed by the Globe Theatre a Japanese tourist asked me to take a photograph. I took the photograph and he bowed, grinned and thanked me. I envied him; he didn't have my problems. Just past the Globe, the path leaves the Thames and goes along by the Clink Prison. I found the change of temperature in that shade-ridden narrow street made me come over with goosebumps. At least I'm sure it was that and not the thought of the word 'prison'. The more I thought about being locked up the more I realised I had to seriously consider some other alternatives. By the time I was walking alongside HMS *Belfast* looking across to the Tower of London, I'd already decided that if it got worse I'd have to disappear. I'd need money and Mumford would have to provide it. The drug money had now completely run out as Sniffy wouldn't supply me now, as he had said it was too risky.

Thinking about Mumford, I realised I'd need some insurance. The obvious course was to write everything down and leave it with my solicitor to be opened only if I died. It all sounded pure melodrama but it would work. Sniffy would be able to get me a new passport. All I'd got to do then was to decide where to go do.

I felt much more cheerful as I walked under Tower Bridge. I'd also started to feel hungry – I hadn't touched the filth at the Swiss Centre. There was a table free outside the Chop House right under Tower Bridge itself. Amazingly it offered a two course meal for seven pounds. *What the hell?* I thought. *As they're practically giving it away I might as well have a decent meal.* I ordered watercress soup followed by some sort of chicken concoction. I liked the idea of wine by the glass and I somehow managed to get through three glasses of a pleasant Chilean Cabernet Sauvignon during the meal. When it came to it I couldn't resist a sweet – it only cost an extra one pound fifty so I finished with a ginger pudding. After the coffee I asked for the bill, expecting it to be about fifteen pounds. I wasn't too amused when it came to over twenty nine pounds. I checked and it was correct. Four pounds fifty a glass of wine adds up, and I hadn't noticed the twelve and half percent service charge. No wonder Conran was so rich.

Even though I'd spent more than I'd intended the meal helped me to sort out my thoughts. I spent the next few hours writing down the information that would finish Mumford should he not co-operate. I put the document into a separate envelope, marked it 'only to be opened in case of my death' and then quickly wrote a covering note to go to my solicitor, Allsop and Jones, 12 Castle Road, Colchester, Essex.

Dear Mr Jones,

I would like you to take care of this document for me which should only be opened in the event of my death and not for any other reason. Thank you in advance.

Yours sincerely,

John Rich

I didn't know what he'd make of it, but after I'd posted it in the letterbox at Dock Head, I felt better. I used a phone box next to the greasy cafe at the end of Mill Street to phone Mumford. As I dialled his number I wondered how co-operative he was going to be. I hadn't really got a lot of time and I did need money.

"Mumford here, can I help you?" Smarmy git, I could just imagine him there at the end of the phone. He always thought he was so smooth.

"Hello Ray, it's John. I'd like to see you privately," I said.

"Sounds serious," he said. "Can it wait? I've got to go to Manchester for the next few days."

I kept my cool.

"Yeah, no problem, Ray. Let's say next Monday. Come to the Angel. You can buy me lunch."

"That's the Angel off Jamaica Road, is it?" asked Mumford.

"Yeah, you know the one. Make it twelve thirty. See you."

I rang off, wondering how much I could get out of him. I needed as much as I could get. It was in some ways lucky that Mumford was not available immediately as I got a strange phone call from Sniffy on the Friday.

"Rich," he said, "complications. Go to the phone box by Dock Head. Be there in ten minutes."

I had to move quickly to get there by the time he'd said. It was clearly going to be very bad news otherwise why all the theatricals? The phone rang and I picked it up, wondering what I was going to hear.

"Rich? Listen, that cretin Goss kept something from the job. I don't know what it was but he's been charged with Maitland's murder. I'm afraid it's not looking good."

"Oh fucking bloody hell," I shouted, "that's bloody great."

"I'm afraid it gets worse. They've also linked him to me, so keep away from now onwards. I don't need to get involved any more than I am already."

"Look Sniffy, I think it's best for both of us if I

make myself scarce. Can you get me a new passport?"

"I can get one but it won't be cheap."

"How much?"

"Ten thousand for a first class one that will get you out of the country."

"How long would it take?"

"About a week. You'll need to give me a good photo. There are plenty of machines around. Put a couple in the post to me care of the Strand Palace Hotel. I'll pick them up from there. Do it today."

"Get it organised and I'll get the money."

"Right, be at the phone box outside the Southwark Council Office on Jamaica Street at seven o'clock on Monday night. I'll get things going but we mustn't phone or meet each other unless we use payphones. They might well have a tap on either of us."

As I walked slowly back to the flat along Jamaica Road I realised I now had no choice. I'd got to go away. It wouldn't be long before they charged me with the murder and then I'd probably be inside for life. Just as I'd reached the Chambers Roundabout a stupid Jaguar pulled out suddenly, misjudged the available space and crashed into the side of a Renault. The Renault didn't come out of it too well. I scarpered quickly as I didn't want to be a witness but it did give me an idea. I ought to die in a nasty car crash. All I'd need was a body and I reckoned I knew where I could get one from. Even better, if I drove the car over a cliff reasonably near to a port I could be out of the country before the 'accident' was discovered. I thought about where I wanted to go. I fancied Australia. The weather was good there and they speak English.

Mumford was not a happy man when I told him that I had to have fifty thousand pounds. At first he tried to laugh it off but when I told him about my document and where it was, he became very pale. In the end he agreed to give me twenty-five thousand, but that was the maximum he could get. He didn't want me caught any more than I did, so I think he thought twenty-five thousand pounds a reasonable bargain. As far as I was concerned it was a down payment; the rest would be payable for the rest of his life but that could wait for another day. He reckoned it would take him a few days to get the money, so we arranged to meet again at the Angel on Thursday at around one, this time just for a quick drink.

I started selling everything I could to raise cash and bought a reasonable Rover 800 on the never-never through a backstreet credit agency. I thought that was quite funny. In this case never-never was correct for it was unlikely that the finance house would get more than a month's payment at their rip-off rates. The car wasn't that good, but it would be fine for the next stage of my plan.

On the Wednesday I drove down to Dover to look for a suitable spot for my tragic accident. I soon found the perfect place in a road up from the Western Dock that ran up the hill and over the cliffs. It was a popular tourist road during the summer but not many cars used it this time of the year, certainly not in the evening. I could fake the accident and walk back to the docks in about an hour. That meant I could be on a ferry easily an hour and a half after the car hit the beach and in France within three hours. I'd worked out I could get a train to the Charles De Gaulle airport which was on the Calais side of Paris. From there I could get a Thai Airways flight to Sydney via Bangkok. This looked to be perfect for my plans and so, pleased with my day's work surveying the lay of the land, I drove back up the M2 to London. I bought an Evening Standard and looked for flights in the classified section. The section was full of cheap flights to Australia and round the world. I found myself spoilt for choice. In the end I phoned Travelbag at their office in Alton. A delightful Aussie girl helped me pick the best flight. I booked a round-the-world ticket with Air New Zealand, coming back via L.A. I had no intention of returning, but it would look better if the Australian authorities could see I was planning to leave.

Mumford delivered the money on the Thursday nicely packaged up into a briefcase. It reminded me of the twenty thousand that I'd packed in a similar way. If only I hadn't panicked I wouldn't be in this mess today. I took the money and hid it in my wardrobe behind my dirty washing. I still had one major problem. I needed a body to stand in for me, one that was male and not very old.

Getting hold of the body proved remarkably easy as it happened. I knew there was a trade in second-hand bodies, a bit like Burke and Hare really. Snatching bodies was very much a growth industry. Not only was there a large demand from universities and hospitals for research, but, believe it or not, artists like bodies to work with. That's pretty horrific. You could go to an exhibition and find your Auntie

Agatha there looking completely different than she did when you last saw her. Believe it or not that happened to someone; I read it in the paper. I'll say one thing for the bastard, he didn't waste bits, some journalists apparently had door handles made out of human thigh bones in their London flat.

I met someone who arranged these things and for the small consideration of a thousand pounds he agreed to find me a male body as near my age as he could. The best bodies, he told me, came from pre-crematorium burials – after all, once a coffin has been burnt who's to know if the body was in there or not? He also told me that they did a good trade in disposals. After all, if you kill someone, where better to get rid of the body? It also made it very difficult for the police. If they didn't have a corpse they usually couldn't start a murder inquiry, only a missing person one.

I drove to his grotty premises on the outskirts of Upminster. I handed him a thousand pounds in notes and the body was put carefully put into the boot of my car. It was at this point the full horror of what I was doing dawned on me, Christ, suppose I had an accident? How would I explain the body? I felt sick and found it difficult even to hold the steering wheel. I drove very carefully back to the flat to pick up what things I could manage to take with me on my disappearance and voyage to Australia.

I felt a bit like the famous Labour government minister John Stonehouse, who did a similar trick off Brighton beach only to turn up later in Australia. It always made me laugh every time we sold a cover signed by him. The joke was he had been the Postmaster General in the Labour Government and as such was entitled to free first day covers. Just think about it, some postman having to address it to John Stonehouse, Her Majesty's Prison, Ipswich. Well that wasn't going to happen to me. No-one was going to find me again.

I collected my new passport in the name of John Roberts from Sniffy, who'd been even more cautious than usual. This time he arranged to meet me as a tourist looking at the ruins of Edward the Fifth's hunting lodge at Rotherhithe. We met only for a few seconds. We bumped into each other, dropping packages in order to exchange them and walk on again. He really was getting twitchy and looked very scared; he also hadn't shaved. This was not the Sniffy I'd been used to dealing with. If he was that worried, I was very glad that I would be out of England by the next day.

I decided to keep my own passport too. Who knew, it might be useful again one day. I hid it along with other personal papers, which I packaged up and put under the floorboards in the flat. It wouldn't be a hard job to break in and get the package should I ever need it again. I could probably just walk in using my key; landlords rarely go to the expense of changing the locks. It was unlikely to be found by anyone else unless I was extremely unlucky.

Not having much to do, I was grateful for finding some short-term pleasure with a girl I picked up in the Angel. By now I was full of hate for Lisa, Cheshire, and Mumford but most of all for myself, for being so stupid. I used the girl to get rid of some of my anger. Each time I took her it was with force; I gave no thought for her feelings. She didn't seem to care and let me do anything I fancied. I had been without a woman for some time and found I could keep going for longer than I could ever remember being able to. It seemed that I fucked her hard throughout the entire night, and near dawn I finally collapsed and fell into a deep sleep. When I awoke at first I thought I was back in Chelmsford and it was Lisa beside me then I remembered and was embarrassed to realise that I didn't even know her name, and I had treated her badly even though she didn't mind. I also had the distinct feeling that she was just a little young but that didn't stop me using her again. This time at least I made it good for her, something she would probably remember for the rest of her life. Afterwards I told her I'd got things to do and she'd have to go. I told her I'd see her in the Angel on Saturday night, knowing full well I'd be out of the country.

The next morning, I drove slowly down the A2, crossing the Medway at the Rochester Bridge. I passed on down through the orchards of the Garden of England. As I was bypassing Canterbury, I noticed the evening sun hitting the cathedral tower. I'd never seen it look more beautiful. It's funny how fear makes you notice things more. Driving down the Eastern Way – the approach road to the harbour at Dover – I felt a pang as I saw the sea, realising I would be leaving England, my home, probably forever. But the alternative of being in a nasty cell and slopping out each day, and sharing it with some disgusting unwashed convict, was not something that I could consider for a moment.

I decided to get the business over and eat on the ferry. I drove along the new road, turning left and heading up for the famous white cliffs. I was feeling very nervous at this stage. It was imperative that I could find a spot where I'd be totally alone and no-one would see me transfer the body from the boot into the driving seat. Luckily, as I'd expected, it was very quiet. I parked the car on a grassy slope approaching the cliff with only a small fence which would break easily. I moved my thousand pound bargain body with some effort out of the boot and squeezed it into the driving seat. I was about to set things going when I realised I'd left my coat in the back of the car. I'd need one for the first part of my journey, particularly as it was an expensive Burberry trench coat. I got it out, put it on, started up the engine, took off the handbrake and put the car into gear. I gave the car a shove to get it going down the slope. It started slowly then gathered pace. I slammed the door but to my horror I'd slammed my coat in the door. The car was now already moving quickly towards the edge. I had to get the coat off. I grasped frantically at the handle but the combined speed of the car and the tightness of the coat made it almost impossible. I found myself falling to the ground and being dragged screaming in terror closer and closer to the cliff edge, and with it, my certain death.

Report from the Dover Herald:

Tragic Accident at a Well-Known Local Beauty Spot

A car plunged one hundred and twenty feet down the cliffs near Dover on Tuesday. It exploded into a gigantic fireball before bouncing on into the sea. It is believed the driver was a John Rich, late of Rotherhithe. Nobody has been recovered and, due to the combination of very high tides and strong winds, it is unlikely that one will ever be found.

The young man's mother who lives in Clacton-on-Sea said it was a dreadful shock. He was doing well in business and was always happy, so it had to be an accident. The police say they have an open mind as to what happened but they are not looking for anyone else in relation to this accident.

PART XV
RAY MUMFORD –
THE FINAL BLOW

Chapter 27

Ray Mumford hated Monday mornings and, to make matters worse on this particular Monday, he had slept very badly and had a hangover. The traffic round Victoria was solid so it took him over an hour to get into work. He arrived at twenty past ten on the first day of what promised to be a very long week. To make his morning just perfect he found that one of his best customers had returned a £6,500 collection. The collector had decided it wasn't quite what he wanted. Stupid bastard! Mumford really needed that money. Life was getting much tougher. He didn't really like the level of debt he had run up. His overdraft at the bank was higher than it should be. He didn't want them to turn nasty as he still owed the organisation extremely large amounts of money.

Trade was really poor. If it wasn't for the Cheshire racket, he didn't know how he'd manage.

He regretted his involvement with Rich, who was too clever by half. It was all very well for Rich to demand money, but it wasn't as easy to get as it had been. On the other hand, his original idea of asking Carlos to eliminate Rich would have to go on a permanent hold. That would have been so easy and in the long run, a lot cheaper. However, if Rich had documented everything as he said he had, and had given it to his lawyers, it would not only be a waste of money, but it would leave Mumford open to into a murder charge. By the time Mumford had thought the whole thing through, he had convinced himself that twenty-five thousand was a cheap price. It seemed the only way of getting rid of Rich for the present.

Mumford's major problem was money, or rather, the lack of it. After he had given Rich the twenty-five thousand, he knew he would have to do something about the bank. There was nothing else for it but to visit his bank manager and explain that he'd got a fantastic opportunity to buy a superb collection at a fraction of its real value. It would be easy, after all, he was more like a friend than a bank manager. He knew Ray would see him all right. The appointment was arranged for the following week. After the call Mumford cheered up, things could only get better.

He arrived at the bank slightly early and approached the information desk confidently.

A very pretty girl smiled the sort of smile he only ever got when on business or if he was paying.

"Good morning, sir. May I be of assistance?"

"I've got an appointment to see Mr Broadbent at eleven. I'm a few minutes early, though."

Her face changed quickly and she blushed bright red. *Hallo*, he thought, *is Jim up to something? If so he's a lucky bastard, she's a good looker.*

"Mr Broadbent? Oh dear," said the girl. "I'll get someone to see you. Er, Mr?"

"Mumford, Ray Mumford."

"Will you just wait here a few minutes, Mr Mumford?"

All very mysterious, he thought, and went to sit at a circular table covered with highbrow financial magazines. Mumford idly picked one up and flicked through it as if he read this sort of magazine every day and not just while waiting in the reception area of a major bank.

"Mr Mumford?" said a whiny, high-pitched voice.

Ray looked up and saw a pompous, young, red-faced, pinstripe-suited ponce looking at him. He looked to Ray to be about twelve years old.

"Mr Mumford? Could you come with me through here please?"

Mumford was shown into an unfamiliar office.

"Please sit down," said the young lad.

Mumford assumed that Jim had been delayed and that the office boy had been sent to entertain him.

"Now, Mr Mumford, what can I do for you?"

"Well, I'll have a cup of coffee, one lump please and just a splash of milk – thank you. Jim's been delayed, has he?" Mumford asked.

"If by Jim, you mean Mr Broadbent, you could say that he's been delayed permanently. He's left the bank."

Mumford was gobsmacked. He just couldn't understand what the youth was saying. He had always got on so well with Jim Broadbent.

"He was there two days ago," Mumford said, trying to think quickly. "Well if he's not here, who do I see then? I'm an old customer, somebody should have let me know." Ray spoke with apparent confidence but he was really dreading the outcome of all this.

"Me," replied the youth, "I'm the acting manager. Now, as I said before, what can I do for you?"

Mumford had to admit that was the last thing he expected. The boy didn't look like he'd started shaving more than a short while ago. He was quite shaken and it took him a minute or so before he could get the words out.

"Ah, well, ah, you see, it's um, it's like this. I've been, um, offered a fantastic collection. It's one of the best I've ever seen. You know what it's like, they always turn up at the wrong time, don't they? It's too good to lose – but I haven't got the necessary resources. They want cash, not an I.O.U. – well you can't blame them, can you?" Ray knew he was making a complete hash of his request. All the time he spoke, the spotty youth just looked silently at him.

"Mr Mumford, I've looked very carefully at your account. You are already over your agreed overdraft limit. Do you honestly expect us to lend you more money? We're living in the sensible nineties, not the careless eighties. Everyone has had to tighten their belts. Mr Broadbent was slower than most managers in applying the bank's policy. I'm afraid it is quite out of the question for us to extend your facility. In fact, rather than lend you more money, I was going to send for you, because I've been instructed by Head Office to tell you that we will be reducing your facility by twenty-five thousand pounds by the end of the year and then by a further twenty-five thousand pounds by March thirty-first next year. As far as I can see you've made no effort at all to pay off the account for eighteen months. No, we all need discipline and in the end, you'll thank me for not lending you more money. Good day, Mr Mumford."

The wretched boy enjoyed his power, that was obvious. He smiled, stood up, and shook hands. Before Mumford had a chance to say anything more, he was shown out into the main part of the bank. He was so shocked he hardly had time to take it in at all. What had been said? No extra money? And then the lowering of the limit by fifty thousand pounds in the next six months.

The horror of his position dawned on him. Because of their help with Hawkins he still had to pay the organisation fifty thousand pounds every six months for the next two years. This meant that he now needed a hundred and fifty thousand pounds in the next six months! He needed to sell something. He needed to sell something quickly. The obvious candidate was the Charing Cross shop. His manager there, Chris Jones, had worked up a good business and Mumford knew he would love to own it. The problem was how much money he would be able raise, and raise quickly.

Ray hurried round to see Chris Jones on the pretext of chatting about their Christmas sales policy. In the course of the conversation, Mumford mentioned the fact that someone had approached him to buy the shop and that, thinking about it, it seemed a good idea. In fairness though, Mumford said that he thought he should at least offer Jones the first chance to buy.

Jones was very excited by the prospect, so Mumford told him to find out what sort of money he could raise, to see whether in fact he'd have a chance to buy it. He thought by rushing through a quick sale he wouldn't get the best price, but the thought of not handing over the fifty thousand pounds to Carlos, which was due in only a couple of weeks, was scaring the hell out of him.

Mumford had worked out that there was no point staying with his present bank. Although they were called the Listening Bank they weren't listening to him, so he wasn't going to listen to them. There was no way he was going to be able to reduce his overdraft as much as they wanted by the end of the year, so it seemed illogical to give them any more money. He decided to take his custom to the bank that liked to say yes. He opened up an account and started banking his takings there. He had an ace-in-the-hole in that he had an enormous amount of Cheshire's stock and Ray knew he wouldn't want that stock dumped on the market. It would harm the collectors' confidence and that would cost Cheshire a lot of money. It wasn't straightforward, though, as Cheshire had refused to deal with him anymore, so he'd have to find someone to act as a go-between. He also knew he would only get a low price for it, as Cheshire was convinced it had all been stolen – which of course it had. Even so, there should be enough to get him through his problems.

Chris Jones came back the next day and told Mumford that he had raised fifty thousand pounds and he made a firm offer for the stock and lease of the shop. It was a ridiculously cheap offer but after thinking it over, Mumford agreed, provided that he was allowed to keep some of the stock back for himself and that Jones would complete the deal within two weeks. Jones didn't think it would be a problem and so at least Ray could see his way to getting the fifty thousand pounds in time to meet the first deadline. As for the Cheshire stock, he managed to find a very small dealer who still had contact with Cheshire who was prepared to act as his go-between. Cheshire, however, played it very tight and offered only fifteen percent of the retail value which gave him just over sixty thousand pounds, which combined with the shop sale, meant that at least he had a year's breathing space before the problems mounted up again.

Mumford came out of his corner fighting. He went to every exhibition he could attend – small or large. Despite the barrage of unpleasant debt letters, he reckoned he could fight his way out of thc problems. All he needed was time.

Chapter 28

Extract from the Philatelic Exporter:

Stop Press

Tragic Death of Young Stamp Dealer

John Rich, who many of our readers will remember and who worked for Cheshire's for many years, has been reported killed in a tragic motoring accident at Dover.

A full report next month.

It would have been hypocritical of Mumford to say he was sorry to hear of John Rich's death. In fact he was rather pleased. In his heart he knew Rich would have come back to him for money again and again and again. Blackmailers always did. Mumford was, however, terrified in case Rich had done as he'd said and documented everything he knew and given it to his solicitor to send to the police.

He didn't have to wait long to find out. Two or three days after he had read about Rich's accident in the Philatelic Exporter, the Essex police arrived and once again arrested him. This time, he was charged with several offences of conspiracy and theft, and was released on police bail. There was one consolation, he thought, at least things couldn't get any worse. But then he hadn't taken into consideration sod's law. Mumford opened the shop a few mornings later. He hadn't been there long, when two official-looking visitors walked in carrying nasty-looking briefcases.

"Mr Mumford?" said the taller, pale-faced man. He was wearing a greyish blue suit. He was one of those really grey people who remind you of a ghost. Mumford had a nasty premonition the man meant trouble.

"My name's Rogerson. I'm from the Customs and Excise. This is my colleague, Mr Smith. We're here to look at your books."

"I didn't know you were coming," Mumford said, trying to sound in control, but his voice came out too loudly and he sounded as if he was shouting. "You normally make appointments."

"Yes, we do, but that is out of courtesy. By law we do not have to give you any notice. I'm sorry if it is inconvenient, but I'm sure you don't mind. You've got nothing to hide, have you? This is just routine. If we could have a couple of hours now, it will save everyone a lot of bother."

Like most businessmen, Mumford was terrified of VAT inspectors and didn't want to appear as if he had anything to hide. He gave them access to his books. They sat at his desk while Mumford continued preparing the stock, getting it ready for the next exhibition.

At about twelve fifteen the man called Rogerson came out to see him.

"Mr Mumford, looking through your records it would appear you don't take much cash in the shop, do you? It appears to be mainly credit card and cheques."

"Yes that's right. People don't use cash much anymore. They tend to use the plastic, well, I'm sure you're the same – I know I am. I much prefer to use my card rather than to carry cash."

"Yes," said Mr Rogerson. "I'm sure that I'd agree with you normally. It's just that we do have a slight problem."

"What's that?" Ray asked.

"As you probably know our department is putting in quite a lot of effort to ensure that funny money doesn't get into the system and therefore banks have to report any large unusual cash transactions. Well, Mr Levy – you probably know him, he runs a stamp business in Colchester – banked rather a lot of cash a couple of months ago. When we queried where it came from he said he sold a stamp collection to a London dealer. In fact that London dealer was you, Mr Mumford. Do you remember the transaction?"

Mumford began to feel very worried.

"Mr Levy... a stamp collection for fifteen thousand pounds..." he said slowly. "Let me see... Ah, yes! I remember now. Although I paid him the money I didn't in fact buy it. One of my customers had a very good win on the horses and he was worried that if he had the money he'd waste it. He'd seen this collection at Levy's and Levy wanted seventeen and a half thousand pounds for it. He reckoned I could get it much cheaper, being in the business. I was a friend of his and I owed him a favour so I did it for him. In all fairness he did give me a hundred quid for doing it and I must admit I didn't put it through the books, so I am guilty of that. I'm sorry about that but I never thought at the time. Of course I should – it was technically a VATable item."

"Oh I see," said Mr Rogerson, smiling. "You realise we'll have to speak to your customer, but yes, that does clear that one up."

"I'm sorry about that, but you know how it is." Mumford felt relieved that he had come up with such a good explanation on the spur of the moment.

"Yes, I understand very well," said Mr Rogerson. "What about the twelve and half thousand pounds which you paid to the Devon Auction House in Plymouth? That was also in cash. Was that also by chance for a friend who'd won on the horses? And also the seventeen and a half thousand pounds you paid to Wickham Stamps, or the nine and a half thousand pounds to the Halifax Stamp Centre – all in cash. No doubt you've got explanations for them all?"

Ray sat down. He'd come over very dizzy and felt rather sick.

"Mr Mumford, it is obvious to us that you've been systematically avoiding VAT over many years by an under-declaration of cash which you have received. Today I'm issuing you a supplementary demand for a hundred and seventy-five thousand pounds, which is the VAT we believe you've avoided on at least a million pounds cash turnover. In my opinion we're being over-generous but we like to be fair. You will also have to pay a penalty of a similar amount which means you owe us three hundred and fifty thousand pounds, payable immediately."

Mumford just sat there looking straight ahead. He could hardly believe it. He was ruined. Totally wiped out. If he told them where he'd got the cash from, he'd be in even more trouble. He could argue the amount, but Customs and Excise worked on a very simple system – you paid them, then argued later.

"I just haven't got that sort of money," he said.

"Well, we'll give you two weeks and if it isn't forthcoming we will take the necessary steps. I think you understand me," said Mr Rogerson. "Well, Mr Smith, our work here is finished. Good morning, Mr Mumford."

At least he didn't say, "Have a good day."

Mumford knew it was the end. There was no way he could get out of this. It wouldn't take long before the other predators descended. If it was proved that he'd avoided VAT on one million pounds' worth of cash takings then the Inland Revenue wouldn't be far behind wanting their pound of flesh. That's all they would get as well, flesh. There was certainly no bone.

Ray closed the shop and walked round to The Coal Hole pub. Later, he could remember starting to drink, but not being put in a taxi and sent home that night. He didn't go into the shop the next day. He didn't feel well. In fact, he didn't go in for the rest of the week.

Customs and Excise served a winding-up notice as promised, but Ray didn't care. He was hundreds of thousands of pounds in debt with no way ever of getting the money. It was far better to go bankrupt and start again. At least he'd then reached the bottom of the pit. Or at least he thought he had.

The phone call which he had really been dreading came just a week later.

He had been drinking, which had become a habit, when the phone rang. He hadn't heard the voice for a long time but he knew it immediately.

"Mr Mumford, I'm disappointed in you. You have let us down."

Ray gulped. The last person he wanted to talk to at the moment was Mr Gunningham.

"I did explain to you right at the start that we had our own way of dealing with things. I'm afraid you've left us no alternative, as we have to keep our credibility. You understand it is important in business. I'm sure you'd agree? I'm sorry about it, of course, as I quite liked you but business is business. Goodbye, Mr Mumford."

The implications of what he said were only too obvious. When Ray thought about it, he was sure that it was simply to scare him. What was the point of killing him? They'd profit nothing out of that. It would be far better to lean on him and try to get money out of him over the next few years. No, it was a bluff just to frighten him.

PART XVI
DAYS OF RECKONING

Chapter 29

James Robinson, known universally as Sniffy, decided the time had come to take his skills elsewhere. He'd always liked the idea of America. He was sure that an entrepreneur of his ability would do well. He bought one of the passports he'd regularly recommended to his friends and was even now heading for the new world to start his new life. He bought himself some rather nice new luggage from Burberry. He was feeling quite pleased with himself as he caught sight of himself in the mirror as he headed for the passport control at Heathrow. He looked prosperous, very much the successful businessman. He knew he could make a new life for himself very quickly. He handed his passport to the rather attractive young lady who was sitting at the desk.

"What's a pretty young girl like you working here for? You should be a model, a beautiful girl like you."

He didn't notice her press a small buzzer on her desk. Two men moved in quickly, one on each side.

She smiled at him. "I'm sorry," she said, "there's a bit of a problem with your passport, sir. Could you go with these two gentlemen?"

Robinson was taken to a small room, where the police arrived half an hour later. He was charged with conspiracy to murder, drug offences, and travelling on a false passport.

*

The news of Rich's death came as quite a shock to Sharon. The old lady had gone to that henhouse in the sky, but Sharon had stayed on afterwards chicken plucking. It wasn't a particularly large farm and the work was hard but the farmer, a big strong Norfolk man, was kind and considerate and gradually, despite the age difference, she had fallen in love with him. They were due to be married the following spring. She was sad about Rich, but it some ways it was a blessing in disguise. She had to admit she really wouldn't have wanted him to turn up at the farm. He was part of her life that she was ashamed of.

*

After Gunningham's phone call, Mumford found himself constantly thinking he was being followed and he became paranoid. On one occasion when a car backfired, he threw himself down into the dirt. He couldn't sleep at night and was scared even to go out to the shops. Time went by and as there was no attempt to kill him, he began to relax. Obviously Gunningham really was just trying to scare him.

He never really believed that Gunningham would

do anything and as time moved on and he got no further messages, he was sure he would be all right. Mind you, he had more pressing things to consider. The bastards from Customs and Excise confiscated everything he had, and auctioned it. He lost his shop, his stamps, and his coins; he had to move out of his beautiful penthouse at Crown Reach into rooms in Tower Hamlets. Still, if Gunningham did come looking, he wouldn't find him here. His lodgings were really just a room in a bloody council house. How his father would have laughed. He'd always said Ray'd come to a sticky end. The final humiliation was losing his car. He loved that Jag. It was the final straw when they took it away. The bloody Philatelic Traders Society kicked him out, and everybody in the trade ignored him as if he'd got AIDS or something. Perhaps failure was catching? Mumford had never even dreamed in his worst nightmares that he would end up on the dole taking state handouts. Another bankrupt, living in a rat-infested slum.

His life turned into one of squalid routine. He got up late. Sometimes he washed and shaved, but often he just couldn't be bothered. He'd taken to walking down to the local for breakfast. He had no place to cook for himself and anyway he preferred a liquid breakfast which helped to take his mind off his pathetic existence. He usually staggered back to his room for an afternoon kip. Then, about six, he'd go out again and if he felt hungry, he'd buy some chips from the local fish 'n' chip shop. Then it was back to the pub for another fun-packed evening.

Take last evening for example. It was pissing down; he got soaked to the skin; the chips got wet and cold, and tasted like shit. Luckily the pub had a fire, so he stuck himself in front of it and steamed dry. As usual there was some stuck-up bastard who got up his nose. Said that he smelled like a public lavatory and asked the landlord why he allowed tramps and scum like Mumford to ruin a good pub. Mumford shouted back at him. The landlord took the snob's side and ordered Ray to leave. Ray Mumford, thrown out of a nothing pub on a nowhere estate, would you believe it?

When he got into the street, it was still raining. He was trying to work out which pub would now get his custom. He remembered a small one round the corner. He was crossing the road when a car started up very close by. To his horror, he saw it was heading straight at him. Everything seemed to happen in slow motion. It was like a nightmare. He tried to run but his shoes were shiny with wear and he couldn't get a grip on the wet road. He slipped and fell into the path of the oncoming Mercedes. He looked up; the last thing Mumford remembered seeing was Carlos' face grinning through the windscreen.

Extract from the Evening Standard:

HIT AND RUN DEATH IN WAPPING

Late last night a man was tragically killed in Wapping High Street. Raymond John Mumford, 49, of 37 Wharf Road, Wapping, was run down by a white Mercedes, registration number L596 CCT. The car had been stolen from Swindon last May and was found abandoned in the Surrey Quays Car Park.

Eyewitness Harry Tate, 74, said, "It was the most horrific thing I've ever seen and as I went through the entire war, that must mean something. The car was travelling at about 60 to 70 miles per hour and as I watched, the body was just thrown over the windscreen then it fell off onto the kerb. The worst thing was when the head became detached and rolled back towards me."

Mr Tate was so distressed that he was taken to hospital suffering from shock.

Police are appealing for anyone with information concerning the Mercedes car or for anyone who was in the area of Wapping High Street between nine and half past nine last night to come forward.

Police spokesman, DC Smith, told the Standard that the police were particularly concerned about the alleged speed of the car. In all probability it was joy-riders, but they were keeping all their options open.

PART XVII

MARK CHESHIRE

Chapter 30

A few weeks after Mumford's death, I met the other two for lunch. Peter's bill for all the detective work he had done, had been far less than I had estimated, so I thought the gathering would in some way go to thank my friends for their help. I chose Le Café du Jardin, a French restaurant on Wellington Street. It was convenient for all of us as Sandy was doing witness duty at the Law Courts, I was visiting Stanley Gibbons, and Peter was close by, busy doing whatever the Peters of the world do.

Neither Sandy nor Peter were great wine drinkers, so for a change I drank their choice, German plonk, or lemonade, as Beth always calls it. Sitting contentedly after eating far too much and generally putting the world to rights, my mind went back to the reason we had all come together.

"Well, I must admit I never saw it ending like this,

with both of them dead in apparently tragic accidents. It wraps it all up," I said.

"I think you're right when you say apparent," replied Peter. "In my own mind, I have no doubts that Mumford was murdered. He kept very strange company for a stamp dealer. What do you think, Sandy, am I right?"

"Oh yes. It was a very professional job, even down to the fact that the car had been stolen nearly a year ago. Still, it saves the taxpayer all that money keeping him in prison. "

"Talking about saving the taxpayer, I've just got a year to go," said Peter sadly. "They won't let me sign on again; I'm too old for field work, so unless I want a desk job, which I don't, I'll be unemployed next year."

"I'm so sorry, Peter," I said. "I know you enjoy your job, whatever it is you do."

"I don't mind that much, it's not the same anyway. It's all this peace dividend, no Cold War, no fun. We will move on to the IRA and suchlike, but that's not the same. Ireland's heading for peace talks, so I'm a dinosaur. I'm thinking of starting a private detective agency. After all, it's all I know, so next year recommend me to your friends." As he said that he looked directly at the Chief Inspector. I suppose you don't approve of private detectives, Sandy?"

"Well not those who bugger about with pipes all the time, but as for the rest, I've never had a problem. I've worked with some very good ones over the years and it's normally worked out very well. Mind you, it's ironic that you should be looking to start up next year, because that's when I'm on the market, too. I retire in April. Perhaps we should team up, but only if you promise to leave your hobby at home, I hate smoke and I don't want cancer."

Peter grinned. "If you can't take the heat, you should stay out of the kitchen. I find I concentrate better with a pipe, but I'm not addicted. Who knows? We could be the new Holmes and Watson."

I raised my glass in a toast.

"Well, whatever you both do, thanks for your help. I couldn't have managed without you. At least Rich got his just desserts. He really was an evil bastard. Here's to the future."

Sandy sat back into his chair and looked at me seriously. Slowly, he dropped his bombshell.

"I'm sorry to be a wet blanket but as far as the police are concerned the warrant for Rich still stands. He may have driven over the cliff at Dover but the question is, what was he doing there? Remember Dover is the quickest exit from the country. When and if his body turns up, then you can be sure he's dead, but my guess is he's alive and out of the country."

POSTCRIPT

James Robinson was found guilty at the Old Bailey and was given a ten-year sentence with a recommendation that he should serve at least four years.

Sharon married her farmer and now has three children and, much to her husband's annoyance, has lost all interest in sex.

Beth confounded all the gynaecologists by having two more children and was delighted when Mark sold his business for a staggering six point five million. He must have had second sight because the collectable market collapsed eighteen months after he sold the business.

Chief Inspector Sandy Neil became the first senior officer to take the police force to a tribunal concerning the discrimination about his promotion. His hunch about being left in his present position was correct and he retired after a successful conclusion to his case when he flew to Sydney, Australia, to arrest the multi-millionaire suspect he'd been tracking for some considerable time. On his retirement, he teamed up with Peter Pyke and now runs one of the most successful private detective agencies in the country.

John Rich's body never turned up, nor did the thousand pound corpse.

Things were looking up for Chris Jones. The Charing Cross Stamp Shop was doing really well since Ray Mumford's horrific death. Even better, some of the old customers were drifting back. One of Mumford's best customers, the one he used to laugh at and call The Duck, was buying heavily again. Yes, he was sure that Mr Gunningham would be the first of many old collectors to start collecting again. Even more exciting for Chris was that Mr Gunningham had suggested he might help him financially with the business and he had arranged to meet him in his suite at the Savoy to discuss the matter further.

THE END

14429007R00179

Printed in Poland
by Amazon Fulfillment
Poland Sp. z o.o., Wrocław